A KIND OF ACQUAINTANCE

A KIND OF ACQUAINTANCE

A Kavanagh and Salt Mystery

David Armstrong

Severn House Large Print
London & New York

This first large print edition published 2008
in Great Britain and the USA by
SEVERN HOUSE PUBLISHERS of
9-15 High Street, Sutton, Surrey, SM1 1DF.
First world regular print edition published 2007 by
Severn House Publishers, London and New York.

British Library Cataloguing in Publication Data

Armstrong, David, 1946-
   A kind of acquaintance. - Large print ed. - (The Kavanagh
   and Salt series)
   1. Kavanagh, Frank (Fictitious character) - Fiction
   2. Salt, Jane (Fictitious character) - Fiction 3. Police -
   England - Fiction 4. Shropshire (England) - Fiction
   5. Detective and mystery stories 6. Large type books
   I. Title
   823.9'14[F]

   ISBN-13: 978-0-7278-7731-4

Except where actual historical events and characters are being described
for the storyline of this novel, all situations in this publication are
fictitious and any resemblance to living persons is purely coincidental.

Printed and bound in Great Britain by
MPG Books Ltd, Bodmin, Cornwall.

For Julia

Sincere thanks to my agent, Vanessa,
and editor, Amanda.

For valued research assistance, many thanks
to Roger Forsdyke of the CWA; Christine
Whittingham at NSC; Neil Holland at the
Forensic Science Service, and New Scotland
Yard.

For reading and invaluable feedback, I'm deeply
indebted to Penny, Andrew, Maureen, Graham
and Clive, and most particularly, my son, Jesse.

Pozzo: Who is he?
Vladimir: Oh, he's ... he's a kind of acquaintance.

> (Samuel Beckett, *Waiting for Godot*)

Prologue

November 3rd 1986

In the distance, down the long, deserted road, Leah could see the boy. She pushed herself back into the car seat, lit a Gold Leaf, and hummed along to the music.

The trees swayed, and the boy pedalled hard against the wind.

Leah could take or leave Van Morrison. Really, she was more a Eurythmics kind of woman, but this was one of the few tapes that was in the car and this morning the curmudgeonly Irishman was at his most mellow. 'Into the Mystic' sounded fine. Just fine.

The boy was out of his saddle now, standing on the pedals as he mounted the little incline against the gusty breeze. A milk tanker trundled up the farm track on the right, puddles glinting in the ruts there.

At sixty miles an hour, Leah swung the old Fiat out to pass the child. Without a backward glance, with no thought of a car behind him, the newspaper boy cut directly across her path.

The sound was horrific as the metals came together for a fraction of a second, before the

11

bike careered into the ditch and the boy's body thudded on the windscreen and then catapulted over the car.

She screeched to a halt, lurching the car into the verge at a crazy angle.

With the engine still running, she ran back along the empty road, crying all the time, 'Oh, God. Oh, God, no. Please, please God, no.'

Even before she reached him, she stopped. He was completely still on the tarmac, the only noise the sighing of the trees.

Blood seeped from a gaping head wound that she could barely bring herself to look at. She forced herself a step closer.

'Oh, God. Oh my God,' she pleaded again.

Why hadn't he turned? Why hadn't he looked round? Why hadn't he stuck out a hand to show his intentions?

She knelt down beside the boy and put two fingers on his neck, feeling for a pulse.

There was nothing, not even warmth.

'Oh, God, what have I done?' she wept helplessly as she knelt there.

She looked back. His newspapers were lying in the middle of the road. She got to her feet and walked slowly back, picked up the bag and laid it in the grass.

The car was still running, her cigarette end smouldering on the tarmac, the music playing, and she heard the gross incongruity of Van Morrison's words. *'I want to rock your gypsy soul/ just like way back in the days of old/ then magnificently we will float/ into the mystic...'*

She leaned into the car, switched off the tape, and then walked round to the front of the Fiat.

There was an ugly scar where the cycle had left its mark on the wing, a dent in the bonnet and a crack in the top corner of the windscreen, but there was no torn metal, nothing violently graphic to show that this car had just killed a boy.

She got back in the car, wrapped her arms around the steering wheel and lay her head there, weeping, unable to look up at the smeared windscreen.

After a while, with the wheels spinning on the soft, damp grass, she reversed off the verge and slowly back down the road to where the child lay.

The wound had stopped seeping, and the pool of red blood was already a brown stain on the tarmac, like dirty water from a burst radiator. She took a plaid rug from the rear seat of the car and laid it on the floor of the boot.

And now the impossible part. She put her arms underneath his shoulders. Was he twelve, perhaps thirteen? A slight boy, his eyes closed, face bruised and his head cut terribly, his long brown hair matted with sticky stuff. She held him to her and lifted him, his blood smudging her clothes.

She eased him into the boot of the car, folded his legs and covered him with the rug. Somewhere close, she heard the engine of a lorry starting.

As she drove away, through her tears she

13

glanced in the mirror as the blue and white milk truck swung out of the farm track and drove away in the other direction.

One

September 2006

Sarah lived alone. She didn't worry about choking on a fishbone – she didn't *eat* fish. Nor meat, nor fowl. And she didn't fear falling down from a stroke. Yes, she smoked cigarettes, and drank quite a bit, but she also swam fifty lengths of steady breaststroke three times each week.

She had lived in flats, in squats, in the countryside and in the bustling city. And now she lived alone, on a sixty-foot boat moored on the Grand Union Canal just outside Rickmansworth.

But even for a writer, the lone toiler at the blinking word-processor, there can be problems with the solitary life. And not just the fishbone in the throat or the sudden heart attack. What happens if you go missing? Who's going to alert the authorities to your disappearance? Who's going to come and try to find you?

Sarah was thin – just this side of anorexic – a condition that she knew all about from her un-happy teenage years when, bullied at school for her boyish looks and outspoken nature, she had been treated for the illness.

Slight, with red hair cut short, astonishingly full eyebrows, green eyes, and still with the bosom of a girl, she was a forty-year-old waif of a woman.

Waif or not, though, she was famous. Well, not exactly famous *now*, perhaps, but she certainly had been. Before she was thirty, Sarah Clement had published a novel, a book so haunting, so precocious and dauntingly mature, that it had sold a hundred thousand copies, been translated into a dozen languages, adapted for radio and the stage and was, even now, occasionally studied as a sixth-form text by the very brightest pupils.

Of course, this triumph had not been achieved without the struggle known to almost every successful writer. And perhaps this demeaning period, the humiliation of rejection after rejection, had had an even more debilitating effect on Sarah than it had wrought on her thousands of predecessors. Who knows?

In any event, she continued to labour and toil.

And finally, after all that endeavour – the endless writing, redrafting and revisions, the sort of thing that only obsessives and sick people can manage – in 1993, her breakthrough title was published.

The House of Loss had met with universal acclaim, and there had been a clamour to pay court to, to heap praise upon the attractive writer and her first book, notwithstanding her reputation for a prickly attitude and rather chippy nature at interviews.

But that early success had turned out to be the high-water mark of Sarah Clement's career. She had done almost nothing since – a bit of TV work where, perhaps with another author or a couple of critics, she'd be invited to chat about her own stellar impact, and to comment knowingly on some new star's prescient work or huge advance.

But these late-night appearances in the public eye were on the back of the success of her early 90's phenomenon, rather than on the strength of anything since. Early on, she'd had a couple of short stories published in literary magazines; there was a second novel – it had, after all, been the standard luminary's two-book deal.

But 1995's *Losing Heart* was at best dismissed as a victim of 'difficult second-book syndrome' by the more charitable hacks; at worst, looking for a bit of vengeful payback after they had lionised her first, the book was cruelly savaged.

In any event, thousands of copies found their ignominious way into remainder shops within only a couple of months of publication.

Later, there was a film script that disappeared into the black hole of 'development' and, finally, a Radio Four play in the afternoon slot that was either ignored by critics or, for those few who bothered to review it, scorned for its 'lifeless writing'.

No, the phone didn't ring much these days. Sarah had fallen out with her agent several years ago, and the only contact she had with her former publisher was the royalty statements and (still) fairly decent cheques that arrived each year in February and August. So out of the loop had she slipped that she didn't even know the name of her current editor.

She still, apparently, wrote. Although she never discussed it with her few friends and immediate neighbours on the canal, it was generally known that she spent hours, sometimes entire days, 'researching'.

The impression she tacitly gave was of a woman who had a surfeit of information, a glut of knowledge, a writer who was constantly accruing, and just waiting for the right moment.

Sarah, it appeared, was bloated with ideas. She was surrounded by floppy disks and card indexes, a library of books with turned-down pages, notes and memoranda. Her boat was filled with Roladex and folders, disks and CDs, stuffed filing cabinets and bulging cardboard wallets. Yet still she did not 'breed one work that wakes'.

Perhaps her fragile confidence had been so undermined by her second book's reception that it was now a millstone around her neck, an albatross that held her back? Maybe she should simply have followed the example of the small but highly impressive list of one-book authors: the Margaret Mitchell and Harper Lee club?

Had these luminaries acknowledged the impossibility of ever writing a second book to compare with – let alone exceed – the merits of a first that has been so triumphant? Or perhaps Ms Mitchell had had no further ambition, was content to bask in American deep-south glory. Perhaps Harper Lee was sanguine about her solitary masterpiece and remained untroubled by the dearth of any further work? Maybe she watched TV, or read and fished all day long?

Alone on her boat, apparently stymied, frustrated, and sometimes close to despair, Sarah Clement was like a woman who has built a huge bonfire, a bonfire piled high with dry timber and broken pallets. But her new novel – if that's what it was – remained cold, dark and unlit. Somehow, she seemed to have mislaid the match that would give it spark and life.

Two

November 3rd 1986

Leah sat huddled on the kitchen floor of the terraced house that they shared in Victoria Street in Stoke. Her knees pulled up to her chest, she lit another Gold Leaf and crushed out the stub of the one smouldering in her fingers in the overflowing ashtray beside her.

Sarah had the front sitting room as her bedroom. Leah's was the large bedroom upstairs. Catherine – who was never there – had the small upstairs room at the back.

There was some muffled movement next door,

a few words spoken. Leah got up, poured water into the kettle, and left the tap water splashing into the sink to mask the sounds from the room next door.

The movements became regular, rhythmic. Giggles and bed squeaks and, eventually, quiet moans as Sarah and her boyfriend had morning sex. Perhaps they were unaware, or maybe they just didn't care that Leah had returned. Now she was murmuring Nick's name. A voyeur's dream. A nightmare for Leah, standing there, hands on the sink, her head bowed over the rim.

She turned on the radio, switched stations from *Today* on Radio Four, with its sober reporting from around the globe, to the seamless jocular inanities of Radio One.

There was a heavy bump, then a fall, followed by a brief silence and then strangled laughter, like that of naughty children behaving badly. Leah felt mocked and ridiculed in her grief and sorrow.

She made tea and started to wash the things that had been piled in the sink. Ten minutes later, the water became a trickle as the bathroom tap was turned on upstairs.

Sarah came into the kitchen, a bathrobe pulled loosely around her. 'Hi, Leah. How did it go? How are you?' she said, and made to give her a hug.

Leah shrank away, didn't want her near her, didn't want to be touched by her warm, sex-sated friend.

'Are you alright?' asked Sarah, affronted and

surprised by her friend's disdain.

'Where's Nick?' Leah replied.

'In the bath.' She nodded upwards. 'Why? What's the matter, Leah? Are you alright?' she asked, and turned her friend towards her.

'No,' she said. 'I'm not alright.' And she started to gasp for breath and weep uncontrollably.

'What *is* it?' asked Sarah, taking her in her arms. 'Leah, please tell me. Is it Ethan?'

'No, it's not Ethan. When's Nick going?'

'Soon,' said Sarah. 'He's playing football ... at eleven. What is it, Leah? What's the matter?'

'Something terrible has happened. I've got to talk to you, Sarah. Please, please God! Something absolutely terrible.'

'Whatever it is, we'll sort it out,' Sarah reassured her. 'Come on, it can't be that bad.' She held her close in her arms.

'It is,' Leah said, 'believe me, it is.'

Sarah took the damp tea towel from the draining board and wiped the tears from her friend's cheeks. 'As soon as Nick's gone, we'll talk. You can tell me everything. I'll make some coffee. Now listen, you go and get changed. And look, what's this on your tee shirt? Put something clean on. As soon as he's gone, I'll call you. OK?'

Three

September 2006

There had been a mini heat wave, with twelve days of sweltering, Mediterranean temperatures throughout Britain, interrupted only by isolated and truly apocalyptic thunderstorms.

Wearing shorts and stripped to the waist, Paul Evison saw the funny side of delivering coal in temperatures more suited to Greece or Morocco.

But these folk, his customers, were creatures of habit, and their steady stockpiling system made sound economic sense: a bag of coal every two or three weeks throughout the year, rather than having to buy a dozen with autumn's first chill.

Sarah's boat looked empty. Evison had developed a sense of these things. Close to burnout three years previously, he'd given up a £100k-a-year job in the City to ply his desultory trade on these still green waters.

He'd read an article in the *Telegraph* about a middle-aged couple who wanted to sell their business. They'd had enough of lugging 25-kilo bags of coal on to the towpath for the folk who had made their homes along this stretch.

Evison and his girlfriend had driven up that weekend in his Audi Quattro and he'd bought them out – boat and all – a fortnight later. In a good year, he reckoned to make ten – if it was a really cold winter maybe twelve – thousand pounds.

Peony, his girlfriend, had gone back south after only a couple of months. Making a living delivering coal on a canal was just romantic twaddle, she said; it was like doing community service for a crime that they hadn't even committed.

She missed the tanning suite, the gym and nail bar, the Screen on the Green, and a dozen decent restaurants within a hundred yards of their Islington flat with its high ceilings and video phone at the front door.

Paul still had a mobile phone, of course, but most of the calls he received these days were for a couple of bags of best nuts. Black Audi gone, flat sold, attractive girlfriend history – the man had never been happier.

Sarah Clement was a regular. He stacked a bag of coal under the tatty blue tarpaulin adjacent to her boat every couple of weeks. He hadn't seen her last time – nothing unusual in that; she was sometimes away – but now the plants on the roof of the boat, plants that flowered in pots and buckets and needed watering a couple of times each day, were wilted, and not just heat-wave wilted, but neglect wilted.

He bumped alongside. The hatch was padlocked. Using his hands on the gunnel, he eased his vessel a yard or two back and peered in through one of the waterside portholes.

He could see tea cups, some brownish scum on one. A glass, and a three-quarters full bottle of Gordon's gin. Books and folders all over the place. The computer monitor switched on, text on the screen flickering there. Overflowing ashtrays, and a big fly bumping the window.

Back on the towpath, he pulled the blue plastic cover back, dropped another bag on the little mound of coal there, and pushed a delivery slip through the tiny crack above the hatch doors.

You didn't really get coal thieves. Very occasionally a boat would be burgled, and there was, of course, a bit of teenage vandalism if the kids from the housing estate could be bothered to walk this far from their street-corner patch. They'd throw a few stones, occasionally chuck a bag of coal into the cut just to see it splash and sink, but really this was as peaceful an environment as you were ever going to find.

Evison stepped back onboard his boat and chugged away up the canal.

At lunchtime, in the pub a couple of miles further up the cut towards Cassiobury, the coalman asked the landlord, 'You seen Sarah lately, Terry?'

'Sarah?'

'Yes. Sarah from *Ulysses*?'

'No, I don't think so. Not for a few days,' he said.

He served a chummy group of tourists, the folk who rented boats by the week, wore jaunty caps and Guernsey sweaters, were gently mock-ed and ridiculed by the locals, and who kept the pub in business.

'Why?' asked Terry eventually as he waited patiently for a pint of Guinness to settle.

'I dunno. The boat looks deserted.'

'It's been so bloody hot, she's probably gone away. But I'll look out for her.'

The landlord thought no more about it. The people who lived along this stretch lived close together, but they didn't bother one another. It was why most of them were living there, any-way. They wanted peace, even isolation, they didn't want to be in one another's pockets. If Sarah wanted to go away for a few days, so be it.

The next day, taking an early-morning walk with his Labrador, Terry peered in at *Ulysses*, and saw that Evison was right. The place *did* look strangely empty. It didn't feel quite right. There was something about it: the difference between a badly parked car and an abandoned one, that kind of feeling.

Terry stepped aboard, and felt the boat roll slightly with his weight. His dog looked on, un-sure whether to make the little leap and follow his master, or to remain on the towpath.

Terry took the metal pail from the back deck, lifted up a bucket of water from the cut and watered the dying geraniums in their pots along the roof.

Four

November 9th 1986

As the hours became a day and the days nearly a week, Leah didn't get better. She hadn't been to a seminar since the day of the accident.

Sarah made excuses for her at college, told her MA supervisor, Tom Hopwood, that she was unwell, had flu, but would be back soon.

But Leah wasn't getting better – in fact she was worse, much worse every day. Unable to sleep, eating nothing, she hadn't breathed the air on the pavement outside their house for days. She had walked no further than from her room to the bathroom. In only a week, she had lost half a stone.

Ethan phoned from the university in Bangor in North Wales. The payphone in the hall of the house in Stoke rang repeatedly until Leah was forced to pick up the receiver.

'No, I'm fine,' said the diminutive woman, her hair tousled and greasy, a bathrobe pulled about her as she tried to summon her strength and a measure of composure.

'You don't sound it, Leah,' he said kindly. 'You sound tired. Are you sure you're OK?'

'I'm fine,' she repeated. 'I just have to work, Ethan. It's my book. It's difficult, but it's OK. I just have to stick at it, you know?'

'If you're sure,' he said.

'I'm not sleeping very well, but I'll be alright,' she added.

'Shall I come over?' he asked. 'Maybe I could rent a car or get a train or something?'

'No. I can't work with you here. Please, leave me alone for a few days. I'll be alright, really.'

He did, just for a second, wonder whether it was a ruse, some excuse not to see him, because maybe she was seeing someone else. But it was only for a second. If Leah was cheating on him, he was crazy, and as a psychology graduate from New England, he knew very well he wasn't crazy. Foolish sometimes, maybe, but not crazy.

Not only was Leah not the kind of woman to cheat, she was the kind of woman who gave the distinct impression that such tawdry behaviour would somehow be entirely unworthy of her. If she didn't want to be in a relationship – with her boyfriend Ethan, or anyone else for that matter – he knew she'd simply tell him. To be unfaithful, unless he was very much mistaken, wasn't in her nature.

Unlike himself. His own behaviour only a couple of weeks previously had been a shabby episode, and a deception not worthy of him, of Leah, or of their love affair.

Why had he done such a thing? Got drunk on English beer, slept with another woman – a nineteen-year-old undergraduate whom he barely knew? Men! He had to agree: their flesh *was* weak, and all too depressingly suggestible.

Why had he slept with the girl? Of course, he knew, as every man knows, that no matter how attractive and intelligent your partner – and Leah was both – there is always something intriguing about the mystery of a new, different woman.

And, for her part, the girl had not been slow in letting him know her wishes. Ethan, with his beguiling accent and urbane Boston manner, was an irresistible prize – like some exotic beast prowling the monochrome North Wales campus.

And, yes, he had to admit, the sex with the youngster had been exciting. They'd both known it was just that: one-off, half-drunk, lascivious, unabashed, hot, sweaty sex.

They had no intention of seeing one another again, and he certainly wouldn't have confessed his crime to Leah. But although he might have been an excellent postgraduate psychologist, he was not even an average liar. It had taken Leah only a few minutes on the phone to deduce that something was wrong with her boyfriend. The shock was all the more terrible to her because she was convinced that what they had together precluded any such thing happening.

In no time he had admitted his transgression. She was completely devastated. She wept, drank a bottle of wine with Sarah and was ill, then woke up and cried some more. He kept phoning, but she wouldn't answer.

Later that evening, when she eventually picked up the receiver, she despaired of his very voice, wanted to hurt him as much as she had been hurt.

To the perpetrator, a fling is so insignificant. The doer of the deed knows the exact worth, the real currency of the transgression. But to the betrayed, this audit of pain, with so little in the transgressor's column, is itself a grave offence. The plea that 'it meant nothing' merely adds insult – if it meant so little, why did you do it? Why are you hurting me so much? If it meant nothing, why am I so hurt?

And yes, of course, what would you feel if I told you that *I* had slept with someone? The difference is all.

And then came the questions. The 'how's and where's and who did what's'. Leah was a writer, and she felt her pain right now was part of the essential experience she sought.

She made him tell her everything and, eventually, replaced the phone receiver with a heartbroken sadness.

Later there were more calls, abject contrition, his pleas for her forgiveness. She needed time to think, she said, and took the phone off the hook for hours.

Some women, simply to avenge the wrong, would have behaved as he had done. She did think about it. She could have walked down to the union bar or any one of half a dozen pubs within the area and fallen into the arms of any man there. But she had no wish to right his wrong in the arms of another man.

At past one in the morning, bitter and hurt, she asked Sarah if she might borrow her car. She had to see him. Now.

In his room in the postgraduates' house in North Wales, they had a night of needful, hungry sex, trying to right the wrong that he had done. They explored one another in ways that, even in their year or so together, they had never done before.

At dawn they had lain together in his room. In the distance the Irish sea was grey beneath Bangor's leaden sky. Their mouths were dry with the taste of one another on their lips, his flaccid penis against her buttocks, a hand across her breast, his face lightly covered in her hair.

A fortnight later, having hardly moved from her bedroom, Leah barely registered the non-appearance of her period.

There was a tap at the door and Sarah asked quietly, 'Leah, can I come in?'

She lay on her side, dressed, the duvet over her and her knees pulled up to her waist. The ashtray was full beside her, Gold Leaf packets on the floor.

Sarah sat on the edge of the bed with her hand on her friend's shoulder. 'What are we going to do, Leah?' she whispered.

'I don't know,' Leah murmured in reply. 'I don't know.'

'You can't go on like this...'

'I know. I know I can't.' Leah looked at her

friend imploringly, then asked a question as reasonably as if there might actually be an answer to it: 'Why didn't he put his hand out? Why didn't he turn round, just for a second, so that I...?'

'Don't, Leah. There's no point. It's done. It's terrible, I know...'

'You *don't* know,' she said quietly. 'No one knows...'

'No, of course,' said Sarah. 'You're right. Of course you're right, but we can't go on like this. *You* can't go on ... Nick knows there's something wrong. I've told him it's you and Ethan. It's the only thing that would make any sense to him.'

'And what about the car?'

'He believes you. He thinks you had an accident at road-works traffic lights. But he knows something else is wrong, *really* wrong.'

'Has there been anything else on the television?' she asked.

'Do you want to know?'

'Yes.'

'Really?'

'Of course,' she said.

'They're still putting out appeals. They talk about people who might have been in the area, on the road where the boy ... this car or that...'

'Mine?' asked Leah. 'I mean yours?'

'No, not mine,' said Sarah.

'So they don't know anything?'

'The police ... they seem to think ... the child ... that he must have been abducted...'

31

'Oh, God! His poor parents, what they must be suffering, it's too terrible...'

Sarah moved closer, lay down beside Leah and held her friend in her arms. 'Yes, it is. But there's nothing we can do now. We've got to be strong. Together.'

'I can't go on.'

'You must.'

'Believe me, I can't.'

'We have no choice,' said Sarah.

'I've got to go and tell them. When I think of what we did to the car, that child's body in it. It's too horrible. I deserve to die.'

Sarah turned Leah's face to her own. 'Leah, you don't deserve to die. It was an accident. It wasn't your fault. The car wasn't insured, but that's not what caused it to happen. That was why you left there, that's all.'

Leah looked at her with incomprehension, the tears streaming down her hollow cheeks.

'But now it's not just you. It's me, too. You pleaded with me to help you that day. You begged me. If you tell the police now, what's going to happen to me?'

'Yes,' Leah acknowledged meekly. 'But I can't go on. Honestly, Sarah. Not like this.'

At the end of the month, Leah's mother and father drove up from Cardiff. They loaded their estate car with her books and clothes, bedding, records, tapes and disks, her word processor and stereo. As they pulled away, Sarah stood at the front door and raised a hand.

Leah sat in the back seat of the car like a child about to begin a reluctant journey, ashen-faced and motionless.

The only thing the college knew was that it was some sort of breakdown, perhaps compounded by ME, that cruel and debilitating illness that often seems to afflict the brightest, the most hard-working young women.

Five

Late September 2006

It was difficult to say just how long Sarah Clement had been missing – and, indeed, whether she was actually missing at all. Contrary to popular belief, the police don't have hard and fast rules regarding 'mis pers'. Every case is judged on its merits: a toddler's disappearance for twenty minutes in the park will spark an immediate investigation and search; a crack user with a muddled lifestyle will not be dealt with in quite the same way.

Some folk, perhaps those who are in troubled or awkward relationships, choose to disappear, and have no wish to be found. It's a sensitive area. If someone goes out for a loaf or a packet of fags and doesn't return, it's just possible that that's exactly what they intended to do.

On Saturday afternoon, a short, generously proportioned PC pressed herself up against the boat's varnished hatch doors and did her best to peer in through the little crack at the top of them, but she could see nothing from the angle that was afforded her.

She and her colleague walked around the boat and, bent double, leaned down and looked in through every porthole that did not have little curtains drawn against them.

Back at the hatch doors, the male PC took the solid padlock in his fist, gave it a shake, and passed on the benefit of his experience. 'If she's come to any harm, it's unlikely that someone's going to lock the hatch after them.' And then, as an aside, he added, 'And she can't be inside with the thing locked from outside.'

'Unless somebody's killed her,' ventured the woman PC quietly, and not entirely joking.

He smiled indulgently, and put the discussion to bed. 'She's not going to be chuffed if we break in and she comes back tonight, though, is she?'

'I suppose not,' agreed his colleague.

They walked back up the towpath to the bridge where they had parked their car outside Sunnyside, a red-brick, Victorian bed and breakfast that straddled the quiet road and the canal.

A man in powder-blue shorts and tee shirt was strimming the rough grass in the no man's land between the end of his nicely kept garden and the verge that fringed the waterside path.

'Hi,' said the policeman above the whining

34

sound of the machine that was scything through the tired grass.

'Hello,' said the man, switching off the strimmer. 'Is there a problem?'

'No, I don't think so,' said the cop. 'Just looking for the woman from the boat down there, *Ulysses*. You haven't seen her, have you?'

'No,' he said. 'We say hello, but I haven't seen her for a few days. Something wrong?'

'No, I don't think so,' said the man, 'just checking. Cheers, anyway.' They walked back up to their car.

'Nice shorts,' said the woman to her companion.

'Very,' he said.

They drove the couple of miles round to the pub at Cassiobury, parked the car on the lane and strolled down to the waterside gardens. Lunchtime trippers and boating holiday-makers were eating sandwiches and drinking shandies in the autumn sunshine, kids playing on the swings and obstacle course.

In the bar they asked the landlord about Sarah Clement. The man told them that he knew her, said she came to the pub maybe once every couple of weeks, usually alone, but occasionally with a younger woman. He'd heard she was a writer. She often sat over there, and he gestured to a table in the corner. She always had a pad with her and was often jotting down notes.

'Have you seen her this week?'

The man thought carefully. 'No. I haven't. But

the coal guy, Paul, he told me her boat looked empty, so I checked it out when I was taking the dog for a walk.'

'And?'

'And he was right: nobody home. Why? Is there a problem?'

'It's probably nothing, but her sister's been trying to reach her. She just wants us to check that she's OK.'

'Right,' said the man. 'Can you excuse me? I have to get these lunches out.'

'Sure,' said the cop and handed him a card. 'Give us a call if you see her, or if you hear anything. Anything at all.'

The man took the card and pushed it into his shirt pocket.

Unusually, Sarah had not phoned her sister. They called each other every couple of days unless one of them had said they were going to be away and, notwithstanding the independent nature of both women, and the slightly chaotic, even addled lifestyle of Sarah, they were sisters who did what they said they were going to do. When Charlotte had tried her mobile, there was no answer.

She tried repeatedly and, on Saturday lunch-time, by now really concerned, she had called the police from her home in Hebden Bridge.

When they reported back to her that evening, Charlotte, a woman who had never been intimidated by authority, made no bones about the fact that she was not impressed with their efforts to locate her sister. 'So all you've established is that the boat is locked? Is that right?'

'We made enquiries. We can't break in without authorization,' said the policeman.

'Please,' said Charlotte categorically, 'break in. I'm giving you permission. Sarah wouldn't go away without telling me.'

On Sunday morning, a sergeant from CID accompanied the woman PC back to the boat. As they stood on the towpath, a hire boat chugged by, the trippers silently peering at the plain-clothes policeman and his uniformed officer colleague.

There was a decent pile of plastic sacks of coal on the verge adjacent to the boat, a cycle chained to the roof, and a few pots of withered herbs and plants on the front deck and along the roof.

They'd brought nothing with them to force the lock and the man sauntered down to the next boat a hundred yards away. A man with a neck tattoo and a couple of piercings lent them a crowbar. The policeman ignored the half-dozen cannabis plants that were flourishing in buckets on his ramshackle houseboat. One good turn...

'Do you know her?' he asked.

'Yes, we say hello,' he offered. 'She keeps herself to herself mostly though. Most of us do.'

'Thanks,' said the cop. 'I'll pop this back in a bit.' And he ambled back down the towpath, swinging the two-foot crowbar beside him as he went.

With a deft motion, he forced the padlock from the hatch, eased open the doors and peered into the stifling boat. He stepped down inside, and suggested that his colleague remain outside.

The place smelled bad. The heat was overwhelming, and the headroom was ridiculous. Living here would give him a bad back in an hour.

He saw papers, books, tea cups, a half-full glass. He picked up the tumbler in his handkerchief and sniffed the flat gin there. There were dead flies on the porthole ledges, several ashtrays, all of them overflowing with thin rollup stubs, lighters, large Rizlas and a lump of black dope the size of an Oxo cube on the table.

He went through to the bedroom; the duvet was lying crumpled on the bed. More books, notepads, some computer disks spilling out of their tray; several CDs lying around the mini-stereo and on the floor; a couple of tee shirts draped over a chair.

In the galley he opened the refrigerator. It was like a laboratory fridge, containing a dozen plastic pots and foil-covered tubs. They looked like samples, cultures, something odd. He feared the worst, prised open the lid on one and brought his nose very warily down to the greenish, watery liquid there. Vegetable juice, just as the smudged hand-written label said. Where were the cans of Stella? The cheese, the butter and Pot Noodles?

He passed back through the main room and glanced at the computer screen with its page of shimmering text, the cursor patiently bumping there in the middle of a line. Amazing: all driven by batteries, he guessed.

As he stepped up into the back deck he banged his head hard against the hatch and exclaimed, 'Fucking hell!'

'You alright?' his colleague asked.

He said nothing.

'Anything to see?' she asked.

'Fuck,' he repeated, rubbing his scalp. 'No, nothing,' he eventually said, and pushed the doors together. He hung the broken padlock on the sturdy hasp. 'Serves her right if someone *does* break in,' he said, and walked back up the towpath to return the crowbar.

Six

Sunday October 1st 2006

The volunteers were a jolly bunch. For one weekend each month they'd travel from all over the country – some from as far as two hundred miles away – put up at country pubs, bed and breakfasts and village halls, and then spend seven or eight hours of each day hacking down undergrowth, digging out mud and marsh weeds and feeding the bonfires that always smoked and flickered along the sides of overgrown canals.

Wearing hard hats and yellow vests over their shirts and jumpers, this disparate crew of bank managers and teachers, IT consultants and shelf stackers, accountants, pensioners and even a student or two had, after years of friendly toil together, developed a warm rapport, their only common denominator being their affection for these largely forgotten feats of eighteenth-century engineering.

However, as train drivers tend to regard train spotters, those dejected-looking men who stand on railway platforms with notebooks in their hands – people who travel the rail network with the Zen-like attitude of those for whom the journey is everything, the destination immaterial – so were canal enthusiasts seen by British Waterways employees: harmless folk, no doubt, but surely a little crazy for all that.

For several months now, through three seasons and all weathers, the group had been working on a long-abandoned branch of the Grand Union Canal, close to the hamlet of Batchworth in Hertfordshire.

They'd cleared the thickest of the matted undergrowth, removed ivy, pollarded the willow, and cut back the elder, thorn and sloe. The former towpath was now discernible, the half-submerged skeleton of a long-abandoned butty revealed, and the huge water-edge wash stones exposed to the pale autumn sun for the first time in decades.

Observing this good-natured toil, it was almost beyond comprehension that, some two hundred years ago, this tranquil place had been the throbbing construction site of its day. With no health and safety regulations, no medical provision, schooling or additional accommodation, and with little prior warning, hundreds of men, women and children had once descended on this place to work, fight, whore, drink and loot.

In the wake of the engineering elite, whose job it was to plan and oversee the progress of their enterprises, trudged the tribe of camp followers: miners to sink ventilation shafts; masons to build bridges and line tunnel walls, and carpenters to fashion massive timbers into lock gates, locks that would facilitate a logic-defying miracle, the movement of water – or at least the craft that floated thereon – uphill.

But most of the workforce were labourers, itinerant workers, puddlers to make the bottom of the cut watertight and, most numerous of all, those men who wielded the picks and shovels and wheelbarrows, the people who shifted the earth and rocks and stones through which the canal was inexorably driven.

Like the biggest engineering projects of today – the M25, a new tube line or a Channel Tunnel rail link – man will not be denied. He sets forth with dogged obduracy and faces down every obstacle until his diligence sees him through. Notwithstanding every setback, the Grand Union Canal had, finally, been driven through these woods and fields and meadows until it had emerged at Paddington Basin in the capital city.

And now, on this Sunday afternoon, an ancient yellow digger was chugging and smoking its way down through the stumps and fires towards the brackish water's edge, to begin scooping out the mud and detritus of a hundred years' neglect.

People's motives are often ambiguous. Many of these volunteers *did* love the canals. But others simply felt sufficiently warm towards wives, husbands or partners to join them in their beloved pastime.

And, of course, like the joiners of a dozen other activities, from amateur dramatics to salsa and skating, from Gilbert and Sullivan to the Open University, there are always people in the group who can actually take or leave summer school, Chekhov and Pirandello, for what they are really looking for is something even harder to find than a decent essay mark or triumphant first-night performance: they are here because they are looking for love.

A widow or divorcee perhaps; a youngster who doesn't care for discos and wine bars, feels ill at ease at the water cooler in the office, or in the bustling staffroom. But maybe here, amidst the sexless banter, the wood smoke, tea and sandwiches, there is a partner to be found.

Just up from Batchworth, not far from the canal-side reservoir that stored the water needed to replenish the canal's supply – a supply that was constantly depleted by leaks, evaporation and, most profligate of all, the thousands of gallons that flowed away downstream each time a boat went through a lock – the volunteers sat around and took their afternoon break.

Schoolteacher Jan, a thirty-six-year-old in a woolly hat and combat pants with half a dozen pockets, went into the sea-container where everything of value on the site was securely stored. There were lunchboxes and wet-weather clothes, scythes and rakes, shovels and bow saws, boots and kettles, gas cylinders to make tea and fry bacon, even a visitors' log to record who came on and off the site, and a sheet of Health and Safety regulations and insurance requirements pinned to the wall.

Jan picked up her cigarettes and wandered away along the newly exposed towpath. One of only two smokers amongst the twenty-odd volunteers, notwithstanding the good-natured mockery that accompanied her lighting up in their midst, she still felt uncomfortable each time she gave in to her 'filthy' habit.

She was a woman who shouldn't really have been a smoker, she knew that. She was too intelligent, wholly aware of the dangers of the habit – and anyway, she was convinced that her life was not so hollow that she needed the prop of tobacco and cigarette smoke about her.

Head of the geography department in a big secondary school in Stroud, a place where she managed the most difficult of pupils, Jan Mc-Avoy had good classroom discipline, achieved excellent exam results, and her colleagues appeared to both like and respect her.

But what Jan McAvoy didn't have in her life was the person that she would have wanted there: a special person, a significant other. Married at twenty, she and her husband had broken up only four years later when he confessed to an affair with his lab assistant at the school where he was teaching chemistry.

Jan hadn't grieved for the relationship: she'd begun to find him as tedious as he appeared to find her irritating. After only eighteen months together, it was clear that they had made a mistake, that they had little or nothing in common. He liked sport, playing it and watching it. She didn't. He never read a novel, only work-related magazine articles. She was a reader who liked the theatre and travel. He didn't. They shouldn't have got married and neither of them was quite sure why they had. Some sort of safety and mutual reassurance, perhaps. It had proven anything but, and now he was with his lab assistant and Jan was alone.

Her few cigarettes a day were an act of defiant independence, a sort of 'screw you!' to a world that appeared reluctant to send her a man with whom she could get along in a world apparently filled with people who did get along together. She felt a little aggrieved: why *was* she alone? Sucking the smoke down was a gesture that allowed her to say, 'You see, I might be alone, but I am in control, and yes, I can even hurt myself, if I so wish.'

Unfortunately, the only male who was within

ten years of her own age, and with whom she could possibly conceive of having anything more than a conversation, was Steve, an IT consultant who drove down from Leamington Spa each month and slept in his campervan. But alas, in the few months that they had known one another, he had shown absolutely no interest in her.

If she were to put the most optimistic gloss on their exchanges, it would be that the man, who appeared shy and withdrawn in the group, appeared to be even more maladroit on those very few occasions when the two of them had found themselves working together on cutting through undergrowth or grubbing up a tree stump.

Maybe he was so smitten with her that he could barely function when they were in close proximity? But she thought not. Even as she had left the big circle of friends and like-minded souls a few minutes ago, Steve had been sitting just a little out of the circle, a computer geek's magazine on his knee, a mug of tea in his hand, ostensibly in the group, but not really a part of it. Oh, well, she thought, maybe he was just as he seemed: another tragic IT case.

Two hundred yards up the path, where the canal branch joined the Grand Union, a couple of young men speaking with eastern-European accents passed her. She sat on the verge beside the pound and lit a Silk Cut.

Jan had pulled so many bits of rubbish from the still waters of overgrown canals in the last

two years that she knew precisely the archae-
ology of a boat's long-abandoned iron frame,
could delineate a broken hull from a forty-five-
gallon rusting barrel.

What she saw now, just beneath the surface of
the water, was neither of these.

She didn't finish her cigarette. She crushed it
beneath her Caterpillar boot and took a step
towards the water. She crouched down to look
across its surface and, without the reflection of
the late-afternoon sun upon it, could see that
something was billowing there, just beneath the
water.

She got to her feet, steadied herself, looked up
and down the canal that stretched away into the
distance, and walked slowly back to her colleagues.

The digger was at the towpath edge, engine
running, still chugging away as the driver sat
with the other volunteers, chatting.

Jan approached the team leader and said
quietly, 'Jeff, can I have a word?'

'Sure,' he said, a little surprised by the formal-
ity of the request. He arched his back as he got
to his feet and they took a few steps away from
the group, mug in hand. Steve glanced up from
his magazine and watched them go.

'What's up, Jan?' he asked as he put the tip of
his index finger into his tea and flicked an insect
away. 'What is it?'

'There's a body in the pound, Jeff. I think
we'd better call the police.'

'A body?' he replied.

'I think it's a woman's body,' she said. 'Yes, we should call the police.'

Seven

Wednesday October 4th 2006

'So, where's the phantom cyclist?' asked DI Frank Kavanagh.

'I'll take that as a hello,' replied Salt.

'How are you, Constable?'

'Not bad, thank you, Inspector. Yourself?'

'Drink?'

'Tomato juice, please.'

'Worcester sauce?'

The couple were pleased to see one another. It had been over two weeks.

'You look nice, Jane,' he said, putting her juice down on the table.

And she did. Her dark hair worn short made her look funky and sort of gung-ho, ready for action in a way that he found attractive.

Anaemic cover girls and fake-tan magazine women these days had the flawless – invariably blonde – featureless beauty that he found entirely resistible. Salt was no freak, but there was something about her slightly quirky appearance that was both sexy and full of character. Especially to him.

'Thank you,' she said. 'You're looking pretty good yourself.'

'Eye of the beholder, I'm sure,' he said. 'But thanks, anyway.' They touched glasses.

The likelihood of an imminent terrorist attack on London had eventually been downgraded by one level. Every sentient being knew that there would be another attack – almost certainly more than one – but for now there was no intelligence to suggest that the current threat was imminent, and so dozens of the detectives who had been transferred to deal with the crisis just a few months ago had now been stood down and returned to normal duties.

And they were needed. Just because Britain was being attacked from within – a frightened, divided nation, no matter what community leaders said on the airwaves – it didn't mean that rapists and murderers weren't still driven by their own rapacious and murderous urges.

No, the domestic crime rate remained constant, even as the headlines were dominated by the arrests and detention of terror suspects throughout the land.

Rickmansworth *was* just about in Kavanagh's outer-London patch, but anyway, with so many cops being redeployed, there was something of the legal fraternity's taxi-rank approach to cases: first come, first served, no matter what the exact nature of the crime.

OK, there were limits. Kavanagh's boss, Assistant Chief Constable Hyland, wasn't going to put Kavanagh and his ilk – experienced cops with the successful prosecution of dozens of serious crimes behind them – on a Harlesden mugging or an Oxford Street shoplifting case, but the fact was, with very few exceptions, the investigation of one murder was conducted very much like another.

Notwithstanding maverick TV cops and lurid, crackpot fiction, with bible-spouting, psychopathic serial killers at their depraved work, it was only in the movies that these things were solved by a lucky sighting or an inspired hunch. They were solved by the book – the patient, thorough, painstaking, costly, time-consuming approach that had evolved over decades. And why had it evolved? Because it worked.

From the witness interviews to the door-stepping; the profiling to the reconstructions; the press conference to the bereaved's staged – and often, as events subsequently proved, fake – TV appearance; the collection of evidence and amassing of computerized data, and the supply of information from the street through the network of informers that *every* cop who was punching his weight cultivated, *these* were the steps in the well-ordered march that invariably led to arrest and, eventually, conviction.

Kavanagh glanced at his watch; the full briefing he had asked for wasn't until two o'clock. 'So, what about Lance Armstrong?' he continued.

'Lance who?' queried Salt.

'Keep up, Jane. He's won the Tour de France about a dozen times...'

'Oh, right,' she offered.

'So who is he, this mystery biker?' pursued Kavanagh. 'And where's he gone?'

'He's certainly a mystery,' replied Salt. 'A day after the news of Clement's death was made public, these two youngsters got in touch to say they saw a man cycling the towpath.'

'Where?'

'Up the canal, towards Tring. They use that route regularly, and they'd never seen him before, and then he completely disappeared, just about the time that we think Sarah Clement was killed.'

'Do you reckon he knows we're looking for him?' asked the inspector.

'We only put out the appeal for him to come forward last night, but it's been very widely covered.'

'Maybe he doesn't watch the news?' suggested Kavanagh.

'Or read a paper?' countered Salt. '*Or* listen to the radio?'

'Cyclists ... you know...' he said inconclusively.

'Know what?' she replied.

'Well, you know how they are.'

'How are they?' she pursued.

'Well, you know, they can be a bit...'

'Bit what? I *like* cyclists. I like bikes,' she added. 'I've got one. You have, too, as I recall, Frank.'

'It's got a puncture,' he said disconsolately.

'The only cyclists I don't like are the ones that

ride like maniacs on the pavement. I'd book 'em,' she said firmly.

'You should, Constable,' he suggested. 'You're a copper, remember?'

'Actually, I don't have time to arrest some dispatch rider trying to run me over outside Blockbuster when I'm trying to catch the guy who's robbing the bank next door,' she rejoined.

'All I'm saying is,' continued Kavanagh, 'I bet when we find this guy, whether he's involved with our body in the canal or not, he'll be some sort of nutcase.'

'It's you that's nuts, Frank. You've been locked away in an office too long.'

'Boris Johnson rides a bike,' he added. 'And look at him. Cameron, too...'

'I think you'll find that two Tory politicians are not *quite* a representative sample,' she said.

'OK, we'll up the ante on tracing him. What else have we got on the dead woman?' he asked.

'Well, initial reports on her background suggest she's done quite a lot of dating – on the internet, personal ads in the paper, that kind of thing,' she said.

'That's gonna be easy,' he mocked. 'They're mostly nuts, too.'

'As I recall, Frank, the first time you and I spent an evening together, we sat in your flat in Crouch End whilst *I* screened the women who'd responded to *your* ad in the previous week's *Guardian*.'

'Yes, I remember that,' he said, putting his hand on her knee beneath the table.

51

'So?' she asked.

'So, that was different.'

'Different? Why?' she asked, mock gauche.

''Cause I'm not nuts. I'm the exception that proves the rule. And anyway, look, I ended up with you. And you weren't advertising!'

'Maybe *I'm* the one who was nuts. I should have fixed you up with one of those *Guardian* woman instead of taking pity on you myself...'

'Pity?' he exclaimed.

'You were – if you care to remember – a complete wreck. You'd virtually had a nervous breakdown, and if you'd not been trying to catch a bloke who was killing his wife's former lovers, you'd probably have killed your *own* ex-wife. You'd have been having porridge for breakfast for the rest of your natural.'

'I like porridge,' he said. 'Right, Sarah Clement,' he said to change the subject. 'She was a writer? What do we know about her?'

'You know the best-seller she wrote?' Salt asked.

'Of course,' he said.

'Did you read it?' she asked.

'Yes, I think so. It was a long time ago. It wasn't quite *Catch-22,* but it was one of those books that everyone read at the time.'

'And still do, apparently,' confirmed Salt. 'Her publisher says it still sells several hundred copies every month.'

'She was pretty well-off, then?' asked the inspector.

'Yes. Not J.K. Rowling, but apparently the

royalty cheques come bouncing along.'

'And what did she spend it on?' he asked.

'Nothing obvious. Didn't go away much. Drank a bit, smoked a good deal of dope—'

'For inspiration?' he interrupted.

'Well, if it was, it didn't seem to be working.'

'How do you mean?'

'She hadn't had much success since *The House of Loss* in 1993.'

'Really?'

'Apparently not. I phoned her former agent. He hadn't placed anything for her for years, literally. There was a second novel, a year or two after the big one, which didn't do much, then a couple of short stories, a radio play, and that's about it.'

She opened her pocket book and flipped through the pages as he watched her closely. 'Giles Curran – that's the agent – he says he's seen it before: writer says everything she's got to say in that first big book, and then spends the rest of her life trying – and usually failing – to match it.'

'Sounds grim,' said Kavanagh. 'Anything else about her?'

'Well, like I say, she was doing quite a bit of dating, and as well as the dope and the booze, apparently she was on Prozac to try and straighten out her moods. And then there was something called...' She checked her pocket book again. 'Zopiclone to help her sleep...'

'And now she's got the big sleep – got herself killed, eh?' he added. He drained his gin and

53

tonic. 'Why do you think someone would want to kill her, Jane?'

'Well, it doesn't look impetuous,' said Salt. 'A burglary gone wrong, that kind of thing. None of the usual signs, and nothing taken.'

'Sexual assault?' he asked.

'Initial examination suggests not. They're checking for DNA, of course, but she'd been in the water for a while, possibly too long for there to be anything useful.'

'So, what about these dating contacts?' he asked, getting to his feet.

'It's not going to be easy,' she said. 'A good deal of them were internet connections. People use pseudonyms, some of them are married, just looking for a bit on the side, and they're often concealing all sorts of stuff, including their real identities. They're not easily traceable, not like newspaper advertisers. But the computer gurus are on the case, trying to uncover traces and footprints from email, mobile-phone records and all that stuff.'

'Rather them than me,' said Kavanagh, a Luddite who could just about buy a railway ticket on the internet, but still preferred to queue at Waterloo or King's Cross and speak to a human being. 'Anything else?' he said, helping her with her jacket.

'Nothing specific. There's a good number of foreign workers employed on one of the farms that skirts the canal – we'll have to look into them. And we're checking out the local low life, anyone in the Watford, Rickmansworth, Berkhamsted triangle with a record of preying on single women – flashers, that kind of stuff – also anyone in the area who's been released from prison recently. Oh, yes,' she added as an afterthought, 'the local force are trying to find out whoever it was she got her dope from.'

'Everybody smokes now,' he said. 'It'll be available in Tesco soon.'

'You should be so lucky,' she said, giving him a disapproving look.

'Oh, yes, last of the big junkies, eh? You know me, Jane. I just like a little joint at bedtime occasionally. But it's getting impossible these days. I can't get anything that's mild enough to just give me a good night's sleep. It's all this super-strength stuff. I can't be doing with it...'

'I'll see what I can do, Frank. Next time I arrest some twelve-year-old with a quarter ounce of Moroccan, I'll confiscate it for you. How's that?'

'Ho, ho. Right, we'd better get over to the briefing. Anything else you've got?' he asked.

'The local landlord was on hello terms; a bed and breakfast bloke nearby was the same, and there's a guy, a sort of boating coalman with a City background, who knows her a bit. Maybe they had something going on? But I think the main man we could do with tracing is this missing cyclist.'

'Are the witnesses reliable? He did really exist, did he, this bloke?' he asked as he held open the door of the pub.

'Two fifteen-year-olds on their way to school,'

55

she replied. 'They seem sensible enough lads. They say he'd got bags on the back of his bike.'

'Panniers?' Kavanagh asked as they stood at the edge of the busy road.

'Well, they didn't exactly use that word,' said Salt. 'It's 2006, Frank. I think they said "bags".'

'Camping gear?' queried the inspector.

'Maybe,' she said.

'There's fields all around,' he shouted against the noise of the traffic. 'If he was camping, he'll have left some trace.'

'Yes, I guess so,' she agreed as they nipped across the busy road.

'Right,' he said as, with professional discretion, they parted a couple of hundred yards away from the police station HQ. 'Speak later, Jane.'

'Bye, take care,' was all she said.

Eight

October 2006

At the briefing, Kavanagh was introduced to the assembled team by the man from whom he was taking over, acting-Inspector Ray Durham.

'I want to thank Ray here for handling things thus far. They haven't brought me in because he wasn't doing a good job; they've moved me over here because, for the time being at least, the threat level on the terror front is down, and they don't want dozens of us marking time and getting up to no good around Whitehall.'

'Thanks, Ray.' There was a desultory round of applause for their erstwhile superior, but it was early days for any kind of glad-handing.

The two men sat together at the front, flanked by their boss, ACC Hyland, whilst the investigating officers gave their briefs. Kavanagh took the occasional note, but there was little that Salt hadn't told him that needed to be run into the mix. Yes, door-to-door was continuing, albeit on a canal – the local shop; the two closest pubs; the bed and breakfast, a former weighbridge and toll house that now looked cosy, snug dwellings dotted along the towpath in the immediate vicinity, and the couple of farms whose fields skirted the area. The workforces of these places, mostly east-European fruit and vegetable pickers, would all have to be interviewed.

A fingertip search of the areas adjacent to both the site where her body had been discovered, and Sarah Clement's boat, was being undertaken under the supervision of one of the few senior officers not actually present in the room.

At that very moment, men and women in forensic suits with tape and markers, prongs and pickers, were examining every blade of grass for two hundred yards in each direction around both places.

Looking for what, no one knew. Anything out of the ordinary: a footprint, a tissue, a bit of discarded clothing, a scrap of paper, an apple core, a cigarette end. Anything. By the book. And that was the trouble. *Everything* had to be ruled in, for the time being, at least.

And then came the pathologist's report on Sarah Clement's actual death. 'We've a reasonable notion of when Sarah Clement died,' began Doctor Rice. 'Her email and mobile telephone records tell us there were no calls or messages made or received after Wednesday evening, September the twenty-seventh. So, we're looking at any time after that.'

'Assuming it wasn't someone else dealing with her mail or picking up her calls,' said Scrivener.

'It's possible, of course,' conceded the doctor. 'Cause of death,' she went on, 'was drowning. Place of death: unknown. Circumstances surrounding the woman's death? The presence of canal water in her lungs is clear testimony to the fact that she was alive when she entered the water. Whilst suicide cannot be entirely ruled out, it seems highly unlikely, unless it was assisted: tightly knotted to the woman's right wrist was a long silk scarf, the other end of which was tied to a piece of steel rail or girder, about a metre long and weighing nearly eighty kilos.'

'What's that in old money?' asked Detective Sergeant Joe Lavendar.

'It's about thirteen stone, give or take,' said Rice. 'It might be possible to achieve this without assistance, but it would be difficult and is, I think, highly unlikely. Especially as we understand that Sarah Clement was right-handed – you wouldn't generally use your "other" hand to tie something to yourself, given the choice. If it was murder, the rail was probably used by her killer to ensure that the woman remained anchored to the bottom of the canal. There is a pile of identical lengths of steel some twenty yards from the canal pound, and it seems likely that the woman's killer took advantage of their presence in attaching one to the woman. He or she must have assumed that the body would, thereby, remain beneath the surface.

'To a large extent the cold water arrested decomposition. If she did die on Wednesday, or possibly Thursday, for example, she would have been in the water for some four days. In more favourable, i.e. warmer, circumstances, the bacteria in the intestines produce gas which would bloat the body and, subsequently, make the tongue, breasts and eyes swell and protrude, eventually pushing the intestines out through the rectum.

'In this case, the process was somewhat inhibited by the temperature, but there was still some accumulation of gas, and this had the effect of inflating the corpse until it eventually tried to rise, ballooning up through the water until, restrained by the anchor, it could rise no further and remained just a little beneath the surface, which is where her body was spotted by the woman who found it.

'Given the considerable amount of alcohol in

the woman's bloodstream, an accident of some kind wouldn't normally be ruled out, but the steel girder attached to her wrist rather puts paid to that notion,' she added drily.

And then came the most startling fact from the pathologist. 'Although there was some deterioration of soft tissue due to immersion, there appears to be little indication of struggle or resistance. There is slight bruising to the woman's left wrist, but apart from that, no evidence of restraint. There were no collateral injuries whatsoever on the deceased's hands, arms, ankles or legs. There is no skin or fibres, no hair or any other human or inert material beneath her fingernails, the sort of thing that we would normally expect to find there if there had been a struggle. In fact, Sarah Clement appears to have died without attempting to fight her killer in any way.

'In conclusion, therefore, whilst the manner of the woman's death can be reasonably conjectured, the circumstances surrounding it cannot.' Doctor Petra Rice closed her folder and sat down.

Kavanagh got to his feet and said soberly, but a little facetiously, 'If anyone has any suggestion as to why Sarah Clement didn't act as every other murder victim in the history of the world has acted, I'd be glad if you'd share your thoughts with us. Even suicides – and I'm not talking fakers, help-seekers, teenage angsters; I mean people who are absolutely intent upon their own self-destruction – they always struggle at the end. It's human nature to "rage against the dying of the light..."

'A few years ago now, a poor sod who'd killed both his young kids when his wife said she was leaving him for another bloke, drove his car into Ullswater. But he *knew* that he'd try and get out. So what did he do? He got hold of the best pair of handcuffs he could from the local sex shop and cuffed himself to the steering wheel.'

'And?' said someone from the middle of the room.

'And when we pulled the car out, he was still held there, attached to the wheel of his Mondeo, but he'd broken both his wrists and smashed his ankles to the bone as he'd fought to escape from that car. Just as he knew he would. And yet he still did it. Still tried to get free. It's human nature.' There was a long pause, and then he added, turning to her picture on the evidence wall behind him, 'Sarah Clement was murdered, so why didn't she do the same?'

There was complete silence in the room.

'Right,' said Kavanagh. 'I'll come to the mystery cyclist in a bit, but first of all, whilst nothing's ever guaranteed, the one thing we can be reasonably sure of here is that we've got a one-off killing. We're not in multiple killer territory: there's no violence to speak of and, as far as we know, there's no sexual assault. The motive for this killing lies elsewhere and, as ever, if we find that we're halfway home.

'Sarah Clement's death is not part of some bigger picture; this is not serial-killer stuff.

61

Leave all that to the fiction writers. We've none of the markers: no souvenirs taken, no degradation of the body and, as I say, best guess is no sexual assault, either. With patient leg-work, thorough background checks and local intelligence, we'll find the motive for what's happened, and that'll lead us to the killer.

'I'm going to get back to the crime scene and search area, see how that's shaping up. You're already in your teams, but before we break, I'm going to hand over to Jenni Clough for a few minutes. She's the psychologist on this enquiry and she's got a couple of things she wants to run by us about Sarah Clement's personal life.'

Clough got to her feet. 'Thus far, from what we know, it seems that Ms Clement had a pretty active dating life. Nothing wrong with that, and I don't want to insult anyone sitting in this room. I know the statistics – policemen and women have more than their share of failed marriages and divorce – but I just want to say that all the research – and there's been lots of it done – points to the fact that excessive promiscuity, like excessive gambling or, indeed, excess of any other sort, is invariably a substitute for something else that the subject feels is missing from his or her life. In a way, it's a sort of self-harm, a longing to fill a void in the person's psyche. It seems that Sarah Clement had taken a lot of lovers but, whatever it was that she was looking for from those people, she doesn't seem to have found it.

'At this very early stage, without wishing to go out on a limb, and certainly not to preclude other areas of enquiry, it would be my initial contention that what we need to find is just what it was that she was looking for. For the time being, at least, that's where I'll be focusing my initial enquiries and doing background research. Thank you,' she said, and sat down.

'Right,' said Kavanagh briskly. 'Let's pick it up again. Back to thorough house-to-house. DC Jackie Marsh and DS Joe Lavendar are in charge of the dating contacts trail. We need to reach as many of the blokes she's been seeing as we can. Put out a media appeal. Give anyone she's been in touch with the opportunity to come forward in confidence – some of them are bound to have been playing away – before we start embarrassing them with a knock at the door. That should flush a few out. Contact as many as you can, Jackie. Go back a year initially, and if that turns up nothing, we'll make it two. Get as full a picture as possible.

'DCs Robbie Hinton and Trish Gregory, you follow through on the family. The parents are both deceased, but the sister who originally contacted us is up in Hebden Bridge in Yorkshire. Get up there and see what she knows about Sarah.

'DC Salt's going over to Keele to speak to her former tutors – in particular a bloke called Hopwood who taught the writing course she did as a postgraduate.

'We've got a couple of translators coming up

to help us get through to the migrant workers on the farms. We'll speak to them as a group and then begin individual interviews with them.

'Tony,' Kavanagh faced DC Tony Mullin, 'will you and Gordon start getting around the canal volunteers? I'm due to speak to the woman myself who found the body tomorrow morning. What's her name, Ray?'

'Jan. Jan McAvoy,' replied Durham. 'She's a school teacher.'

'Right,' continued Kavanagh. 'I want you to do thorough checks on the backgrounds of these canal folk, make sure they're all kosher and don't have anything going on that we should know about. Any questions?'

'Yes, what about the cyclist?' asked DC Pat Scrivener.

'Yes, right now he's our priority,' replied Kavanagh. 'It might be nothing, but this bloke's spotted a way up the towpath from Clement's boat, and then he seems to go AWOL. For obvious reasons, he's the one we need to speak to.'

Kavanagh turned to Phil Jervis, the young press officer who was taking responsibility for his first full case. 'Phil's briefing the media for the six o'clock TV and radio broadcasts. It's time for us to go public on some of what we've got – not everything, of course, but a deal of it, to keep the thing hot, and flush out anyone we can who's got anything that might help us with our enquiries. Phil, dangle a bit of a carrot. Tell your press contacts we'll give 'em a bite of something special if they'll run big with the

64

story for another day or two...'

'Yes, Inspector,' said Jervis. 'And what *will* we give them?' he asked, pen poised above his yellow legal pad.

'Fuck knows,' said Kavanagh.

'Thank you,' said Jervis. This was no Hendon Police College training stint. It was very early days of the real thing, and the young man in the nifty suit, gelled hair and decent tie was already seeing his reputation for fair dealing with the press go out the window.

Kavanagh went on, 'Hopefully we might jog someone's memory, or even get Bikerman himself to come out from wherever he's lying low. There's got to be some reason for his disappearance ... let's just hope he's not in the cut, too.' He turned towards the door. 'OK, let's get on with it.'

'Frank?' said ACC Michael Hyland quietly, and with a familiarity that always made Kavanagh feel deeply uneasy.

'Sir?' said Kavanagh as he stood there and shuffled reports into his briefcase at the front of the room.

'Just a quick word, please, if you don't mind. My office, when you're ready.' The ACC extended his arm, implying that he expected him to be ready right now.

With some people, it was easy to identify what grated, but Kavanagh could never quite nail just what it was about his boss that made him feel so discomfited. The man was, truly, unexceptionable. You could rarely quarrel with what he said, and he was invariably courteous to those around him, whether taking part in a TV studio debate or giving evidence before a House of Commons select committee hearing.

Perhaps that was it, thought Kavanagh as he followed the man's straight back, immaculate uniform and measured stride from the room. Perhaps it was the very fact that, although his boss irritated him, the inspector couldn't quite put his finger on *why*.

A couple of years previously, Hyland had been widely tipped as successor to the first UK drugs tsar but, almost overnight, the government's then position on drugs – to whit, zero tolerance – had been discarded in favour of an altogether more liberal approach, a change of policy that left almost everyone confused, and left Hyland exactly where he had been before: as an Assistant Chief Constable.

You could now buy skunk at Brixton tube as readily as a ticket for the Ritzy Cinema across the road or a pint of Grolsch, something that appeared to have made little difference to anyone, with the possible exception of Hyland who had seen his putative position – quite literally in this case – go up in smoke.

For the time being, then, the ACC was in a sort of limbo as he bided his time and awaited developments. Perhaps there would be yet another change of policy when a new Home Secretary was in post. In any event, in this hinterland, the man presumably felt that the most expedient thing he could do would be to continue to look smart, speak quietly, with both authority and due deference, and do nothing at all that might draw attention to himself in any kind of negative light.

This was a murder enquiry, and the victim, whilst no longer exactly in the public eye, was someone whom some of the more thoughtful movers and shakers had actually heard of, albeit a few years ago now. Hyland therefore wanted there to be no doubt that he expected it to be handled expeditiously. Hence his need for a word with DI Kavanagh.

The men sat opposite one another at Hyland's immaculately ordered desk.

'Frank, you're sure?' he began reasonably. 'This murder of Sarah Clement, a one-off?'

'Well, as you know, sir, nothing's ever certain,' said Kavanagh. 'But given all the evidence, I'd certainly say it looks like it.'

Hyland nodded sagely and eventually said, 'Well, if you say so, Frank. So, let's get it dealt with, eh? Keep up the pressure, motivate the staff, and let's get a result. Sooner rather than later is what we'd be looking for. Anything you need, and of course if there's anything you want to run past me, I'm here.'

The man seemed to think that his few words of encouragement would sprinkle some kind of investigative fairy dust over proceedings and facilitate the enquiry's speedy conclusion. Perhaps he was expecting a word of thanks, thought the inspector as he continued to sit there.

'And, Frank? Good luck,' Hyland said. 'That will be all.'

'Thank you, sir,' said Kavanagh as he left the room with a barely contained sigh.

Nine

June 2006

The coach had left at dawn, seven hours previously, from the shipyard city of Gdansk, right up on the Baltic coast.

Just after two o'clock in the afternoon, Katrina passed her suitcase to the driver, who stowed it away but didn't utter one word to her or any of the other dozen passengers who joined the vehicle at the bus station in Poznan in central Poland.

She made her way up the aisle. No one moved; the other passengers, all of them young people, mostly in their early twenties, stayed curled up in their seats, lolled awkwardly in their places, obdurately refusing to move the newspapers, magazines and drinks cans that littered the vacant seats adjacent to them.

It was a battle of wills: one concession to civility now, and you jeopardized that (possibly) free seat all the way to London, some twenty-one hours away.

Halfway up the coach, Katrina stood in the aisle and looked down at a pale youngster who stared stonily out of the window. The older woman didn't deign to speak, nor even summon a facetious cough. She just stood there, looking down as the girl stared out into the bleak space of the gloomy bus station. Eventually, tacitly accepting defeat, the young woman removed her magazines and little rucksack, and Katrina took the seat beside her.

Despite their inauspicious start, the women could hardly sit this close together and travel in silence. As they trundled through the pine-forest-fringed roads towards the border with Germany, they made desultory enquiries of one another. Where was each of them heading? Did they have work? Friends? Relatives? Was accommodation lined up for them in Britain and, equally importantly, just how well did each of them speak the language of their soon-to-be adopted country?

Some clichés, it appeared, were true. The young girl knew several of the others on the coach, and there was, indeed, a plumber on board, as well as a couple of plasterers. But most of them were headed to the farms of East Anglia where work was plentiful and the cost of living cheap.

Hanna, Katrina's travelling companion, had worked in an import/export office in Poznan, had spoken English on the phone daily, sent faxes and emails in that language, and was clearly proficient.

The more they talked, the more Katrina felt inadequate. She was not without education. She had a college degree, but she'd graduated twenty years ago, when everything in Poland – when everything everywhere – had been very different. And what had she done with her degree? She'd got married and worked behind the counter in her former husband's paint and wallpaper shop in a remote suburb of the city. For her, this whole venture – moving to a foreign country, looking for work, staying, initially at least, with friends of friends, people much younger than herself, and whom she barely knew – was a daunting prospect.

Yes, Polish newspapers and magazines had had a surfeit of articles for years now about the riches to be found in the UK. The country was crying out for reliable labour, the wages were good and the natives, apparently, were friendly.

And yes, of course, to speak the language would be a bonus, and anyone travelling to Britain would be well advised to learn English but, frankly, Katrina, desperate to escape her impoverished country and the legacy of a second failed marriage had wondered how much English you really need to be able to pick lettuce or serve coffee and burgers in a bright McDonalds.

But this was no magazine article: this was stark reality, an airless bus heading inexorably west at a steady eighty kilometres an hour; a forty-five-year-old woman surrounded by confident youngsters. For her, there was no sense of excitement; Katrina only felt anxious, ill-prepared and not a little afraid.

In fact, the tide was just, almost imperceptibly, beginning to turn. And one or two prescient reporters, rather than continue to file more lazy stories that echoed the party line, had started to write the kind of copy that made less comfortable reading for would-be migrants. Stories of a warm welcome, good wages and comfortable living had started to metamorphose into a more ambivalent account of life in the UK. Many of the natives, it now seemed, were finding themselves less engaged by the novelty of foreign accents in the supermarket aisles and post office queues. The person called into the GP's consulting room was as likely to be from Hungary as Hounslow, Krakow as Kettering. Soon, those overheard snatches of conversation on the street no longer beguiled, but began to irk.

The new arrivals' reputation for reliability, due diligence at work and a propensity to accept any overtime that was offered might have endeared them to their hard-pressed employers, but the indigenous workforce were more inclined to regard them as some sort of threat.

In Rickmansworth, when an enterprising woman from Bydgoszcz rented premises and opened a Polish shop there, importing the jam, sausage, barszcz, black bread and meatballs that the immigrants hankered after, for some of the town's residents, this wasn't an example of retail diversity and innovative multi-culturalism; it was the last straw.

People actually began to articulate their thoughts: 'We don't want a Polish shop here. We don't mind these people, but if they want to be here, why don't they buy pizza and Indian take-aways like the rest of us?'

The simmering antipathy of only a year or two ago was in danger of turning into overt hostility, and nowadays the window glass of Angelika Patula's shop was smashed so regularly that the woman had been forced to put crude plywood shutters to it every evening when she closed.

Just after lunchtime on the following day, after an hour on the choppy English Channel and a couple more spent driving through the fields of Kent, the new arrivals began the stop-start final stint into the city.

The traffic-clogged A2, the streets of east London and the eerie light of the Blackwall tunnel didn't look quite like the promised land that most of them had imagined. Where were the horse guards and palaces, the domed churches and golden-stone parliaments, the broad and leafy Malls?

At two o'clock, when the bus finally pulled into Victoria bus station, many of them made their weary way down Buckingham Palace Road to the tube station. Katrina rode out to Baker Street, and from there took the Metropolitan line to Watford.

The friends of friends, nine of them sharing a terraced house in the outer-London town, felt a little sorry for the older woman, but the fact was

Katrina's manner conveyed not the timorousness that she actually felt, but an apparent self-assuredness that made her appear not so much shy as forbidding. Very soon the consensus was they would all be relieved when the woman was gone from their midst.

By the end of the week, having scoured the classified ads in the local newspaper, lodged her details with all of the employment agencies in the town, visited the Job Centre twice each day, and phoned several of the numbers that appeared on postcards and scraps of paper stuck in the window of the Polish shop, Katrina was offered work on a nearby farm. She could live in, as did many of the other employees, and she could begin work the very next day.

At seven the following morning she stood at the junction of Rickmansworth Road and Milton Street with half a dozen day labourers waiting for the minibus that would take her out to the farm, just outside Rickmansworth on the Grand Union Canal a few miles away.

Ten

September 2006

Marcus Breese was a man with ideas. And it had been a *good* idea.

With a degree in media studies, Breese had begun work only eighteen months previously as a researcher on a Midlands TV lunchtime news programme. Today he had his own slot on *Monday through Friday*, the station's early-evening magazine show, one of a couple of programmes that bridged the awkward gap between the horrors of the six o'clock news and the reassuring theme tune to the bleak *EastEnders*.

As consumer affairs presenter, Breese spent five or six minutes on Mondays, Wednesdays and Fridays – wedged in just before the sport and the local weather – covering stories of wrongdoing in the region.

OK, yes, at the behest of the show's editor and her insistence on balance, there was sometimes an item featuring a local factory boss having his head shaved to raise money for a stricken youngster, or a cat that survived a two-hundred-mile round trip to the coast beneath the bonnet of the family Honda. But for the most part, the items that viewers clearly wished to see were stories of the heartless theft of the presents from beneath the Christmas tree, or a newly-wed couple's home burning down as the deep-fat fryer overheated, especially if one of them had only just come out of hospital.

'It's not *my* fault,' Breese would often plead as he pitched that week's items, including yet another scandal of a dodgy builder who'd replaced a couple of slates on a pensioner's roof and charged her a grand, or the corner shop that was selling cigarettes to kids of twelve. These were the stories that he wanted in his slot. And he wanted them there because they were the stories that would get him noticed, and if he was noticed often enough, he wouldn't be on a regional six thirty programme for much longer, he'd be wending his way down the M1 to join the demigods on *Watchdog* or *Rogue Traders*.

Breese knew very well he wasn't Woodward or Bernstein. A local water shortage, maybe, but Watergate, no. Breese was never going to be the next Michael Moore, but he very much felt that he *could* be the next Nicky Campbell.

In pursuit of his single-minded ambition, he'd already contrived to get himself hit on camera – not once, but twice – by people who, confronted with a film crew and an overweeningly self-righteous presenter, cared more about giving rein to their feelings of anger than continuing to feign any kind of innocence.

A couple of decent swipes were par for the course, all essential for the Roger Cooke type of

CV, and worth every bruise and scrape, just so long as they were recorded on film and broadcast in that week's show.

There was only one problem with Breese's career-path trajectory: his crusading zeal smacked of a piety that proved more offensive to many viewers than the misdeeds of the unscrupulous people that he was actually exposing. Was it the lengths that he was prepared to go to? The elaborate disguises, the hidden cameras, the actors pretending to be householders? And all this just to catch a dodgy plumber who could barely fix a bathroom leak?

Yes, of course these people should be brought to book in some way, and yes, of course they were doing wrong, and yes, the Trading Standards people did seem to take a very long time to cut through bureaucracy and bring their prosecutions. And then, even if they got them as far as a magistrate's court, what did the wrong-doers get? A fine of two hundred pounds and a couple of paragraphs in the local rag, a finger to the waiting film crew for good measure.

Better then, reasoned Breese, to expose them on a six-thirty TV programme, even if, as they actually waited for *Emmerdale*, most of the viewers were watching in the most desultory fashion, chatting, eating supper or sniggering at the appalling fit of the weather girl's garish jacket.

Breese might have been pious, and he was certainly smug, but he was not stupid. As a presenter, he looked like a man who had already outgrown his regional remit. There was something just too right about the knot of his tie, the spikiness of his hair, the cut of his suit. He exuded more attitude than was decent for the modest show, but alas none of this *savoir faire* endeared him in any way to the viewers of Dudley, Great Barr and West Bromwich.

The sheer simplicity of Breese's idea made him smile anew as he strolled through the glass-fronted building that housed the TV studio on Birmingham's Broad Street.

His girlfriend, Bernadette, an account manager with an ad agency in Soho, lived in Primrose Hill. At weekends, unless he was filming, he drove to her flat in the city. Alternatively she took the train out of Euston up to Birmingham New Street, where he would meet her and they would drive on to his home in the village of Shebdon, just outside Market Drayton.

From his bedroom window, across a couple of fields, he could see the Shropshire Union Canal a hundred yards away. Of course! What a cracking idea. He'd get on his bike, sometime soon, and he would cycle the two hundred miles to London: flat towpaths, a traffic-free environment, and the whole stretch more or less deserted.

OK, it was hardly a polar expedition or a tricky hack through the sweltering rainforest. He wasn't going to have to do a Bruce Parry – hunker down with some remote tribe and eat unspeakable things in an attempt to ingratiate himself with these people who, given half the chance, would doubtless skip the goat's testicles and dive into a burger and chips; people who given the choice might well eschew the itchy loincloth and slip instead into a decent pair of Levi's – but a cycle ride would do nicely, especially if he did it for charity.

Not for him the stay-at-home would-be celebrity's chosen route to upping one's shadowy profile – the excruciating labour of retailing hoary anecdotes on some daytime TV chat show with a C-list presenter and even worse guests, or cringe-making appearances on third-rate quiz shows with recovering alcoholic stand-ups.

No. A long-distance cycle ride was an interesting, completely do-able undertaking which, pursued properly, would go some way towards redressing the negative publicity that, in spite of his best efforts, he seemed destined to attract.

He often wondered just what was the matter with these people, this wearisome, lumpen public who were so obdurate in their antipathy to him and who appeared wholly impervious to his not inconsiderable achievements on their behalf. This little enterprise would cast him in an altogether more favourable and compassionate light. Yes, indeed, even Max Clifford himself would have been proud to have come up with this wheeze. It was, he felt, nothing short of inspired.

And, at the end of it all, only a couple of miles from the canal basin at Little Venice would be his girlfriend Bernie's welcoming Primrose Hill flat. Oh, yes!

During the next couple of weeks, Breese sorted out the route details, bought and equipped his bike and camping gear, and planned the overnight stops.

He also collected money. Lots of it. By the time he was ready to leave in late September, friends, colleagues and associates had pledged over fifteen thousand pounds for the hospice in Edgbaston that was going to be, according to a very brief item on his own TV station, the beneficiary of Marcus Breese's high-riding achievement.

With tags like that, he groaned to Bernadette, he began to feel like he was appearing in one of his own show's more desperate items.

Eleven

May 1982

Of course, early promise does not always portend later success. How many three-year-olds bump around the paddock on a docile pony, never to become teenage three-day eventers? How many youngsters in the park, coached by zealous fathers, fail to emulate the Williams sisters, having abandoned racquet and balls at the first sniff of a neighbourhood romance?

Infant daydreamers, barely able to wield a

crayon, scribble a story beneath the kitchen table, never to write another thing when, as adolescents, they put on the white face paint and black eyes of a Goth, or play bass guitar in a rock 'n' roll band.

But Leah Porter had been none of these girls. She had shown no particular promise as a youngster, hadn't penned anything at all until, as a late-developing fourteen-year-old, she started to write poems, but poems that were for her eyes only.

At fifteen, without even telling her parents, she submitted a story to a competition in the *South Wales Echo*, and was more mortified when it won – and was, of course, published – than she would have been had she heard nothing but the silence that she fully expected.

She passed nine O levels with good grades at the school a mile from her home in middle-class Roath. She was liked by the other fifth-form girls for her open, friendly manner, but didn't have pretensions to being any kind of social star. She was also liked by several of the pupils in the adjacent boys' high school, but their admiration had more to do with her shoulder-length blonde hair and nicely developing figure than her personality.

She didn't actually date anyone until she was nearly sixteen, and even then, notwithstanding the peer pressure of the day when it seemed everyone was 'doing it', she didn't have sexual intercourse with Robert for the first four months of their slow-burn romance.

Robert was hardly conventionally cool, but, given the notion that fashion's a kind of circle, and the very furthest edge of extreme cool is always just within touching distance of major ineptitude, Robert was tantamount to some sort of bespectacled icon. Like a kind of Jarvis Cocker before the Sheffield singer had even arrived to make gangling dyspraxia a statement of performance intent.

Robert was clearly part-geek, of that there was no doubt. But just how much was something of a mystery. His general reticence made it difficult to fathom, and his lack of transparency made Leah incline his way, rather than to some of the more conventionally attractive boys who would certainly have obliged her.

He didn't play football, he read Hardy and Lawrence for pleasure, and was said to be writing a book himself, something about which he was suitably circumspect.

If pressed – unlike his sixth-form peers, who were always ready to reveal their latest enthusiasm for this or that band – Robert would simply and unequivocally state that The Smiths were the best band in the country, and he would then quietly argue a case for Morrissey's being right up there with his most revered literary heroes.

As far as Leah was concerned, the fact that he was from the wrong side of town only added to his charm and attraction. He didn't appear embarrassed about his humble background, but he never sought to make any crass political point about it either. He was doing alright at school, and now here he was in the sixth form, and later he would go to university. His dad was a painter and decorator and his mother worked at the hospital as a cleaner. His background didn't even seem to register with him. When he first came to her house in nicely appointed Roath, Leah felt inclined to apologize for her schoolteacher parents' income, their sofa and TV, the cars on the drive.

When they did finally consummate their relationship, it was she, not he, who initiated the sex. Her parents were out for the afternoon, down at the Magnet showroom in Canton for the umpteenth time arranging the delivery and installation of a new fitted kitchen.

Given Robert's apparent restraint regarding her burgeoning charms, Leah had even begun to wonder whether some of her friends were right, and that he was, in fact, less interested in girls than he might have been expected to be. Perhaps their kissing and tepid fondling was no more than a reflection of a closeness borne simply of their shared affection for certain poets, bands and books...

But that afternoon in her bedroom at the back of the house, he embarked on the business of their first complete coupling with enthusiasm and a certain, apparently easy familiarity with both her body, and his own.

She didn't have an orgasm that first time, but he was a considerate lover and did his best not to hurt her in any way. He asked her several times whether she wanted him to continue, whether she was alright. She appreciated this care, although it tended to lower the sexual temperature, but in truth she could perhaps have done with just a little less solicitude, and a little more urgency, even if it had meant a lack of the self-control that he was clearly exercising.

No matter. Things improved and, as their A level exams approached, they found the opportunity, in between fairly heavy revision timetables, to do it a couple of times a week, usually at her house, whilst her parents attended after-school meetings or supervised detention classes.

Come August, Leah got three As – in English Literature, Sociology and History – and Robert passed Literature, Geography and Psychology with two As and a B.

It had been assumed by her parents that she would apply for Oxford, and her headmaster father felt sure she would get in. He'd taught for thirty years, and had a pretty good measure of the youngsters that left his care to go off to university each year.

When Elwyn had gone to college himself it had been a financial struggle for his parents. Now, his own daughter was destined to take a similar step, but this time, it would not be the trip that he himself had made, down from the valleys of South Wales to the capital of the principality. Nor would it be across the Severn Bridge to Bristol, or even Bath. It would, he felt sure, be along the A40, to Jesus or St Anne's, Somerville or Trinity – to Oxford itself.

But it wasn't to be. Leah didn't even want to

apply for a place. The daughter whom they had nurtured in Wales wanted to remain in the country of her birth, and her father was touched by what he saw as her constancy.

In fact, whilst there was some truth in his surmise, there was something else, something that the young woman valued even more than her birthright.

She was just a little fearful, and the thing that she was afraid of was that the naked ambition that she would be surrounded by in thrusting Oxford, the place where tomorrow's cabinet ministers would be jockeying for position with the luminaries who were destined to inhabit every other sphere of cultural and political life, would be too rich a soil for her modest talent to flourish in.

Yes, she wanted to read the books – the novels, the plays, the poets – she wanted to attend the lectures and blossom in the seminars, but she wanted also, perhaps more than anything else, to nurture the nascent talent that she believed she had: her ability to write.

In a hothouse environment that spawned Booker and Orange and Whitbread prize-winners as a matter of course, she feared that whatever ability she herself had might well be swamped and overwhelmed, her still-emerging voice rendered mute by the atmosphere of competition, an atmosphere in which she had never thrived.

She therefore declined the university admissions advice that she was given and, in September of 1982, began her degree in English and American Literature, not at Oxford or Cambridge, but at St David's, Lampeter, in west Wales, the smallest, most rurally situated university in the United Kingdom.

An added bonus of this course was that a part of the third year would be spent at a college in America – and not just any university, but Smith College in Northampton, Massachusetts, the women-only institution which counted amongst its former alumnae Sylvia Plath, Margaret Mitchell and Gloria Steinem.

That same year, Robert went to Birmingham to read Geography. Their sixth-form affair, it transpired, had been just that. As friends they still met occasionally, and spoke often on the phone. At one of those meetings, back home in Cardiff during his second term at university, Robert confided to Leah that he'd met someone of whom he was very fond. He and Clive stayed together for the next ten years.

Twelve

October 2006

University tutor and MA supervisor Tom Hopwood had seen better days. Much better. Retired from Keele ten years previously on health grounds, he now lived a few miles from the place where he'd spent the better part of his working life, and within sight of the Derbyshire Peak District National Park, a place in which he had never set foot.

No longer needing to be near the centre of the university town, he had sold the first-floor flat he'd lived in for twenty years before buying an unprepossessing two-bedroom bungalow in Leek on a recently built development half a mile from the centre of town.

His tutor's salary had been reasonable, and his outgoings few. Now his pension was adequate, and his outgoings even lower. He didn't even run a car. The one that he had once used sat in the drive, its tyres half flat, the paintwork tarnished and the windscreen growing moss in the corners. Every now and again someone who'd spotted the Volvo saloon sitting there for what seemed like forever would knock at his door and offer to buy it. He always declined to sell.

Salt had been volunteered to go up to speak to the former academic. She was the obvious choice: the previous winter, she and a dozen other female officers from around the country had been seconded to the Potteries force as the local CID struggled in vain to track down a rapist.

The man proved difficult to identify. With no previous convictions, and therefore no DNA identification record, he turned out to be a middle-aged car dealer who, instead of watching *Match of the Day* on Saturday evenings, assumed a token disguise and, driving any one of the many vehicles available to him from his own forecourt, impersonated a mini-cab driver before violently raping his – frequently drunk – young fares as he drove them home.

Two of the rapist's victims had been students on the widely spread, and therefore difficult to police, university campus.

Yes, DC Jane Salt knew the area well.

Hopwood drank huge amounts of alcohol, but he rarely went to the pub. He watched with a certain fascination the motley crew gathered in the newly opened Wetherspoon's, sandwiched between Blockbuster and Argos who by 9.30 in the morning were drinking pints of lager, chatting, and sucking on cigarettes.

For Tom Hopwood such social interaction had nothing whatsoever to do with drinking. Drinking alcohol in the quantity that he took it was a serious business and, like most other serious pursuits, it was a solitary one.

He drank barley wine for breakfast, and had smoked three or four cigarettes by the time he walked to town for his *Guardian*, a newspaper which he read, every single day, from cover to cover.

By ten a.m. he was back home and drinking the blended whisky that fuelled his days. He was hollow-cheeked, as thin as a proverbial rake, and the whites of his eyes were bloodshot. And no wonder: most days he ate nothing but a few cream crackers, a bit of cheese and perhaps half a tin of milk pudding if he had happened to get that far down the supermarket aisle and had dropped some Ambrosia into his basket.

His GP, a pretty girl who looked as if she was just about old enough to be in the sixth form, told him when he'd come in for a routine check-up for his high cholesterol statins that if he continued to drink this much, let alone smoke forty Marlboro a day, he'd be dead within a year.

Hopwood had smiled the smile of the benign drunk. 'Maybe you're right,' he'd said, 'but my last doctor told me that eighteen months ago, and I'm still here,' he wheezed. 'Well, sort of. Didn't he have a heart attack? Fell-running or something?'

It was true, and the sixth-former GP had to smile. 'Take my advice, Mr Hopwood. At least cut down, even if you can't give up. And try to eat a little something, otherwise, whether I'm dead or not, you certainly will be.'

'Thanks,' he said. 'Will that be all, Doctor?'

And then he shuffled out of the consulting room and straight down to Sainsbury's, his one-stop shop where he collected a carton of two hundred cigarettes, two bottles of own-brand whisky and his newspaper.

'Do you have a Nectar card, sir?' asked the checkout girl.

He smiled, put his booze in one bag, and that bag inside another. 'No,' he said, 'I'm afraid I don't.'

Salt rang the bell now but didn't hear the man's footsteps approach the front door.

'Mr Hopwood? I'm DC Salt. We spoke on the phone. You remember?'

'Oh, yes, of course I remember,' he said, standing aside. 'Come in.'

The smell – of cigarettes, a solitary male, thick fitted carpets and centrally heated airless rooms – was cloying. 'Thank you,' she said and followed his slight sway through into the sitting room.

He moved a few books and newspapers about, rearranged things from the sofa to the floor and gave the armchair a little exaggerated flourish of a brush with the back of his hand. 'Please,' he said.

Salt sat down.

'So, my dear, would you like a drink?'

'No, thank you. I stopped for a coffee on the motorway.'

'Right. Don't mind me. I like a little something mid-morning.'

'Of course,' she replied.

'So, what can I do for you? It's about Sarah

Clement?'

'Yes, I'm afraid so, Mr Hopwood.'

'How old would she have been?' he ruminated. 'Don't tell me,' he interrupted himself. 'Let's see.' He picked up his tumbler and swirled the spirit there.

'Mr Hopwood, please, don't think me rude but would it be possible to open the window? Just a little?'

'Of course.' He got up and forced open the top window of the bay a couple of notches. 'Let's see,' he began again. 'Unless I'm mistaken it's 2006. I reckon Sarah Clement was in the first intake of the MA writing course. *Creative* writing,' he added scornfully. 'Is there any other kind of writing, Ms Salt? An epistle to the milkman? A lover's note? If they are not creative, carefully chosen words that speak of nuanced deeds, the right words for the task, what are they, pray?'

'Yes, I suppose so,' said Salt, and sniffed the fresh air that had started to contend with the smoke and dry atmosphere in the room.

'I think Sarah would have been with me in ... 1986? Possibly a year later?' He lit another cigarette, blew the plume of blue smoke across the room. 'How did I do?'

'Spot on, Mr Hopwood. 1986 it was.'

'And what is it you want to know about her time up here, Sergeant?'

'It's Constable, actually, Mr Hopwood. Detective Constable, but my name is Jane. Jane Salt.'

'Jane,' he said.

'Well,' continued Salt, 'she was an under-graduate for three years, and then a postgraduate for another two. Yes? It's a significant amount of time in anyone's life.'

'Of course,' he concurred.

'And given what she went on to do – her writing career, I mean – I think it important that we look at the time that she spent here.'

'I see,' he said, and then added thoughtfully, 'And now she's been killed?'

'I'm afraid so.'

'Reason?'

'Sorry?' said Salt.

'Motive? Reason? Frost, Morse, Dalziel, even that tiresome Rebus, I watch them all. Never guess the killer, of course; I've never got one right yet. But what I do know is that the resolution's always a big let-down after the set-up. People with butterflies in their mouths, scrawlings on the wall in blood, it's just so much tosh, icing on the cake to keep the punters amused. At the end of the day, in real life, it's always just another squalid killing done by the next of kin. If it's planned at all, the best we can hope for is a love rival despatched by a hired hand from the badlands of Manchester for five hundred quid.

'But I do know there has to be a motive. Real life or fiction, there has to be a reason. There's random violence, but that's Saturday night down in the town, isn't it? From what I've read in the press and seen on television, Sarah Clement's death wasn't random.'

'No,' said Salt. 'You're right, her death appears to have been no accident, and possibly premeditated. But we're not sure why. Not yet, anyway.'

'Poor girl,' he added. 'What would she have been? 1986 ... 2006 ... About forty, I suppose?'

'She was forty-two,' Salt replied.

'Well, at least she'd had some life,' said Hopwood.

'Is there anything you can tell me about her, Mr Hopwood?'

'Please, Jane, call me Tom. I feel as if I'm being told off when you call me that.'

'Of course. Tom, what do you remember about Sarah? Anything at all would be useful. We're trying to fill in her past to see whether there are any clues to her murder there.'

'She was a bright girl, of course. But they all are on the MA. Young men and women, all keen, all fresh and eager. As the years went on, I saw it as a large part of my job to try and put as many of them as possible off.'

'Really?' said Salt, not a little surprised.

'The thing is, Jane, by any reckoning, there are far too many writers in the world, especially now. Who needs 'em all? Is there really that much that hasn't been said? And all that enthusiasm gets so wearing. People are always going on writing courses and returning home to announce to their shocked spouses and horrified children that they are giving up the tax-collecting or accountancy. They're going to go into the attic and write that novel.

'Couldn't we have a few more writers who, fed up with being skint, humiliated and rejected, shut down their Apple, put away the paper and announce that they have decided to give it all up to become a plumber, or at least something useful? Anyway,' he said, betraying just the slightest smile, 'they generally ignored my advice. The women were generally better writers than the men, I found, but they could all pen a line. They wouldn't have been there otherwise.'

'I'm sure.'

'But I used to tell them, you need two things to be a published writer.'

'Yes?' she said, intrigued.

'And neither of them is talent,' he continued.

'Really?' said Salt.

'Well, yes, of course you need to be able to turn a phrase, but heavens, anyone can do that. All that education, all that reading, yes, everyone can turn a phrase these days. No, what you need is a little bit of what nothing can buy and no one can learn...'

'Yes?'

'A little bit of luck. The right desk, on the right day. That was my mantra. It's what I used to tell them until they were sick of hearing it, but it's true. You come up with a half-decent idea, you turn a phrase – well, a lot of phrases for a book, fewer for a story, not many at all for a poem. And then you try and get lucky, and the way you do that is by sticking at it. But get a bit of luck and you're away.'

'I see,' she said. 'I believe you are a writer

yourself, Tom?'

'You've done your research,' he said.

'Not really,' she acknowledged. 'The university told me and then I just Googled you.'

'I did a bit once. A few comic novels. Howard Jacobson out of Tom Sharpe; Malcolm Bradbury with just a dash of David Lodge. You know the sort of thing, campus malarkey. Students no better than they should be, staff even worse, plenty of booze –' he tapped his glass – 'a bit of soft drugs, all very innocent of course. It was all very different back then: no danger, no tragedy, and lots of people either falling over or falling into bed, always with the wrong person.'

'Do you no longer write?' she asked.

'No, not any more. I did about half a dozen in the late seventies, and that was it. I ran out of luck, I guess.' He glugged a large measure of whisky into his tumbler from the bottle that stood in the hearth beside him. 'The publisher turned the last one down. I tried again, did a lot of rewriting, even tried a whole new area, tried to do a serious piece, a literary novel,' he sneered. 'But once the train's moved on, you've had it really. And I had. Are you sure you won't have a drink, Jane? Just a little one?'

'No, really, thank you.'

'So, what can I tell you?' He swallowed a disconcertingly large measure of scotch, took a cigarette from the box and then noticed the one already smouldering in the ashtray beside him. 'It's a long time ago, that's for sure. Books out of the word processor – water under the

94

bridge, eh?'

'Yes, it is,' said Salt. 'A very long time.'

'Right, Sarah Clement. I knew nothing about her social life, her friends, nothing at all. Work? She was a decent writer. Nothing exceptional, at least I didn't think so. And then, lo and behold – as the angel might have said – she came up with that big book in, when was it? In the early nineties?'

'1993, I think,' added Salt.

'Was it?' he said thoughtfully. 'Completely surprised me. Every year – well, almost every year – there'd be one. Someone who'd have that little bit extra. But I didn't know it was Sarah, didn't think she'd got it in her. There again, you can't always tell, not with writing. Nothing, and then something really decent. She's not the first and she won't be the last, but it was a surprise.'

He threw his cigarette end into the cold ash of the fireplace and immediately lit another with a plastic lighter. 'Do you remember matches, Jane? Swan Vestas? A match named after a Roman goddess? Not quite like today, eh? I can smell them now, as you pushed open the box, wood and sulphur...'

'Yes, I remember matches,' she said.

'And now you get these. Ten for a pound. Thank God my pension fund didn't invest in Swedish timber, eh?'

'I guess so,' she said, humouring the man.

'Where was I?' he asked. 'Oh yes, Sarah's big book. She didn't do a lot afterwards, did she? But after all, who knows where the stuff comes

95

from? The whole thing's a bit of a mystery.'

'I think there were other books, but nothing very successful,' said Salt.

'Brain cells,' he said, touching his forehead, apparently apropos of nothing in particular. 'Remind me, what was it called?'

'*The House of Loss*,' she confirmed.

'That's right, *The House of Loss*. Can't remember a word of it now, of course, but I do remember it was a decent book, a real achievement. Poor thing,' he added, and then, 'Really, I'm sorry, but I don't think there's much else I can tell you.'

Salt got up. 'Don't worry, you've been very helpful,' she said. 'I'd best be on my way. I have to speak to a couple of people over at the university before getting back down south.'

'Of course,' he said, easing himself from the sofa and steadying himself on the mantelpiece.

'If anything else occurs to you, would you give me a call?' She handed him her card.

He escorted her down the hall to the front door, put his cigarette in his mouth and extended his hand.

'You know, I've no right to interfere, but perhaps if you got back to *your* writing, maybe a bit of luck would come your way?'

He smiled, raised his hands in the resigned but hopeless gesture of one for whom the train is already disappearing from the station platform. 'Thank you,' he said. 'We have choices, Jane. I've made mine.'

'I'll look out one of your books,' she said. 'On

eBay.'

'I suppose some nice man has the benefit of your kindness?' he said. 'I just hope he appreciates you.'

'Thank you,' she said. He opened the door and she took a couple of steps down the path.

'You know, the funny thing is,' he said, flicking his cigarette end into the long grass, 'the one person I would have thought really had it in them wasn't Sarah, but her friend. What was her name?'

Salt stopped and turned.

He went on. 'Lily? No, it wasn't Lily, it was an unusual name for that time, nice name ... Leah. That was it, Leah. Leah Porter, I think.'

'Really?' said Salt, jotting down the name.

'Another tragedy,' he added. 'She didn't even complete the course. A slip of a thing. A very pretty girl. Can one say "pretty" any more, or is it an offence? She had some sort of breakdown, I think, and then, apparently, a year or two later, committed suicide. Terrible. But she was the one I reckoned might do something. Just shows you, eh? What do I know?'

'Yes, that's awful,' said Salt. 'But thank you, anyway, and goodbye.' She took a few steps down the path and then turned. 'Incidentally, Swan Vestas might be struggling, but Nike seems to be doing alright.'

'Sorry?' he said. 'Nike?'

'Gods on boxes – they're not all dead,' she said.

'Good point. Goodbye, Jane.'

Thirteen

July 2006

There's nothing like a job to give a person a sense of belonging. A role. The teacher's authority in the classroom, the doctor lording it in her surgery. No matter that once back home with his family, that same authoritative teacher is as readily cajoled into removing his soiled shoes or fixing the patio door as any other hen-pecked spouse.

The GP whose diagnoses are treated with due solemnity in her practice, once home, is no more immune than any other wife from being castigated by a peremptory husband for chatting over the football on TV.

A job – no matter how low the pay, nor how unpleasant the work, or unsocial the hours – bestows you your place. The labourer on the building site, the bar girl behind the pumps, the bus driver down the crowded streets, the fruit picker in the strawberry fields: they now belong.

Actually, on this summer's day, Katrina's work was neither unpleasant nor unsocial. Yes, the day was long, and the fruit had to be picked with great care and at the optimum time to meet the supermarkets' exacting standards. But the weather was sunny, the tea and cigarette breaks regular, and all the time, every moment, Katrina, just like her colleagues, was earning over five pounds for each hour that she stood on the back of the machine that crawled across the acres and acres of strawberry fields.

Five pounds in zloty was a lot. As she snipped each plump berry from the crown of the plant and lay the scented fruit in trays, she calculated what fortune her labours in this Hertfordshire field was amassing back home in the country she had left only a few weeks ago.

The accommodation on Uplands Farm was spartan but clean. Katrina shared a room with three other women, two young Polish friends from Krakow, and a Hungarian girl who had travelled over with her boyfriend for the summer. Each of them had a little wardrobe, a set of drawers and a bedside table. A communal sitting room with TV and games, books and music was down the corridor and across in an adjacent block. There was a redundant pay phone just off the kitchen – everyone owned a mobile – and a white-tiled shower room with high, wide windows was just twenty feet down the hall.

Philip Ellis, a quietly spoken man in corduroy trousers, checked shirt and sleeveless body warmer, tended to avert his rheumy eyes whenever he exchanged a greeting with his workers. The word amongst the migrant labour was that the wiry farmer, rather than engaging directly with his workforce, preferred to drive around the farm on the surrounding lanes in his Range Rover, invariably walking the fields at dawn and dusk, before and after the workers had come and gone.

Ellis lived alone, had apparently been divorced for several years. The couple had been childless, so it was said. But, frankly, who amongst these people cared? It was merely gossip, idle chat, wholly devoid of context or meaning, like passing someone else's grave misfortune on the motorway.

The farmer had spent his working life in the company of the beasts of the field. Only a few years previously the land had been grazed by cattle, but when the price of milk became terminally depressed, and the catastrophe of BSE made the return on beef unsustainable, Ellis had come within an ace of doing what half a dozen other farmers in the area had done, and selling up completely.

But for a man who had lived on the land all his life, it was a daunting prospect, and he hung on for a while, gradually slimming down the herd and eventually phasing out milk production completely.

And then, wholly unexpectedly, on account of the accession to the European Union of several financially depressed eastern European countries, there was, almost overnight, a cheap, reliable workforce available just as there had been immediately before the First World War. This workforce once more made the planting and harvesting of labour-intensive crops not only viable, but profitable. Fields that had only a few years ago been pasture to dung and steaming kine now bristled with soft fruits, spinach, beans and, for the first time this year, several acres of cut flowers, from early freesias to midsummer anemones, right through to autumn chrysanthemums.

No matter how fair the weather, nor how many zloty were amassing in her Polish bank account, it was not in Katrina's melancholy nature to either whistle or sing as she stood on the back of the harvester as it inched its way through the fields of fruit. Not for her some heady reverie in this pastoral idyll. Rather, diligently, and with only a token word to the other two women who rode the machine with her, she simply did her work.

The driver, a Hungarian boy in tracksuit bottoms and a bare chest, looked over his shoulder repeatedly, watched the lines of fruit, and made sure that the women were harvesting it correctly. But he could see that the new woman – there was always a new woman, as people came and went on a weekly basis – was competent.

A couple of hundred yards away, adjacent to a line of white poplars that fringed the huge field, Ellis leaned on the big square bonnet of his Range Rover, and watched. The farmer wasn't above a surreptitious glance at the handsome youngsters working in his fields. He was flesh and blood. In another age – in another country, possibly – he might have sought to take advantage of his position and try his patron's luck, but the man was fifty years old, and most of the folk working in his fields were in their twenties. The new Polish woman, though, was much closer to his own age. Perhaps she was forty, or forty-five, maybe even forty-eight, he reckoned.

Her dark hair was short. She wore blue shorts, a washed-out yellow tee-shirt and sturdy boots. He watched her at work as she bent and straightened. And then he drove away.

Ellis liaised with his workforce via his English foreman. The farmer spent his time either in the little room attached to the former barn that served as an outdoor office, or examining fruit, checking pallets, delivery notes and weights. He had little direct contact with his workers beyond a cursory greeting, and even then he usually left before receiving an answer.

He was a man with dozens of employees, but employees who, for the most part, spoke an alien tongue. On his own farm, in his own fields, he often felt a stranger amongst these strangers.

On Wednesday lunchtime, as a little group made their way to the canteen, he ventured a few words to Katrina as she passed. 'Sorry?' she said, the single word heavily accented.

'How are you getting on?' he repeated, a little embarrassed, as the others in the group moved on.

'Thank you,' she replied. 'All is good, thank you.'

'Good. Good,' he said, and walked away.

A week later, just as the forecasters had predicted, the weather turned. Ellis knew his business and his land very well, and of course he sowed his different crops in succession for staggered harvesting. But no matter how much science he applied, how intermittently he sowed, and how accurate the weather forecasts, he was still, to a large extent, at the mercy of the vagaries of the weather.

As the midsummer rain poured down, making harvesting impossible, the day labourers were laid off, and the few who were contracted to the farm were found other work. Some of the experienced hands were redeployed on maintaining machinery, machinery that was often in use twenty hours a day during the longest days of summer. Most of the women were assigned to gather the flowers that were now blooming in the acres of poly tunnels.

'Robbie,' said Ellis to his foreman, 'I need someone to do some work for me in the house...'

'Yes?' replied the man, a little surprised by the unprecedented suggestion.

'Someone reliable,' Ellis went on.

'OK,' said the foreman.

'And trustworthy,' added the farmer.

'Of course.'

'How about the new Polish woman?' suggested the farmer. 'I think her name's Katrina.'

Robbie glanced at his boss. Ellis wasn't the sort of man that you shared a nod and a wink with, but had he been, the foreman would have done so. 'Sure,' he said, with the faintest suggestion of a smile. 'Do you want me to speak to her?'

'Yes, if you would. I've let the place get in a mess these last few months. It needs a good clean, and I've got stacks of ironing piled up, that sort of thing. Just for a few days,' he said. 'And if the weather improves, perhaps she could do a couple of hours for me in the evening? See what she says.'

'Right. Will do,' said Robbie.

Fourteen

October 2006

Jan McAvoy looked very different in her classroom. Kavanagh had never seen her down amongst the weeds and thickets of overgrown canal banks, but here in Stroud, with her hair tied back, and wearing sensible shoes (she was five-feet-seven and never wore heels) she looked every bit the school teacher, not at all the woman who – in North Face jacket and Caterpillar boots – hacked and sawed, pulled and prodded most weekends and who, only a few days earlier, had discovered the body of Sarah Clement anchored in her watery grave a hundred miles away.

Jan was reckoned to be a nice woman. It was the adjective invariably used about her. 'Jan?

Oh, yes, she's nice.' And she was. The word said it all. It's not too difficult to be nice, generally, if you don't make too many waves. You may not be *first* on the list – 'Oh, we *must* invite so and so, he/she's such good company' – when the dinner-party guests are mustered, or when people think about the little group to accompany the half-term ski trip, but, all other things being equal, be nice-ish, and you'll probably make the cut.

Jan had been on lots of ski trips and fifth-form theatre jaunts. She also ate supper with miscellaneous friends at least a couple of times a month. She was not without self-knowledge. She knew very well she was 'ish' woman, really. Quiet-ish, retiring-ish and, actually – and this was not known by her friends and colleagues – resentful-ish too.

Unlike a couple of her similar-aged friends, she certainly didn't resent not being a mother. In her mid-thirties, she'd taught for some fifteen years now, and found the idea of having a child of her own entirely resistible. In fact, *not* to bring another child into this world, she reckoned, was tantamount to an act of public-spiritedness that bordered on philanthropic. Her rationale did not extend to the thought that her own child – were she ever to have one – would almost certainly be one of those whose destiny it would be to swim against the increasingly barbarous tide of humanity, a barbarous tide which was, of course, the very reason for her decision.

No, based upon her own experience of classroom and playground, to say nothing of a close reading of the Murdoch press, she reckoned the battle for civilization was already pretty much lost and she was reconciled to her decision to abdicate from that particular conflict.

When it came to birthdays and Christmas, she was content to indulge her nieces, nephews, and the children of one or two of her closest friends with gifts. But even that munificence was likely to falter soon, for she had become increasingly weary, and not a little hurt, at choosing something for this or that niece, only for that child to fail to even acknowledge her kindness.

But Jan's resentment wasn't about ungrateful nephews and unacknowledged gifts; it was entirely to do with what she saw as the discrimination against being single. She was no longer, as of a few months now, in a relationship, but in truth, she was not exactly discomfited by this.

Her relationship with hearing therapist Roy, a man whose name she had now come to associate wholly with a kind of blandness, had never been quite as fulfilling as Jan might have hoped. In fact, from the first evening that they had met, introduced at dinner by her colleague and friend, French teacher Alice, there had always been a lack of passion in their romance.

When, that first evening, as they went through the awkward goodbye moments in the hallway of Alice's house in Gloucester, and Roy asked Jan whether he might offer her a lift home, it was, she was sure, no more than a polite gesture, a selfless act without ulterior motive.

If he had noticed the woman across the table, who was two inches taller than himself, he had made no effort to endear himself to her in any way. As the conversation had flitted and flickered amongst the eight folk present, he had neither elaborated on nor developed a single thing that she had said, far less initiated any specific enquiry of her.

What was the man even doing here amongst the several teachers and couple of social workers? She imagined that he must be bereaved or, more likely, recently divorced and be out testing the social waters as he gathered himself to ward off the inevitable ordeal of a future of lonely microwave meals.

On the awkwardly quiet drive to her home, though, she did tease out of him where he had been on holiday the previous year (the Scilly Isles), and whether he liked his well-cared for Saab 93 (he did), which she thought he drove just a little too fast.

A week later, when he phoned, she couldn't actually recall knowing *anyone* called Roy. He reminded her of their meeting the previous week and, the embarrassment over, without mirth or acknowledgement of the faux pas, he doggedly drove through to the end of his mission and asked her out for the following Saturday. She said yes without either excitement or expectation.

And she was not disappointed. Even by her own modest standards, for the next six months their affair – just when, she wondered, does an affair actually become a relationship? – was decidedly lukewarm. It was clear from the start that they had very little in common, and that their going here and there together was an alliance against what might otherwise have been an intimidating social world.

To say that the sex between them was humdrum would be to describe it in overly exciting terms. At first it was simply awkward, reflecting the lack of passion on both his side and hers. He had never shown any interest in undressing her, behaving instead, she imagined, as a long-time married man might do, wending his desultory way upstairs, spending an inordinately long time in the bathroom, and then emerging with sighs and groans and an apparent indifference to the woman lying there on her side of the bed.

But in fact he wasn't indifferent. Or at least, not entirely. And she wondered whether his marathon thrustings reflected simply a sexual endurance that he had always been blessed with, or rather whether his disinclination to actually ejaculate was in fact a complete lack of excitement and arousal when with her.

When, eventually, in the interests of getting some sleep – as well as a justifiable concern for her own health – she faked her climax, he continued to thrust away until some very rapid and heavy nasal breathing suggested that he, too, was replete.

The end of the affair came when he asked her, some six months into their time together, what she thought about their putting their relationship on a 'new footing' and becoming 'friends'. This stuck her as odd, and contrary to the usual course of such matters.

'People usually start as friends, and then become lovers,' she said, 'not the other way around.' He didn't smile or laugh. 'What do you mean, Roy, "friends"?' she added, intrigued.

He told her that he liked her company very much, but that for some time now he had felt increasingly anxious when he knew that their evenings would, invariably, end with their going to bed together.

She was affronted. Yes, the sex had barely improved one jot from the time that they had first tried it, and yes, she now regularly faked her orgasm and contented herself properly up against the washing machine as it shuddered through its final spin cycle.

She said yes, of course. If it was a companion that he was looking for, she fully understood, and she would be happy for them to have supper together or go to the cinema occasionally.

But the more she thought about it, the more hacked off she was, and a couple of weeks later she told him that she thought that she would prefer to be free to look for someone with whom she could have a full relationship. Judging by his complete silence, Roy appeared to have taken the news in his stride; she hadn't heard from him since.

To be dumped by someone she didn't even care for was very depressing indeed, and she was aware that, for these last couple of months, she had not been quite as nice and accommodating as she was generally perceived to be.

Jan had long suspected that many people, including several of her own married friends, stayed together not because of any real affection that any longer existed between them, but through a kind of indolence: the prospect of being alone was a good deal more alarming than the notion of continuing to spend their humdrum time together. After all, something, she reasoned, must account for the couples in restaurants who ate their meals in silence, or stood arguing in supermarket aisles about pasta or oil.

She'd read recently that the average couple, after only five years together, were having sex no more than twice a month. Twice a month. Even she and battering-ram Roy had been doing it more than that.

The same survey suggested that the average person would own eight cars in their lifetime (of 78 years), and have ten lovers. Jan was on schedule on the vehicle front, but certainly needed to put in the hours if she were to make the carnal stakes.

So, she was out of a dull relationship and knew that there was little point in complaining to her chums at the gym, at the salsa class, and certainly not to the motley crew at the weekend canal camps that had now become an even more important feature of her not very busy social life.

The fact was, you moaned to your friends

about your solitary state and they had two responses. Those who had actually met Roy couldn't but disguise their antipathy to the man. He was quietly spoken and yet self-regarding. He was bland, yet managed to be irritating, too. You couldn't quite put your finger on what it was about him that irked, so reasonable was he, but that wasn't unprecedented. If Paul McCartney was the Monty Don of popular music, then Roy Cunningham was his twin in the rarefied world of hearing therapy.

Jan had never heard the erstwhile Beatle utter a single word with which she disagreed – she even owned a couple of his CDs – and gardening guru Monty Don was clearly a very nice man: you could tell from his soft, blue linen overalls, curly hair and quietly spoken manner. So why on earth did she find herself shouting obscenities at the TV as McCartney exchanged pleasantries with Michael Parkinson on a Saturday night? And why did she want to slap the gardener's kindly face as he planted, pruned and spoke tenderly of all things lovely in the earth? It was a mystery, indeed.

The other response, after two or three glasses of wine in the Friday-evening wine bar, from those friends of hers who *were* in relationships, was to tell Jan that she was better off on her own, and rather callously to remind her of the fact that, even when she was in a relationship, all she did was moan about it, which, in the case of her relationship with Roy, was entirely true.

But none of this was the cause of her current

resentment; it was rather that, these days, at school, you got six months off when you had a baby. Even fathers, apparently, were now entitled to a few weeks away from the classroom

There was funeral leave; leave for the demise of a parent, a child, of course, and probably even a sibling for all Jan knew. (Did animals qualify, she wondered?) You got a couple of days off to move house; and no one ran into the back of your car at ten miles an hour these days without your taking at least a month off with whiplash. The only thing that didn't appear to qualify for a day or two of paid leave, as far as Jan could see, was the trauma, to say nothing of the unwelcome notoriety, of finding a woman's bloated corpse in a canal.

On the Monday morning following the gruesome find, and ready to go straight back into the classroom, Don Grayling, the head teacher, had taken her aside and asked her if she was alright. She'd thanked him and assured him that she was. But not content with this reassurance, he immediately began to ask her questions, questions which, in spite of his affected solicitude, she knew very well were voyeuristic, bordering on plain salacious.

'Thank you, Don,' she had replied, 'but the police have asked me not to say anything at all just now.'

It was sort of true, but frankly she wasn't going to indulge the man's morbid curiosity. If that was his thing, let him watch *Crimewatch*. She wasn't going to tell him anything. And anyway, like a kid in the playground with the promise of secrets he shouldn't reveal, she actually had very little *to* tell.

Just as she'd told the policeman who'd arrived on the scene late that Sunday afternoon, she had drifted away from the group for a cigarette. She'd noticed something just beneath the surface of the green water, and had looked more closely. Recognizing at first what looked like merely a floating, slightly billowed dress, she'd eventually had to walk back and tell Jeff, their leader, that she was certain that there was a woman's body in the pound. Jeff had stayed calm, called the police and spoken to them at some length. On her mobile.

When they had arrived, she'd led them to the place but was then escorted from the scene as a uniformed officer muttered something about forensics, and told her rather sharply that he hoped that she hadn't touched anything.

'No,' she replied, a little affronted, 'of course not.'

Ms McAvoy now sat at her desk at the front of the room beneath the whiteboard and invited the policeman to sit in front of her. If she saw the funny side of things as Kavanagh wedged himself into the seat at the child's desk, she didn't show it.

He asked her how she was feeling now.

'I'm OK,' she said. 'What have you been able to find out about the woman?'

'I can't say a lot, you understand,' he said, 'but, as you probably know, she was a writer, local to the area.'

'Had she taken her life?' asked McAvoy.

'Please, keep this to yourself,' he said, recognizing correctly someone who could be trusted. 'It'll be out soon, in the press and the media, but just for the moment?'

She nodded assent. 'Of course.'

'We're almost certain that she was killed, and then her body moved to where you discovered it.' He paused. 'Do you want me to go on?'

'Yes, please,' she said.

'Her corpse had been loosely anchored to the bottom, but as the...' He paused again as she winced.

'Please. It's alright,' she said.

'Well, the gases there led to the body rising and, in spite of the ballast, she obviously came up to the surface just far enough for you to see her there.'

'Oh, dear,' said the woman.

'Yes,' added Kavanagh redundantly. He knew the feeling. How *do* you react to a person's death? Let alone their dying in such a grotesque manner. The emotions were so complex, such a heady amalgam, and most difficult of all was having to deal with the outward display of those feelings, something which often left you unable to ascertain exactly what it was that you *were* feeling.

To his own considerable shame, though, he knew that as well as horror at the heinous nature of the crimes that he had often been tasked with investigating, one of the things that he knew he felt, and had never shared with anyone, including Jane Salt, was that John Donne had told only a part of the story when he had asserted that 'Each man's death diminishes me.'

Kavanagh had also been forced to acknowledge that another person's death – even a complete stranger's – awakened in him an appetite for life. No matter how tragic the case, no matter how appalling the circumstances, as well as shock and sorrow, Kavanagh often investigated the crime with a renewed zest for life.

A week later, maybe watching a game of football on TV, enjoying a cigarette and a pint in the pub, exchanging forehands with a friend on the tennis court first thing on a summer's morning, these were very good things. The all-too-clear recollection of an unknown person, cold on a mortuary slab, was a salutary reminder of that fact, no matter how ashamed he was of acknowledging it to himself.

Driving to work in the BMW, singing along to something on the CD player, there was little doubt, even in this frequently dispirited, often bad-tempered, middle-aged policeman's mind that, in spite of everything, it really was a pretty good thing to be alive.

And anyway, notwithstanding that he'd had this conversation with Jan McAvoy – or one very much like it – so many times before, because of his professional role, he could no longer always tell exactly what he *was* feeling. Of course he was aware that this was a woman's life cut short. He was aware, too, that she was someone's sister, daughter, friend and lover. But he was a cop, and first and foremost it was his task to find the reason for, and perpetrator of, her violent death.

'Yes,' he said again, and this time added, 'It's very tragic.' There was an awkward silence before he eventually said, 'I believe you spend a good deal of your time with the canal volunteers, Ms McAvoy.' It sounded as if he might be interviewing her for a job and enquiring about her pastoral life.

'Yes,' she replied, 'most weekends, when school work permits.'

'What is it about canals?' he asked briskly. 'I don't imagine it would be everyone's idea of fun.'

'Oh, they're wonderful things,' she said. 'You think about it, Inspector; the people who made them were just like us, you know, and they had nothing but pickaxes and shovels...'

'I suppose so,' he said.

'The only mechanical thing you would have seen would have been a wheelbarrow.'

'Yes, I guess,' he said.

'Hundreds of miles of waterways – eighteen or twenty feet wide, six or seven feet deep, towpaths, bridges, tunnels, locks and aqueducts – they really are absolute marvels of...'

'Engineering?' he offered.

'Yes,' she concurred, smiling. 'Of course. But the thing that's always fascinated me is the sheer doggedness of the people who dug them. Can you imagine what it must have been like? It's the mid-eighteenth century. Almost everyone works on the land, and it's quiet but for the beasts of the field, threshing and planting, winnowing and harvesting, and the village clock tolling the hours. When suddenly –' she banged her hand on her desk, as if to wake up some imaginary pupil dozing at the back of the room – 'out of nowhere, hundreds of brawny, illiterate, complete strangers arrive in your parish. They're here to burrow and toil, to fornicate and drink; they have to sleep and defecate, but they will also steal and pillage and rape. Some of them will get injured, some will become ill, and some will die.'

'Blimey,' said Kavanagh, 'you paint quite a picture. I think if you'd taught me history instead of old duffer Jones, I might have got a decent pass! Your kids,' he said, gesturing to the empty desks, 'they're lucky to have such an inspiring teacher.'

'Oh, yes, I bet they feel lucky,' she said.

'No?' he asked.

'A man in breeches with a pickaxe is not much competition for a Play Station or an Xbox, Inspector. Nothing surprises them any more. I doubt that these men will really cut it for them,' she added wistfully.

'Anyway, you're happy to be involved?' he added rather superfluously.

'Yes, I love it,' she agreed.

'I'll never see a canal in the same way again,' he said. 'But to return to Ms Clement...'

'Of course,' she said.

117

'We're trying to interview everyone who might have been in the vicinity around the time of her death. We have to fill in all we know about her last-known movements, and account for everyone who might have seen or spoken to her...'

'I see,' said McAvoy.

'You discovered her body that Sunday afternoon. Did you often leave the group?'

'Occasionally. For a cigarette. You know how it is these days. Filthy habit, social leper, all that stuff...'

'I know,' he agreed, and tapped the tobacco pouch in his pocket as a sign of solidarity. 'What about the others?' he asked.

'How do you mean?'

'Is there anyone else in the group who tends to spend time away? Anyone you're aware of who might go off on their own?'

'You don't think one of our lot was involved?' she replied, aghast.

'We can't rule anything out at this stage,' he said. 'Sarah was killed sometime during the previous several days. I believe some of the volunteers were on site as early as mid-morning, Friday. They could have been in the area before that. We'll need to check and account for everyone's movements and whereabouts during that period. It's the way we do these things.' He sensed a little unease in her. 'What is it?' he asked.

'It's not my place to suggest anything about anyone, but...'

'Please, go on,' he urged her.

'One of the newer people, he does spend a deal of time on his own. We've tried to make him welcome. They're a friendly lot, really, but this young man tends to work on his own, and he does wander off site a bit. Of course, people come and go all the time. To their cars; they pop to the shop to get milk or a paper, or back to their B and Bs if they've forgotten something. It is work we do, but it's not *employment*. We're volunteers; we don't have to be there.'

'I understand,' said Kavanagh.

'I'm not suggesting anything about him, but he is a bit of a loner...'

'What's his name?' he asked.

'Steve,' she said.

'Steve what?'

'I've no idea,' she said. 'You'd have to speak to Jeff. He's the one with all the contact details.'

'And where does he stay? Do you know where he's from?'

'He comes down from the Midlands some-where. And he sleeps in his van. I think it's, you know, one of those conversions. At least, he's got bedding and stuff in there. Look, I hope I haven't said too much. He's probably perfectly alright, but just a bit shy...'

'I'm sure,' said the inspector, 'but any bits of information might prove useful.' He eased him-self up from the desk where he had been wedged in for the last twenty minutes. 'Right, Ms Mc-Avoy. You've been a great deal of help. We'll speak again, no doubt. But meantime, one of my officers will come down and take a detailed statement from you. And please, just for now, don't pass on any of what I've told you.'

'Of course,' she said. 'You have my word.'

Fifteen

July 2006

Farmer Philip Ellis stood beside the curtain and watched as the woman approached. She looked at her watch. It was just before eight o'clock, and she waited at the box hedge at the front of the garden for a couple of minutes. As the clock chimed eight in the hall, there was a tap at the front door.

He invited her in and showed her the polishes and cleaning materials, as well as the ironing board and vacuum cleaner in the downstairs cupboard. He then took her through to the sitting room with its big open fireplace where they stood awkwardly. He put out his hand. 'Incidentally, I'm Philip...'

'Katrina,' she murmured, extending her hand.

'Would you...' he gestured to the cold ashes in the fire.

'Light?' she asked.

'Yes. No. Just make ready. Not light. Not yet.'

120

She parted her lips in a smile, and he smiled too.

'Sorry,' he said.

'Sorry?'

'It's alright,' he offered. 'Would you like a cup of coffee, Katrina? I'm going to have one.'

'No, thank you,' she said, unzipped her fleece and began rolling newspaper to lay the fire.

As she busied herself, he brought down several shirts and a couple of sets of sheets and pillowcases from the airing cupboard.

A couple of years previously, some three years after his wife had left him, fed up with microwave meals, evenings in front of the TV, and a drink at the local pub on Friday evenings, the man had joined a dating agency. They'd taken his two-hundred-pounds subscription and made all kinds of promises about the women on their books.

He'd spent hours filling out forms about his likes and dislikes, had half a dozen sets of photographs taken at the booth in Boots in Rickmansworth, but in a year and a half he'd had only three introductions, one of which had gone no further than a disastrous, tongue-tied phone call.

He wasn't even sure that he was looking for a woman: he knew that what he didn't need was agricultural advice or a farming partner, some Ruth Archer with a ballsy attitude and harebrained schemes about doubling the spinach crop. He knew perfectly well what he was doing on the farm. No, what he imagined he wanted was simply to have someone around to talk to about how his day had been, maybe to occasionally eat supper with in the evening, someone to come home to sometimes.

He had money in the bank, but that was just a problem, for he was wary of attracting a gold-digger, some woman who'd spend all his cash without so much as making an apple pie or putting fuel in the Aga. Was it too much to ask?

The couple of women he'd taken out for the evening had liked the Range Rover and the meals in the decent restaurant well enough, but they'd shown no interest whatsoever in his daily work and life. The fact was, Ellis had concluded, it might be miserable being alone, but it was better, surely, than being with someone with whom you had little or nothing in common.

A little chastened by his dating-agency experiences, he'd put his energies instead, that early spring, into working on the extensions to the accommodation for that season's soon-to-be-arriving workforce, accommodation that had formerly served as a shippen and milking parlour.

Even now, some eighteen months later, every couple of weeks, the agency would send details about some wholly unsuitable woman – twenty years too old, hugely overweight (he was agile, slim and fit), or living five hundred miles away in the Scottish Highlands. He'd grown used to chucking the pictures and the women's profiles in the bin before getting back to his daily work.

'Katrina,' he said now, standing in the doorway.

'Yes,' she said, turning from the ironing.

'I'm going out. To the fields.' He spoke slowly, judging her level of understanding from her look back at him. 'Please, make yourself at home, and do have a cup of coffee...'

'No coffee,' she said seriously. 'I here for work.'

He smiled. 'Thank you, anyway.'

'Sorry?' she asked. 'Why "thank you"?'

'It's alright,' he said. 'It's nothing.'

She turned back to the ironing as he sat on the stairs and pulled on his boots.

He got up and put on his Barbour jacket. As he passed the open door of the sitting room, with arms akimbo she folded a double sheet. She might be forty or forty-five, possibly even a little older than that, he thought, but she had a very nice figure.

Sixteen

October 2006

'Joe, let me speak to Frank,' said Salt down the line.

DS Lavendar called out across the crowded incident room to Kavanagh and motioned to him to pick up the phone.

'What is it?' Kavanagh called back.

'It's Salt,' said Joe. 'They've found something down at the canal. She wants to speak to you.'

'It'll be the cyclist,' he said, and picked up the phone.

'Frank,' said Salt.

'Jane? What you got? I'll give you six-to-four it's Lance Armstrong. Go on, you've found the phantom cyclist...'

'It's not a cyclist, Frank,' she said.

'No?'

'You'd best get down here.'

'What have you got? You know I'm not good with surprises,' said the inspector.

'A ladder.'

'A ladder? What? You've found a window-cleaner? Have him get round to my place pronto – they're filthy.'

'No window-cleaning here, Frank. We think this one's been up a tree.'

'Up a tree?' he said. 'I've no idea what you're talking about, but I'm coming down. Give me half an hour.'

The thing about even a relatively small search area is that it requires a huge undertaking in manpower and resources. A little unfairly, perhaps, just one aerial photo by a tabloid newspaper makes the same space look tiny. But look more carefully, and you will see just how many houses and garages, sheds and outhouses there are in that little picture.

And in every one of those houses and outbuildings there are dozens of rooms with very many cupboards; there are lots of cellars and hundreds of loft spaces and attics. This is hide and seek for very big stakes and no party bag for the loser, just widespread opprobrium and ridicule. And if, a day after a killer is eventually convicted, it is revealed that the police had initially missed something obvious, the cops can be made to look very foolish indeed.

The other thing about searching is that you can only go so far; there have to be prescribed limits. It's not like the village team looking for the cricket ball that they know has been hit into the long grass beyond the boundary. The cops don't even have the luxury of knowing whether it is indeed a cricket ball that they are looking for, and so must collect every single thing – every tiny scrap that sits on leaf or lies in earth or is speared by grass or twig.

After the initial examination of two hundred yards around the scene of the discovery of Sarah Clement's body, and the same area around her boat, notwithstanding the number of officers who had spent two days crawling through the undergrowth on their hands and knees collecting every scrap of detritus, nothing material had been found.

Just as the cricket ball goes undiscovered, and yet may be lying only a foot further on, so – had the police extended their search by only a few yards – they would indeed have stumbled upon a clue to their enquiry almost as good as if a suspect's name had been scrawled on a piece of paper and left pinned to a tree there.

But they didn't.

A day later, aware of the search team's lack of success, Kavanagh authorized his team to widen the area. It was more an act of desperation than inspiration for, frankly, apart from a missing cyclist who was declining to come forward and identify himself, they hadn't a great deal to go on.

And, of course, to make matters worse, every senior officer in the country was haunted by the memory of the high-profile mistakes that had been made in the past, like the search for an Oxford student's missing girlfriend, whom he claimed to have escorted on to a bus after a lover's tiff, but whose decomposing body was found in the boy's flat a week later when they eventually prised away the bath panel.

No, if Kavanagh missed anything on this enquiry, it wouldn't be through lack of diligence.

In an age when video cameras used in covert surveillance are the size of fountain-pen tops, there was something touchingly old-fashioned about the rough ladder that had been clumsily concealed in the scrub.

It didn't take a survival expert or an aborigine tracker to deduce that when the thing wasn't lying concealed in the undergrowth, it had been carried the few yards to a nearby beech. And, from twenty feet up the mature tree, courtesy of several neatly lopped boughs, there was now a pretty much unimpeded view of the shower block on Philip Ellis's farm fifty yards away.

'So, who found it?' asked the inspector.

'One of the boys on the search team,' said Salt. 'He's cock-a-hoop. They widened the area, as per your instructions, were about another thirty metres inland from the canal for a new, extended sweep, and, lo and behold.'

Kavanagh grinned as he looked from the ladder across to the farm buildings.

'What is it?' Salt asked.

'Well, two things,' he began. 'Is it just me, or is there something innately funny about a ladder?'

'How do you mean?' said Salt.

'A ladder, you know? Does it not have all the wrong connotations? Somehow, I just can't associate a ladder with tragedy...'

'Meaning?' she said.

'They're things that you walk under at your peril, but always in a funny way; in cartoons, a pot of paint falls on your head. I don't know ... they're just a bit Laurel and Hardy. You know what I mean?'

'OK,' she said, clearly unconvinced. 'And secondly?'

He looked about him a little shiftily. There was no one within earshot. The forensics people were absorbed in their work, examining the rough-built orchard ladder, carefully picking through the grass and brambles where it had been concealed and dusting the bark of the tree with aluminium granules for fingerprints.

'Off the record, of course,' he said quietly.

'What, Frank?' she said a little sharply.

'Well, I don't know what it's like for women, but, you know, show me a bloke who wouldn't...'

'Wouldn't what?' she said sternly.

'You know ... it's pretty harmless, a bit of...'

'No, I don't know. What exactly do you mean, Frank?'

'So, somebody's climbing a ladder, and having a dekko in through the shower-room window. I'm not condoning it, of course...'

'It sounds to me like that's exactly what you're doing,' she said uncompromisingly.

'Look, at the end of the day,' he said, 'what harm's he doing? Himself or anyone else? The biggest risk is him falling off and breaking a leg.'

'You amaze me, Frank.'

'Really?' he said.

'Really,' she reiterated.

'This won't be anything to do with Sarah Clement's killing, I guarantee you. This is just some guy from the farm having a bit of...'

'A bit of what?' she asked.

'A bit of fun. Not exemplary, maybe, but it's hardly a hanging offence.'

'You ought to find yourself a therapist, Frank.'

'Thanks. Jane, you know, sex, it's a funny thing...'

'You're telling me?' she said.

'What people do, what they get off on, it's up to them. If there's no harm done...'

'Frank,' she said, as if speaking to a recalcitrant child, 'this is 2006. Whoever's done this, they're committing a crime. It's not a bit of fun. This is one person spying on another. It's not mutual; there's no consent. It's an invasion of privacy.'

'Well, technically, yes...'

'Technically? What do you mean, "technically"?' With that she stalked away.

He followed her, and spoke to her back. 'Look, some bloke's far from home, and he's getting a bit of a thrill watching a woman having a shower. We're here to investigate a murder, not to occupy the moral high ground about a peeping tom. Really, at the end of the day, what's the harm? Is it any worse than him going down to the local massage parlour?'

She turned and faced him. 'Two wrongs, Frank. And anyway, what's the next step? What

129

about when watching's not enough? What about when he wants to touch? What about when he wants the woman for himself?'

'I think there's a bit of a jump there, Jane, a want of logic. Lots of blokes watch stuff. They're not rapists. I've watched the odd bit of stuff myself; find me a bloke who hasn't. I'm not a rapist.'

'I'm disgusted, Frank. I really am.' She picked her way through the marker tape strung between the poles, back towards the canal.

He walked after her, as irked by her high-mindedness as she was with his lax morality. 'You know, Jane,' he said quietly, 'the sexual urge is very strong in men. That's a fact, it's official, not an opinion. The most powerful man in the world had a woman half his age go down on him in the Oval Office. He's the Commander in Chief of the armed forces; on his desk he's got the button that can begin the destruction of the entire world. And yet, at that moment, he will not be denied. At that moment, Bill Clinton's the same as a man in a field here who sticks a ladder up a tree to watch a naked woman. That's all I'm saying.'

She stopped, turned and looked at him with total contempt. 'And do you know what I'm saying, Frank? Clinton, and whoever put that thing up a tree, might have all the urges in the world. The fact that we're supposed to be civilized means that we don't just give in to them, we deal with them.'

'Yes, maybe, Jane. In a perfect world,' he

130

rejoined.

'And to be honest, if I didn't know you better, I'd report you,' she said.

'Yes? And do you know what? I actually think you would,' he sneered. 'And just how fucking sad is that? You *do* know me, and that's why I'm trying to tell you how it actually *is*, not how you up there on your high horse would like it to be.'

'I don't believe I'm hearing this,' she said. 'I really don't.'

'Look,' he said, 'given the situation here, given Sarah Clement's murder, we'll find the Tarzan who's done this and bring him in. But you wait and see; he'll be the same as any other bloke looking at a few pictures on the internet.'

'Men!' she said with real feeling, and strode away.

Seventeen

May 1986

It wasn't like being in a new city, it was being in a city that she'd seen a hundred times before, but could now experience with all of her tingling senses.

Leah smelled the hot-dog stands as the lumbering yellow cabs rolled by and the gleaming fire trucks swayed and sirened; she watched the horse-mounted police amble down Fifth Avenue, relaxed yet imperious and, in the following days, she splayed her fingers over the Indian limestone and granite of the Empire State Building, stood in wonder at the echoing marble caverns of Grand Central Station, rode the Staten Island Ferry and walked the boards of Brooklyn Bridge.

They'd driven by bus down the east coast from Boston, through Connecticut and the Long Island Sound, as America stretched 3,000 miles away on their right, all the way to California and the Pacific coast.

OK, the view from the concrete highway was, for the most part, as much like the M6 in Birmingham as anything distinctly American, but there were enough Chevrolets and Pontiacs cruising by them to remind her that this was neither the M6 nor the A48 Newport–Cardiff trunk road. This was *America*, and twenty-year-old Leah was thrilled to be here.

Ethan was the man she was in love with, and – not always the same thing – Ethan was the man she loved to *be* with.

He'd been to New York half a dozen times, had driven this unprepossessing highway with his parents, with his older sister who now worked out of Washington and, on his first ever trip to the place, he'd gone by bus with three dozen school friends way back in 1977.

But right now, he was sitting beside a young English woman who was seeing the Atlantic seaboard of his country for the first time, and he knew exactly when to tell her this, point out that, and fill her in on the other, and when to keep quiet and let her experience these things for herself.

The bus pulled into the Port Authority terminal on 42nd Street at three in the afternoon. How could such a prosaic street sign be so evocative? It wasn't even a *name*. How could a sign that said simply West 42nd Street be so incredibly ... What? 'Stirring' is the word she wrote in her workbook that night. But frankly, 'stirring' didn't even come close to what she felt that day.

She'd met Ethan halfway through her sandwich year at Smith College in Massachusetts, ninety miles west of Boston. A rangy young man, a year older than herself, Ethan was halfway through his postgraduate doctorate in psychology. He'd driven over from Harvard to see a former school friend, Kelly, who was also studying in the college's English department.

Kelly introduced him to Leah and, unlike in Britain, where mating rituals more or less decreed that one was obliged to ignore the very person in any group that one actually liked the look of, here, these two immediately and unselfconsciously took a deal of pleasure in one another's company.

At Ethan's clapboard house in the Boston suburb of Somerville a fortnight later, whilst his mother and father were away for the weekend just across the border in Québec, the young couple slept together for the first time.

Cardiff sixth-former Robert had been – until she began her undergraduate studies at Lampeter and had a couple of relationships during that first year – Leah's only real lover. Sex with pensive, bisexual Robert had involved very little laughter, and no endearments. And although the laconic Morrissey fan had said to her one winter's afternoon, 'Anything you want me to do, Leah, just say,' it was an offer that had been made with such detachment that it was like being handed a menu in a Japanese restaurant for the first time: faintly exciting, but rather alarming, too.

If sex with Robert had been sushi, for Leah, making love with Ethan was an English fried breakfast, an overflowing plate of bad-for-you, high-cholesterol, fat-saturated food that left her sated, slightly ashamed, and feeling absolutely wonderful.

Theirs was a closeness that was unlike anything she had ever previously known. Lying beside him in bed one afternoon, his heart beating steadily against her back, they played out their future together with lovely dreams and wilder schemes, and she told him something that she had never told anyone before in her life: she whispered that she was going to be a writer. Not that she *wanted* to be, but that she was *going* to be. He squeezed her hand, lifted the hair from her nape and kissed the back of her neck.

And now, just a couple of months later, on a beautiful day in spring, here they were in New York, the very name of which thrilled her to the core.

They stayed a hundred yards from the Chelsea Hotel on West 23rd, and during the next couple of days, visited the New York library, the Post Office building with its proud declaration etched in the stonework there: *Neither snow nor rain nor heat nor gloom of night stays these couriers from the swift completion of their appointed rounds.*

They photographed each other on the water in New York Harbor before the Statue of Liberty, watched the chess in Washington Square Park, bought tee-shirts in Canal Street, ate in Little Italy and walked the length and breadth of Central Park.

At night, in the big hotel bed, Leah sat astride him as he held his arms around her. 'And after all that, we're having sex in New York, Ethan,' she said, and they both laughed.

'We sure are, Leah. We most certainly are,' he said.

Back in Wales in their sixth-form days, she and Robert might have had some mawkish notion of themselves as a sort of embryonic Plath and Hughes, a couple of awkward, intense and essentially unhappy people, *artistes manques* who burned hot only through their work.

This couple, Ethan and Leah, were an unaffected pair, a mid-80s incarnation, perhaps, of a fresh-faced Bob Dylan and Suze Rotolo, wrapped in each other's arms in a 1963 New York street, warm lovers in a cold world.

But where to go from here? All they knew was

135

that this was no transatlantic, term-time fling. In September, Leah would be beginning her MA in creative writing at Keele in Staffordshire.

The idea that Ethan wouldn't – at the very least – be in the same country, was not for either of them even a remote possibility.

Eighteen

July 2006

He wasn't wrong. He was diffident, but he wasn't wrong. After a week of self-consciously manoeuvring past one another in the kitchen, along the hall, Philip Ellis was almost certain that he wasn't wrong.

Katrina stood just a little *too* close as he asked her whether, when she'd dusted the book-shelves, she'd mind fixing the tear in a shirt or put a button on a jacket.

Didn't she? He couldn't afford to make a mistake, for all sorts of awkwardness could result.

But they had so many misunderstandings when they tried to communicate in anything but the most rudimentary language, it would be better, safer really, to write to her instead.

She always had her dictionary to hand. If he wrote to her, not only could she take the time to absorb everything he wrote, but anything she didn't immediately comprehend, she could check. And there'd be no question of his being, at some time in the future, accused of having abused his position as an employer. A man who forced his attentions upon a reluctant foreign employee, with issues of harassment and even exploitation. Especially if he kept a copy of the letter. Most importantly, though, it would avoid the embarrassment if he had misread the entire situation.

But he didn't think he had: he was a man, and she was a woman, and whether Polish, English, French or Dutch, her proximity to him at the sink, at the cooker, near the washing machine, surely these things told their own story.

But then he'd agonize. Perhaps in Poland everyone smiled when you said something considerate, or made the most routine request of them?

But did everyone laugh – as they now often did – when there was yet another of their linguistic gaffes? She'd told him on the second day that her degree was 'in Freud and horticulture'.

'That's an unusual combination, Katrina. In this country, I think students do philosophy and politics. Or English and sociology.'

She took a step towards the fruit bowl, picked up a banana, then an apple. 'Freud and horticulture,' she repeated.

'*Fruit* and horticulture,' he said, then put his arms around her, and immediately sensed her soften against him.

There was something about this woman that might suit his needs much better than any number of women who could conceivably come to him via a London dating bureau. Yes, she was quiet, and yes, she was often very serious. But Ellis wasn't looking for a comedian, some life and soul of the party flibbertigibbet, as his mother might have said.

At school, as a fifteen-year-old, he'd had to do some Wordsworth poems for O level English. They were mostly stupid, of course, poems about daffodils and a woman singing while she cut the hay. Some chance! And he'd mocked them along with all the other lads. But there was one he liked, about a boy stealing a boat and rowing across a lake until he gets terrified as the rocks come up behind him. And there was another one that he now remembered as he watched Katrina going about her tasks, a woman who 'dwelt among the untrodden ways'.

Yes, thought Ellis, Katrina was exactly that kind of woman. Someone who might have been good with the docile cattle in the old days when the farm was teeming with heifers, a biddable woman, someone who for him would be ideal.

Maybe he wasn't such a bad catch after all. He had money, and he didn't want much: just a woman who would do for him, help him with this and that, keep the house clean and cook a little.

After that day, when he had placed his hands on her shoulders, there was a new intimacy between them, like the bond that links any couple who have slept together.

But she didn't take advantage of their new relationship in any way. She was just as diligent in her work. He came home the next day to find her on the floor in the bathroom, the blinds stretched out before her on the oak boards there. She was cleaning each slat with warm, soapy water. In the twenty years that the blinds had been at the windows, they had never, as far as he was aware, been cleaned beyond the most cursory wipe.

The bed sheets were just as nicely ironed, his shirts pressed and hung. She was always punctual, and left his supper not only cooked, but the table somehow considerately laid, almost as if the cutlery and the water tumbler and little vase of flowers there carried a message for him as, later, he sat and ate alone.

When she came in to work the next morning, she found little yellow Post-its all over the cupboards and work surfaces – the tea caddy and sugar bowl, the milk jug and colander – almost every utensil was labelled in English.

She thanked him when he came in for mid-morning coffee.

He asked her if she would do the same for him, in Polish. Actually, he didn't want to learn her language. Not really. His half-dozen words – *tak*; *prosze* and *dzien dobry*, enough to say good morning – were all he'd ever needed to make civil gestures towards his workforce, but he felt it right that she see their wholly unequal relationship in more egalitarian terms. He didn't want to exploit her.

'I no want,' she said, turning away.

'No want?' he repeated, a little affronted by the rebuff. 'Why not, Katrina?'

'I want learn English. Is no necessary you learn my language,' she said, and went about her work.

The next evening, as she made ready to leave, he asked her, 'You have a boyfriend, Katrina?'

'Boyfriend?' she railed gently. 'I am woman.'

'Yes, of course,' he added. 'It's just a phrase, in English.'

'Phrase?'

'Something we say. Yes, you are woman. Do you have, then, a man? At home, in Poland, perhaps? Or one of the workers here?'

'I don't like Polish man,' she said. 'My husband, in Poznan, he is Polish. I don't like.'

'I see,' said Ellis, quietly pleased to hear this dismissal of an entire nation's men, especially as quite a few of them were now here, working in his fields. 'Katrina, would you like to stay for a drink?' he asked.

She hesitated for a moment as she appeared to consider the offer, and then glanced down at her sweatshirt, her baggy tracksuit bottoms, and said, 'No, thank you, Mr Philip. Tonight, I go back.'

As he ate his supper on his lap, the volume of the television turned down almost to inaudibility, he conjured the phrase, 'Tonight, I go

140

back.'

Even he understood that it admitted the possibility that, on *another* night, her answer might well be different.

Or maybe that was a conclusion too far. He was no linguist, and she was a woman who could barely construct a grammatical sentence in his alien tongue. But if there wasn't a real warmth, even an affection between them, why did he feel so much happier than he had done in ... well, in years?

He felt relaxed and content. He was glad to see her every morning when she tapped at the front door before letting herself in. And even that tap at the door was done with an innate decorum, a sort of reserve and polite consideration that was all the more welcome for its absence in just about every English person he ever met these days in the supermarket or garage. She seemed to be born out of her time, living out of her place.

The letter he wrote was straightforward.

> Katrina, I am writing to you because I want you to have time to consider what I am saying, and I think you will have more time to think about it, and understand it properly, if I write rather than say these things.
>
> I have grown fond of you since you have been working in my house, and the way we talk and laugh makes me think that, perhaps, you might feel the same way

about me?

Please don't tell anyone else what I have written here. These thoughts are for you alone.

Yours sincerely,
Philip

He left the letter propped up on the kitchen table and, the following morning, made certain that he was out by the time that she arrived.

When he returned, just after eleven, having spent the morning – and all the previous evening and night – thinking about what he had written, he bitterly regretted what he had done, and had convinced himself that he had made a foolish mistake and would soon be a laughing stock amongst his own workforce.

This time, it was he who tapped at his own kitchen door before entering. Katrina was on her knees, emptying the washing machine. She turned and smiled. 'Please, Philip, come in.'

Nineteen

Late September 2006

There had been quite a fanfare for Marcus Breese's departure on his two-hundred-mile cycle ride. The press came – the local press, anyway. And, of course, his own TV station sent along a cub reporter and a cameraman.

There was bit of bunting strung across the marina's chandlery, and a few balloons blown about on cotton in the overcast morning. The south of the country might be experiencing a heat wave, but here in the Midlands, it was grey and showery.

The Mayoress donated a cheque for £25, written on a piece of cardboard four-feet long, which was received by the director of the local hospice who gave a gracious vote of thanks, not only for the cheque, but also for our 'pedalling hero', his dedication and fund-raising sponsorship.

Local onlookers – a couple of men walking dogs, and women on their way home from taking children to the nearby primary school – were chivvied by girls with yellow sashes

143

around their shoulders, Market Drayton cheer-leaders whose skin goose-pimpled in the Sep-tember chill, into putting a few more coins into the collecting bucket.

And that was it. There was a countdown and Marcus Breese pedalled off down the towpath, turning just once to wave to his girlfriend, Bernie. Unfortunately, in looking back over his shoulder, the cycle, laden with camping kit, clothes and food, wobbled alarmingly, and the *Midlands Today* cameraman wondered whether the story of yet another local fund-raising event might not be going to become a decent story after all: 'self-serving consumer affairs reporter falls headlong into Shropshire canal'.

But Breese regained his balance and dis-appeared out of sight down the muddy towpath. The camera crew and press went on to their next assignments at the local infants' school, the crematorium and the Magistrates' court. The staff from the hospice went back to their sombre work, and a few glum teenagers returned to their earnest, spitting business.

For all his panache in front of camera in a TV studio, Breese was glad to leave the gaggle of onlookers behind and get on with his long-planned ride. He'd done his research: flat tow-paths, no traffic, few people and a good number of possible camping spots identified for over-night stops during the next five days.

And he wouldn't even have to file a story. He *was* the story. OK, he wasn't crossing the Alps in a flimsy balloon; it wasn't even the London marathon but, no matter, the publicity would do his career no harm at all.

And his career *did* need a little realignment. It seemed that, in spite of his own best efforts – the public righting of others' wrongs – many viewers saw his zealotry as an all too transparent self-aggrandisement.

In the course of exposing folk who brought a few cartons of tobacco from Belgium or France for sale in the local pub, or flogged counterfeit DVDs at the local car boot sale, Breese was perceived by any number of viewers as being rather more off-putting than the hapless folk that he was supposedly exposing.

Of course, very few things go exactly as planned, and Breese's pedalling trip was no exception. After less than an hour, the plans that he had made sitting at his table, the maps of Shropshire and the West Midlands, Northampton and Buckingham and Hertfordshire spread out before him, seemed absurdly ambitious.

Planning and mapping, listing and printing-out was one thing; but the reality was already proving very different. Only a mile or two from the town's little marina, the path which had been described on his map as 'negotiable' became a quagmire. The canal had been driven through a sandstone ravine and trees overhung the whole cutting. It was a sunless place, and surface rainwater collected there, unable to drain away.

Further recent heavy rain had made the path a swamp and the cycle slithered and strayed beneath him. Having lost control and nearly fallen into the water, he dismounted and began to push his unwieldy tourer through deep mud that had the consistency of coffee-coloured ice-cream.

He checked his watch: he'd been underway an hour and was already sodden and mud-spattered. He'd not brought boots with him, merely trainers suitable, as he imagined, for the cycling that lay ahead.

A canal boat chugged up alongside him as he squelched on a few more yards. As the craft passed, the helmsman looked back and said, 'Rather you than me, mate,' and puttered away.

Twenty

October 2006

Kavanagh's notion of a farm, in as much as the Birmingham-born inspector had a notion of a farm at all, was of concrete yards, deep in mud and ordure, five-bar gates and arcane machinery littering the corners of dilapidated buildings, the main feature of which was rusting corrugated iron.

And, although Kavanagh didn't say as much to Salt, since the BSE crisis of the late eighties, and the nationwide culling of hundreds of thousands of cattle – just like some vile joke that, once heard, can never be eradicated from consciousness – the abiding image in the police-man's mind was of stumbling, slavering beasts, a terrible preamble to the apocalyptic television pictures of piles of cattle, their legs in the air, smouldering on funeral pyres throughout the land.

In fact, as he parked their BMW outside the accommodation block on Philip Ellis's farm alongside a Skoda on a Czech plate, the only machinery in sight looked pretty new, efficient, and very clean.

As for dung, or even the sight of country mud, the man might just as well have been wearing carpet slippers, a pair of which he had not owned for over thirty years.

Ellis's foreman escorted Salt and Kavanagh past a minibus, a couple of stacker trucks and several towers of ten-foot-high timber pallets. They went through the yard, past the little office and up to a wooden, five-bar gate that led across to the farmhouse.

'We'll be fine from here,' said Salt. 'Thanks a lot.'

The solid front door was wide open and they stood there and called out a couple of times to the farmer. Eventually Ellis padded towards them down the wide hall as the sound of a vacuum cleaner started up somewhere far away in the house.

'Hello again,' he said. 'Just battling the paper-work. Please, come in.'

He led them through to the kitchen, offered them chairs around the farmhouse table and put the kettle on the Aga hot plate.

'How can I help you?' he said.

'You'll have heard, Mr Ellis, there've been a couple of developments,' said Kavanagh. 'The ladder that's been found is with forensics right now. We're awaiting the results.'

'Yes?' said the man. 'And what are you hoping to find?'

'Who knows?' said Salt.

'That ladder's been on the farm since God knows when,' said Ellis. 'It'll have my fingerprints on it, of course. Probably my late father's, too, if they last that long.'

'Yes, of course,' said Kavanagh, 'we'd expect that. But we should be able to isolate other users' more recent prints.'

'I see,' said the man.

'Do you have any idea when you last saw it?' asked the inspector guilelessly.

'No, not really,' he replied. 'It's an orchard ladder, virtually an antique. Belongs in a farm museum, really.' He paused and then added, 'You don't think this business with the spying's got anything to do with the murder of the woman, do you?'

'I'd personally have thought it unlikely,' volunteered the cop, glancing at Salt, 'but it's possible, of course.'

'We'd be unwise to discount any line of enquiry at this stage,' added Salt more conservatively.

'And so what can I help you with?' Ellis asked.

'Well, as well as the ladder, it's routine for us to do follow ups, check people's recollections, that kind of thing,' said Kavanagh.

'Recollections?' queried Ellis, pushing his hands into the pockets of his body-warmer and leaning back against the work surface.

'People sometimes forget things the first time we speak to them,' said Salt. 'Given a little time to think, they often become clearer.'

'And of course, it gives us the opportunity to pick up any inconsistencies in a person's story,' added Kavanagh. 'When someone's telling the truth, they can relate something a dozen times. The sequence might be different, there'll be omissions and additions, no doubt, but there won't be any holes. Truth stays watertight; liars always leak.'

'You're not referring to me, I hope?' said Ellis defensively.

'Your foreman supported the account that you gave us of your movements surrounding the time in question, but...' Kavanagh began.

'Good,' he interrupted. 'I'm here virtually the whole time. As I told you, at this time of year we're often doing eighteen hours a day. It's like a military operation just to make sure the thing runs smoothly.'

'But as I say,' continued Kavanagh, 'while your movements are accounted for during the work periods, the problem is, like many people who live alone, there are always times that can't be vouched for.'

Ellis straightened himself up, turned and

shook tea leaves from an open packet into the glazed teapot. It was the first loose tea that Salt had seen since she'd left home a lifetime ago.

'Actually, I haven't been alone at night for quite a while now,' he began and, walking to the kitchen door, called out, 'Katrina?'

The vacuum cleaner ceased and there was the sound of footsteps descending the oak boards of the staircase.

'Philip?' said the woman from the foot of the stairs, facing him.

'It's OK, Katrina, please, come.' The woman took a couple of steps towards the kitchen door. 'Police,' he gestured. 'You must tell,' he said very slowly, 'we spend all nights together. *Tak?* We in bed, all night, since we are together...'

'Of course,' she said. 'Always. Always together at night. *Tak* ... It's OK?' said the woman from the open doorway to Kavanagh. 'It's good?'

'Thank you,' said Kavanagh politely.

'It's good,' Ellis reassured the woman, smiling. 'Would you like some tea, Katrina?'

'No, I go back to my work,' she replied. 'Goodbye.'

'Goodbye,' said the police officers.

Kavanagh turned to the farmer. 'We'll need to get her story ratified with the translator, of course, but why didn't you say anything about her being with you when we last spoke?'

'I didn't want to involve her. She's a long way from home. And I didn't think it would come to this. I really didn't think you'd be checking every detail of what I had to say.' The kettle started to boil, and Ellis picked up the packet and shook a few more leaves into the pot. 'You like it strong?' he said.

As he made the tea, Salt went on, 'You know we're in the process of interviewing your workers, and arranging translators for those who speak little English?'

'Of course,' said the man, bringing cups and saucers to the table. 'And have you turned up anything useful?'

'Not really,' said Kavanagh. 'Not everyone can account for every hour, but there's nothing that looks suspicious yet. We'll probably arrange some DNA testing during the next few days.'

'DNA? I thought you told me that the body had been immersed too long?'

'Not on the murder victim,' said Salt. 'From the voyeur's scene of crime.'

'I don't follow,' said the man, perplexed.

'That kind of behaviour – peeping toms – it's obviously sexual,' said Salt, 'and of course, it ends in ... well, you can imagine what it ends in, Mr Ellis. There might, therefore, if we're lucky, be DNA evidence.'

'I see,' he said soberly, and placed on the table a pretty china bowl with a yellow Post-it stuck to its side.

'Sugar?' queried the constable, indicating the little label.

'It's for Katrina,' he said. 'I'm trying to help her with her English. She wanted me to.'

'And how's it going?' asked Salt.

'It's OK,' he said. 'Except that some of her colleagues seem to resent her being here, you know. They are not as friendly towards her as they might be,' he added as he carefully poured the dark, hot tea.

Twenty-One

October 2006

There was very little upon which bed and breakfast proprietor Terence May did not have an opinion, and he was not at all reticent about sharing that opinion with DI Frank Kavanagh and DS Joe Lavendar, the two officers who were doing their best to interview him following the initial brief statement that he had given.

'Gentlemen,' he said, 'show me any half-decent chef who would send something out of his kitchen without tasting it first.'

'Sorry?' said Kavanagh, mystified by the man's rhetoric.

'The only way to run a bed and breakfast establishment, in my own opinion, is to sleep in every bed in this house. At least once a year. It's what I do.'

The officers glanced at one another. It was, indeed, very warm this early-October afternoon, but the man's shorts, thought Kavanagh, were remarkably short. And unfashionably tight.

'And why would that be?' asked Lavendar, rather beginning to doubt the sanity of the proprietor of Sunnyside.

'Fear not, gentlemen,' May sought to reassure the officers wedged together on the wicker sofa in the sweltering conservatory. 'The man you see before you is not mad. What's the first thing you do when you check into a hotel room, Inspector?' he continued.

'Sorry?' said Kavanagh.

'Think about it,' continued May. 'You've just checked in. What do you do?'

'Look for the fire escape?' suggested the ever-cautious Kavanagh.

May looked disappointed. 'Then?' he encouraged, just a little petulantly.

'Feel the bed?' tried the inspector, glad to see that the question was a multiple choice.

'Ta-da!' exclaimed May, clearly delighted to have elicited the answer that he required to prove his pedantic point.

'I see,' said Kavanagh, keen to move on.

But before he could, the man started up again, 'And it's not only beds. What about the duvet? Has all the down ended up at one end, leaving nothing but cotton cover at the other? It might not be the way that *some* people do things, but it's what I do. Sleep in the bed, check the duvet; boil the kettle, flush the loo, take a shower, open the windows. It really is the only way,' he concluded as he stretched his neck out of his tee-shirt. 'Anyway, gentlemen, my guests seem to

153

appreciate my efforts, judging by the way they come back year after year...'

'I'm sure they do,' said Kavanagh, keen to truncate this impromptu forum on the best way to run a guest house. 'Mr May, you'll forgive me, but to get back to Ms Clement...'

'Of course,' said the man.

'It's just that we're very busy, and time is short...'

The man sat forward in his chair, his back straight, his knees together, and signalled his readiness to engage.

'Incidentally, how long have you been here, Mr May?' asked the inspector.

'Six years,' he replied. 'Six years, last June.'

'And before that?' asked Lavendar. 'Your accent's...'

'London. I've always wanted to live in the countryside, and when I sold the business, I was able to come out here.'

'I see,' said Kavanagh. 'And in London? What were you doing there?'

'I had a gallery. Contemporary painting, but mostly modern sculpture.'

Kavanagh read a bit, went to the theatre now and again, and loved cinema, but apart from a trek around the National and the Tate every six months or so, he wasn't really up to speed with the visual arts, especially those in three dimensions.

'But I never go there these days,' added May. 'It's filthy and noisy, and there's nowhere to park, nowhere at all. Frankly, I don't know how

154

anyone lives there any more. And anyway, everything I want is here.'

'Yes, it's a lovely spot,' added Kavanagh. 'Unfortunately, as you know...'

'Yes, of course, the murdered woman,' said May.

'Did you know her at all? Her boat's moored only about half a mile from here,' said the sergeant.

'I saw her, of course, at the bottom of the garden, on the towpath sometimes. But she wasn't the chatty sort. Tended to keep herself to herself. She might wave. Say hello if I was strimming down by the bank, but she didn't seem bothered to chat. And that's alright. I get more than enough of that from the guests, you know.'

'How about other people?' asked Kavanagh. 'Have you noticed anyone in the area that is not normally here? Anyone at all out of the ordinary?'

'Well, of course, most of the visitors are not normally here. They pass by on the water, stop at the shop for an ice-cream and a paper, some bacon, that kind of thing. Or they might be here for a holiday, a little break. A weekend with a bit of walking and sight-seeing. Most of them I never see again. Of course, when you chat to them, they say it's the best place they've ever seen and they'll be back, but most of them don't. There are exceptions, of course. I have some couples who come every summer, but mostly it's new people every year. Either through word of mouth, or I sometimes place an ad in *Gay Times* if things are quiet. Of course, I have a web site.'

'Can I just ask you about the volunteers – the canal restorers? They've been working in the area for quite a while,' said Lavendar.

'I have very little to do with them,' he said. 'They're a bit, you know ... what shall I say? They don't exactly throw their money around. They tend to stay with friends. A couple of them bring mobile homes, and I believe the parish hall lets them sleep there sometimes.'

'And that's it?' said Kavanagh.

'There's very little happens here, really, Inspector. It's why I like it,' said the man.

'And you've seen nothing out of the ordinary? No one unusual?' asked the sergeant.

'What is to see?' he said very precisely. 'Narrow boats; a fishing person; a canoeist paddling by. The odd cyclist, perhaps. Couples walking the towpath.'

'What about the cyclists?' said Lavendar.

'Yes, we see a few. Towpath cycling has become quite popular.'

'In particular? Recently?' pressed the sergeant innocently.

'There was one on the path a week or so ago. Got the bicycle in the air. Must have had a puncture, I suppose. The hedges have recently had their late-summer cut, and I imagine there were plenty of thorns on the path. She must have picked one up...'

'She?' said Kavanagh.

'Yes,' replied May.

'Are you sure?' pursued Lavendar.

'Definitely a woman,' he confirmed. 'I know the signs, gentlemen,' he smirked. 'She had all the female things. Anyway, Inspector, Sergeant,' he said, getting to his feet. 'Will that be all? I've guests arriving in an hour, beds to make and a lawn to mow.'

'Of course,' said Kavanagh, getting up from the creaking sofa. 'Thank you for your time. If you remember anything else, anything at all,' urged the policeman, 'please, give me a call.' He handed him his card.

As they passed through the gate at the bottom of the garden that led directly to the towpath, and May began pushing his elderly Suffolk Punch up and down the grass, Lavendar said above the noise, 'Who the fuck dyes their hair these days, Frank?'

'And what about the neck?' added Kavanagh. 'What price vanity, eh?'

'I can live with that,' said Lavendar. 'My missus wants her tits done for her birthday. But the hair, fucking hell, you might as well just hang a sign up.'

Twenty-Two

July 2006

The first time Philip Ellis had seen Katrina naked in his bedroom was not the first time he had seen her naked.

He felt a little ashamed, and just a little disappointed, as if the currency of the legitimate, genuinely affectionate transaction that had led to her being there at all, had been devalued by his earlier, counterfeit approach.

Maybe he should tell her? Not now, of course. But sometime. Sometime in their future together, perhaps.

Ellis was a beachcomber of a voyeur, like a man with a metal-detector, for whom really the pursuit is all. When the languid sunbathers and frolicking children have all gone home, this is the quiet Philip Ellis time.

He cruised the ground in a desultory way, an arbitrary thrill seeker who experienced a passing frisson of pleasure at finding even a drinks can ring pull. His midnight rambles would take him through the fields of his farm, down the surrounding tracks and lanes and on to the towpaths, and there he would stand and watch as the careless and carefree holidaymakers went about their bedtime tasks.

Often, he would be rewarded with no more than an indistinct shape passing the curtain en route to bathroom or bed. But sometimes he would see a little more: someone removing their clothes, and even, occasionally, their undergarments. Young trippers, especially, careless of their modesty, curtains barely closed, afforded him more than enough satisfaction in his quest.

And of course, the same young people – much more inclined to spend the evening drinking in the pub down the path than older folk – would invariably return to their craft and do exactly, and uninhibitedly, what he really thrilled to see and hear them doing.

Whilst passing holiday trade was often worth a summer's midnight ramble, just as good in many ways were the year-long residents, the local boat-dwellers who could be depended upon to follow their nocturnal routines: the dreadlocked man up the path who always took a leak in the hedgerow last thing at night and in particular the insomniac Sarah Clement, a woman whom he had watched perhaps more than any other.

Often, he had waited hours for her to retire, standing there silently in the hedgerow bushes, the summer breeze in his hair and billowing his cotton shirt. When the first of autumn's chills arrived, of course, the lamps inside would be lit, and the view afforded be so much better.

He had watched as Sarah had swayed and

rocked to the drinks cupboard in the galley. He had watched her stumble to the little cabin loo, take more drink, and loll on the sofa there, entirely careless of her state of dress.

But, alas, often so incapacitated was she that the man had returned to his own bed before she had made ready for her own. Frequently, too, she would fall asleep in her clothes, exactly where she lay on the sofa bunk, a glass in her hand, a cigarette smouldering in the ashtray beside her.

And what was he supposed to do, he wondered, if she did, one of these nights, as she surely must, set the boat on fire? Wait for it to be in flames, and claim a passing interest? Or rush in before the fire took hold and, in alerting her to her folly, reveal himself?

Oh, well, it hadn't happened. Yet.

He returned repeatedly because twice he had seen her slip her top off, remove her brassiere, push down her jeans and pants and crawl beneath the duvet. And it had been worth the long, long wait, for Sarah Clement naked was surely a thrilling sight to any man, let alone this nocturnal voyeur. With her taut body, small but shapely breasts of a much younger woman, and heart of rust pubic hair, she had made his wait worthwhile.

When, this last couple of years, he had taken on his foreign labour, the expansion of his illicit interests seemed the natural and fulfilling thing to pursue. The shower block was in line with a copse, the trees there adequate cover for his activities. All he needed was access to one of those trees and the removal of a couple of inconvenient branches, something which the dexterous man achieved with ease. He then concealed the ladder in the long grass nearby, and all would have been well but for the tragic and inconvenient death of Sarah Clement.

By the time Ellis was aware of her murder, the place was overrun with police and there was no opportunity to remove the thing. He had little option but to bide his time and await the questioning which would surely follow as to just what the ladder was doing there.

And he was right, of course: on the second, extended sweep of the area, the crudely made orchard ladder had come to light, a barely discernible track through the long grass leading directly to the tree where its purpose was all too clear.

Forensics officers had swarmed around the spot, quietly euphoric at the patient task that lay ahead of them. And they had every cause to be optimistic. The warm, dry weather would certainly assist them in identifying the unusually athletic voyeur. As far back as 1920, Edmund Locard, director of the world's first crime laboratory, had declared in *L'enquête criminelle et les methodes scientifiques* that, 'If there is contact between two items, there will be exchange.'

The white-suited officers, perched upon their carefully erected tented scaffold, dusted the rough bark of the beech tree and the uprights and rungs of the ladder as they sought evidence of that exchange.

Now, in Philip Ellis's bedroom, Katrina wasn't naked. Not yet. She was wearing a cream, silky top. What were they called? Was it a basque? Ellis thought not. It was a slip, really, a cream silk slip with narrow shoulder straps that came down to her thighs.

The man associated his east-European workers with the austerity of the former Soviet Union and their gloomy satellites. The idea that this woman could have emerged from one of those dour countries and look so enticingly sexual confounded every notion that he had.

Of course, her breasts were not the breasts of a young woman, but they were full, and they rocked slightly and most beguilingly against her top as she took a step towards the bed.

He said to her quietly, 'You look very nice, Katrina. Please, come...'

She took another step towards the bed, and he turned down the duvet for her.

'I take off?' she asked, gesturing towards her top.

'Yes,' he began as she lifted her slip over her head. 'Please, take off,' he murmured, wholly unnecessarily.

Twenty-Three

October 2006

'So, during the last few years, Clement's had at least a dozen relationships,' said Kavanagh.

Salt knew her man – and her boss – well enough to know that the apparently neutral comment carried with it just a hint of traditional, male censoriousness.

'Well, you know what they say,' she replied, refusing to rise to the bait.

'What do they say?' he asked.

'That a new relationship allows you to re-invent yourself.'

'Yes?' he said. 'So Sarah reinvented herself quite a few times?'

They sat together at his desk in the incident room and, in the light of their still-fresh wounds after the testy exchange about the activities of the voyeur out at Ellis's farm, at least a part of their aim was rapprochement.

She let his comment pass and said, 'So?'

'So nothing,' he replied, and continued to scroll down the screen through just some of the many hundreds of pieces of information that had thus far accrued about the deceased woman's life.

These days, on any big enquiry, the Home Office Large Major Enquiry System (HOLMES 2) software was routinely employed. Apart from a little disquiet about the obvious redundancy of one of the two adjacent adjectives, Kavanagh, like every other senior officer in the force, recognized the value of the beast.

If the recollection of abortive searches haunted senior officers, catastrophes caused by failure to adequately cross-reference incoming information positively scorched them.

The investigation a couple of decades earlier into the activities of the so-called Yorkshire Ripper was seared into the minds of every copper in the country, not on account of Peter Sutcliffe's heinous crimes and eventual imprisonment, but for the fact that, swamped with information that could not be adequately cross-referenced, the police had repeatedly failed to identify him as the main suspect.

Oddly, the multiple killer shared his birthday with that chronicler of Dorset melancholy, Thomas Hardy, but even if officers might not have been expected to identify this detail as anything but eerie coincidence, surely his being interviewed no fewer than *nine* times should have given them pause for thought?

Rather than let an enquiry become overwhelmed with thousands of testimonies, witness statements and related documents, the Home Office was now equipped with HOLMES 2.

'And you buy into what Jenni Clough said

about promiscuous women like Clement trying to fill a gap in their lives – their psyches?' said Kavanagh.

'I'm not sure she used the word "promiscuous",' said Salt. 'And I'm also pretty sure she said people, not women. But yes, what she was referring to is accepted fact.'

'Her relationships generally appear to have lasted a few months,' he went on. 'A couple of one-night stands that we're aware of – one, quite recently, with an east-German guy that she got friendly with one evening in the pub. But generally speaking she seems to spend a few months with a bloke, and that's it.'

'All blokes?' said Salt.

Kavanagh looked up, gave her a quick glance. Was it that she simply didn't care for his assumption and was, like any good cop, covering all the bases before moving on, or was she making some gender point?

He played it with a straight bat, 'Yes, all men, as far as we know,' he said. 'There is this one bloke she went out with for quite a long time,' he continued, pointing at the man's details on the screen. 'A playwright, someone called Adam Shaw. You ever heard of him?'

'No. Never,' said Salt. 'Where's he based?'

'Altrincham. Outside Manchester. I had a girlfriend there once,' he added, just a touch wistfully. 'It's where the footballers who can't afford Knutsford and Wilmslow live.'

'I'll hear about the girlfriend some other time,' she said, lightening the tone of their staccato exchange, and added, 'Wasn't Sarah originally from up that way?'

'Yes. Born in Didsbury, and went back to Manchester after her stint at Keele.'

'And where did she and this playwright meet?' said Salt.

He scrolled down several pages. 'Doesn't say,' he replied.

'Maybe they were just writers from the same area?' she suggested.

'Could be,' he agreed. 'They went out for a good while. Nearly three years. But then it got stormy, apparently.'

'How come?' she asked.

'Well, according to the correspondence that we took from the boat, it seems to have been pretty full-on for a good while, then it gets so-so, and it seems they both talk about calling it a day. But then it looks like she suddenly takes the initiative and blows him out, just suddenly says she wants to sever all contact with him.'

'Really?' said Salt.

'Yes,' said Kavanagh.

'And he was chuffed, no doubt,' said Salt.

'You bet. He cuts up rough. He pleads with her to see him. In his letters he says he understands, that he doesn't need them to be lovers any more, but what he can't cope with is her cutting him off, the total separation that she's insisting on, after what they've had together, all that kind of thing.'

'Right,' said the DC. 'And? Where does it go from there?'

'She refuses to speak to him; she won't answer his letters or take his calls – all this is before most people had email – so what's he do?' said Kavanagh rhetorically.

'Tell,' she said.

'He only starts to stalk her.'

'And?'

'Court injunction, final warning,' said the inspector.

'What are we waiting for?' she asked. 'Why haven't we had someone get over to talk to him?'

'Well, for a start, we've only just uncovered all this. We've been going through her letters retrospectively, most recent first. The good news is she never seemed to throw anything away.'

'And the bad?' she said.

'Well, there was about a ton of this stuff, so it's taken forever to get back to things that happened over ten years ago. And anyway, there's the question of why Adam Shaw's suddenly going to come into the picture again after all this time. To say nothing of nipping down and killing her.'

'Leopards? Spots?' she said. 'The man's clearly got the unpredictable gene.'

'Maybe,' he agreed.

'Have you spoken to him yet?' she asked.

'Briefly,' he said. 'On the phone. He knows we're due a visit.'

'I think we should get up there as soon as possible,' she said. 'At the very least, even if his attentions were not always welcome, he seems to have known her as well as anyone.'

'We've got the TV reconstruction this afternoon, and then tomorrow's update briefing. As soon as they're done, we'll speak to him.'

That afternoon, Kavanagh and Salt looked just like any other couple out for a stroll as they leaned over the red-brick footbridge and watched as the young director prepared for shooting a reconstruction of Sarah Clement's last-known movements.

Making a film, any kind of film, Kavanagh reckoned, was just about the hardest thing in the world: paint a picture, write a poem, even dance *Swan Lake*, with all that toe-breaking, ankle-wrenching, body-stocking pain, they really were as nothing compared with this business.

This tranquil afternoon in rural Hertfordshire was quite some way from Hollywood, and yet there were still myriad opportunities for getting the whole thing wrong. Continuity, keeping the microphone out of shot, the camera steady, the lighting consistent and the focus just right, all had to be managed and synchronized at the same time as trying to elicit convincing performances from the Sarah Clement look-a-like and the extras who'd been recruited to play a couple of migrant workers as they ambled down the towpath, chatting and smoking.

It might not end up being a BAFTA-nominated performance but, rather more importantly, do a good job and this youngster – sent along from the agency to make a few hundred quid for an afternoon's filming – just might help catch a killer.

As they watched the umpteenth take being set up, Kavanagh looked down into the still, green water beneath them and said, 'What we need, Jane, is a break...'

'Tell me about it,' agreed Salt.

'You know when we were talking about Sutcliffe this morning?' he asked.

'Of course,' she said.

'You remember how they got him in the end?'

'No,' she said, 'remind me.'

'He had false number plates on his car,' said Kavanagh. 'It was nothing to do with all the routine police work they'd done; it was just that lucky break. If a couple of sharp-eyed cops hadn't spotted those plates, God knows how many more killings he might have got away with.'

'Action,' declaimed the director as the clapperboard operator held the thing in shot and called, 'Take four, scene two...'

Twenty-Four

October 2006

'Hello, Neil,' the man whispered.

Most people's worst nightmares never come true. But bed and breakfast owner Terence May's just had. He knew the voice, and the voice was the one he never wanted to hear again.

'How are you?' rasped the breath so close to his ear, he could feel it.

How do you answer such a question? May, in his own bed, in his own guest house, and the man asking after him not interested in his welfare, except in the very worst sense.

'David?' murmured May.

'That's right,' said the man.

'What do you want?' said May.

'Want?' replied the man, his mouth still close to May's ear on the pillow.

The man's shoes bumped to the floor as he pushed them off with his heels and swung his legs up on to the bed.

He lay next to him, spoon-style, May beneath the duvet, the other man on top of it. May was afraid to move for fear of provoking any

170

reaction in him.

'I'm sorry, David,' he ventured. 'I really am...'

'Yes?' said the man.

'Really,' added May.

'Go on. Tell me about it. About your being sorry.'

'I didn't have a choice. The police, they gave me no choice.'

'Really? That must have been difficult. You or me, eh? No choice.'

The man moved his arm, eased the duvet down a foot, and placed the object in his hand against May's naked back. May flinched as he felt the cold metal lie between his shoulder blades.

'I didn't have a choice either, Neil,' the man continued. 'Twelve years. No discussion and no choices. "Take him down," and that was it. Twelve years.' He paused. 'I didn't do twelve, of course. As you can see,' he sniggered, and pushed his crotch up against May's buttocks. 'Good behaviour, good parole board, very good Governor's report. But even six, you know, in a category A – category A, mate, it's home to some very bad people. It really was not the best six years of my life, I can tell you. Not at all.

'Still, they're not going to put me in an open prison with Jeffrey fucking Archer and half the Tory party, are they? Expensive works of art. Big fraud. Very big bucks. Make an example. It's those equal-opportunity Labour fuckers, they don't like people like us, Neil. They don't have a problem with a bit of blagging – Essex

171

bank robbers, all that sort of stuff – but a couple of queens in nice suits and a dodgy auction house, oh, no, they didn't like that at all.'

The man swung his legs down from the bed, stood up. 'No, it wasn't good inside. Not at all. Really, Neil, people on the outside, they would not believe what some of those people are capable of. They're barely human, I can tell you. Especially with people like me. People like us. You know what I'm saying? Still, you only have my word for it, don't you? It was me who had to go away ... What you calling yourself these days, Neil?'

'Terence. Terence May,' he said.

'Terence? What they call you down the shop, then? Terry? That's fuckin' daft that is. Who made that up then? Did you? You're no Terry, Neil. I can just about go with Terence. Yes, Terence is alright. But Terry? No, it's not you at all. Terry sounds like a footballer or something, flash and a bit wide, you know. No, not Terry, Neil.'

'I'm sorry, David. I really am...'

'Yes, I bet you are,' said the other man.

May turned his head a fraction to watch him standing at the window, a little moonlight shining through the bedroom curtains.

'How's ... what was her name?' he asked.

'Robbie,' said May.

'Robbie. How is she?'

'He died...'

'Really?'

'Two years ago...'

'So sorry. The usual?'

'Yes. He was ill for a long time,' said May.

'Uum,' said the man. 'Too bad.' He parted the curtains a fraction, looked across to the canal fifty metres away. 'Chilly night, eh, Neil? Especially on your own.'

'I'm OK,' said May.

The man looked down at the glowing red dot of the electric blanket switch. 'But you still get cold, eh?'

'It's alright,' said May.

'You shouldn't sleep with them on, you know. Health and safety.'

May reached down towards the plug.

'Leave it,' said the man abruptly. 'I bet you haven't even had it checked, you tight arse.' He moved over towards the bed. 'You haven't asked after Lenny. Or did you hear? On the grapevine?' He sat down on the edge of the bed. 'He did pretty well, actually. I'd have given him a year. No more. Up and down to see me every fortnight. Twelve months at most. He stayed the course for nearly eighteen, actually. Nobody's gonna wait six years, are they? Certainly not my little Lenny. Other fish to fry. Who can blame him? I didn't. But that didn't mean I wasn't hurt. Very.

'Of course, eventually, he took up with some other fucker. Usual story. He's a good-looking boy. Young, too. I'd probably have done the same. But it still hurt. Yes, he gave me some very sleepless nights, did Lenny. Not that you sleep a lot in jail. Too afraid to close your eyes most of the time. And the noise is terrible. Not like out here, nice and quiet. No one around here, eh? He's with some fucking Turk now, some dick from Green Lanes north London. I thought I might look them up some time, you know, nip down and say hello. He's got one of those veg stalls they all run down there. A bit of fruit and veg as a front while he's flogging smack.

'I'll give him a call one of these days. When I've got a minute. And I won't be there for the avocados, I'm telling you. By the time I've finished with Ahmed, or whatever his fucking name is, he'll wish he'd never put his fucking face near my boy's cock.' He breathed deeply. 'Anyway, where was I? Oh, yes, with Lenny gone, I didn't hear a word. From anyone. Not a word from you, Neil. Not even a fucking post-card. I couldn't believe it when I saw you on the telly. What on earth did you do that for? I mean, a stupid fuckin' haircut – and have you had something done to your mug, or is it your neck? Fuck me, Neil, I couldn't believe it. I'd got it into my head I'd never see you again, and there you were, fuckin' about with your geraniums just off camera as some local's telling them this and that about the woman who'd been killed down here. You should take more care, mate. I didn't exactly get the next train down, but I knew it wouldn't be long, and here I am ... You're very quiet, Neil. What's the matter? Are you sure you're pleased to see me?'

'David, can we work something out? If it's

money, I've got a bit now. When Robert died, he'd got a big life insurance. You could have ... you could have most of that...'

'Most, eh?'

'You could have it all. I don't need it. Really.'

'Well, you're certainly right about that, mate. You don't need it,' he sneered.

'Really, David, I'll do anything. I'll make it up to you,' May pleaded.

'Yes, I bet you would,' said the other man. He leaned across and pushed his fingers through May's hair. 'This is a fucking disaster. I mean, look at it, it's a fucking joke, mate. Blokes of our age, they shouldn't dye their hair. It just looks stupid.' He righted himself on the bed. 'What's this, then?' He carefully picked up the plastic measuring jug that was nestled beside the bedside table.

'It's for the night,' said May.

'What? Like in jail? You do it in a bucket? Why? You got a problem down there?'

'I had cancer.'

'Shame.'

'Prostate.'

'Really?'

'I had an operation. It's left me ... you know.'

'What? You have to take a piss in the night?'

'Yes. A couple, at least.'

'You certainly do, mate. There's a good bit in here.' He picked up the jug, three quarters full of urine. 'Phew, it stinks,' he said. 'Turn over.'

'What?'

'You heard. Turn over.'

'Please, David...'

'Fuckin' turn over or I'll shoot you right now.'

'You're not going to—'

'What? Fuck you?' he said. 'You are joking? I wouldn't have fucked you if you'd been the last queen in Camden. But I'll shoot you if you don't turn round.' And he snatched the pillow from under his head and forced it down against his temple.

May turned over, buried his face in the other pillow, and waited for the shot.

The man pulled down the duvet, exposing May's shoulders, then his back, his buttocks, and eventually his knees. His body shook from head to toe as David O'Connor poured the urine over him in a steady, even stream.

For a moment it collected in the small of his back, then overflowed on his waist, spilled down around his buttocks and between his upper legs.

In a moment more it soaked the cotton sheets, and finally, a millisecond later, came into contact with the wires of the old electric blanket.

There was a blue flash, and May convulsed as the electricity coursed through him.

Twenty-Five

Late September 2006

Marcus Breese had never been quite so lonely. Normally in the evenings, at home in Shropshire, electric light filled almost every room in his house, music played from radio or CDs, and at least two of his three TVs – one in the bedroom, one in the kitchen, and the big plasma HD set in the sitting room – were on constantly. 'Got to be connected,' he'd say to Bernie. 'Have to keep in touch. It's my work.'

Each email in his inbox was a minor triumph to him, an affirmation of his place in the world, a world at whose centre he sat. Naturally, he rattled off replies like a man in a hurry, which he very often was.

There were landline sockets all over the house and handsets aplenty. A couple of cell phones were never out of reach, and he would no more have left home without his BlackBerry than without cleaning his teeth.

Now, cycling a silent, little-changing canal towpath for some seven or eight hours was proving to be in marked contrast to all that reassuringly artificial light and colour and noise.

The first day had begun inauspiciously with his struggle and slither through the deep mud only a few miles outside Market Drayton. Although his trousers were mud-caked, things had improved by the time he reached that evening's destination, the hamlet of Brewood, just north of Wolverhampton, thirty miles down the route.

As the tedious hours passed, the cycling might have become easier, but a growing feeling of melancholy had enveloped him. Unpacking his camping gear and pitching his little tent in the autumn dusk, he was filled with gloom and a sense of foreboding about the lonely night ahead.

He wasn't even sure just what it was he was afraid of. Did he think some village lunatic was going to be hiding behind the hedge, or in the next little copse, just waiting for a hapless cyclist to pedal by so that he could attack him? Hardly.

Or was it some more preternatural fear that stalked him? Notions of a towpath ghoul, some incarnation of a long-dead navvy who would now waft from the motionless poplar branches and terrify him into the moonlit water?

He knew these were irrational thoughts, but that helped little. He felt more afraid in this field a hundred yards from the lighted windows of a nearby bungalow than he had felt since, tucked up beneath his Batman duvet, he had been terrified of the shadows on the ceiling of his childhood bedroom.

His pre-trip notion of sitting beside a glowing

fire, the twigs crackling, the warmth and colour a tangible comfort, bore no relation to this reality. He was loath to make any kind of fire for fear of attracting unwanted attention, and the tiny cooking-gas cylinder sputtered and blew in the evening breeze, giving off a blue flame that offered no warmth to his spirit.

At just after eight, when Bernadette called him on his mobile, he tried in vain to sound positive. Eventually, she asked him directly, 'Are you alright, Marc? You sound ... a bit fed up.'

'Long day in the saddle,' he tried to jest, but it was hollow, and their subsequent 'Sleep tights' and token 'Love yous' were barren affairs.

The night was, indeed, long. He'd not felt comfortable enough in the alien surroundings to even go to the loo (where, anyway?) and his half-cooked packet-pasta supper lay heavily on his stomach.

By six the next morning he was pedalling through the deserted landscape of the west Midlands towards Birmingham, the only sounds the squawking waterside ducks and the distant hum of heavy goods vehicles on the M6 a mile away.

The second day had been uneventful, but increasingly bleak. The towpaths through the Birmingham canal navigations were wide and shale-covered and made for easy cycling. But the proximity to urban populations meant that there was also plenty of evidence of 'civilization': the canals were now wide and filmy, the water an oily, lifeless blue-grey that hosted plastic bottles, forlorn carrier bags and stray bits of timber. The remnants of a smashed bedroom wardrobe lay marooned at one lock gate.

Around mid-morning, he passed a group of truanting schoolboys who at first merely called abuse and spat down from the bridge above him, but then, as he drew away, threw stones after him from where they stood.

He was relieved, at last, to be through the densest part of this conurbation and out on to the Grand Union Canal, heading towards genteel Leamington Spa. But then, a couple of hours from his planned evening stop, he had the sinking sensation that he recalled all too clearly from childhood: air-filled travel on a buoyant tyre became a bumpy grind as the tube deflated and the rim of the wheel made contact with the stony towpath.

There was still a little daylight and he found a decent spot to unpack his heavily laden panniers, but finding the puncture proved less easy, the tiny thorn prick elusive in the gloaming. But eventually he sealed the spot and sat quietly in the growing darkness as the adhesive set on the tube and patch. An hour later, he reassembled the wheel and fixed it to the bike.

He felt a sense of achievement, notwithstanding his oily hands and grease-filled fingernails and, with only a few miles to travel, gingerly remounted, and pedalled on.

He camped a couple of hundred yards up the path from a pub and, as he lay in his sleeping bag at only nine o'clock that night, felt mocked by the distant tinkle of laughter from the place.

What on earth *was* he doing?

He woke to shouts and the sound of car doors slamming, turned on his torch and looked at his watch: it was eleven-fifteen.

By two a.m. there was a heavy thunderstorm, and the rain beat down relentlessly on his tent and seeped in and over his groundsheet as it ran across the bone-hard ground.

The following morning he packed his sodden tent, clammy sleeping bag and damp clothes and was ready to be away before the sun was properly up. But as he tried to stuff the unwieldy equipment into his panniers, the sight that greeted him was of a flat tyre on his rear wheel. 'Fuck,' he said with feeling. 'Fuck you, bastard.' And he kicked his water bottle twenty yards away into the hedge.

An hour later, completely miserable, he was on his way again, cycling south. Maybe a trek through the desert or an Arctic sledge pull wouldn't have been so bad after all, he reflected. The thought of an appearance on some daytime TV show with a washed-up comedienne or ex-Priory clinic soap-star was positively alluring compared with this misery.

When, the next day, he spoke to his mother, he told her the trip was going 'very well'. He didn't mention the punctures – by this time, he'd had another one and had used one of his three spare inner tubes – the horsefly bites on his wrist and ankles, the cold nights, nor his sodden clothes.

She wished him well and asked him to excuse her as *Coronation Street* was just starting on TV.

Twenty-Six

April 2006

To be well loved, and yet bereft, was an oddly disconcerting combination for Esther Porter to have experienced throughout her young life. And yet it was exactly what she had always known. Being deprived of her mother when she was only two years of age was something that would, surely, leave scars that no amount of love from her devoted grandparents could possibly eradicate.

Never knowing her father, and brought up by grandparents who were always going to be fifty years older than their young charge, was never going to be easy. And so it proved. Aged twelve, Esther's protectors were in their sixties; by the time she was in her teens, they were elderly people, people who were now living in a world that they could barely comprehend.

As a child Esther had, of course, asked about her mother's illness and subsequent suicide. When Leah, her mother, was a young woman, they told her, she'd had a disastrous love affair with Esther's father; the man had hurt her tremendously by his infidelity, and Leah, like many another broken-hearted woman, had never recovered from the felling blow of his treachery.

As an adolescent, she had repeatedly asked about getting in touch with her unknown father, the shadowy figure from New England who had broken her mother's heart, and been the cause of her suicide. Her grandparents refused to help. They had lost their only daughter to this man's cruelty; they had no intention of facilitating their granddaughter's search for him.

And, anyway, they assured Esther, as if this information might make up for her sense of abandonment, her sense of loss and rejection, it seemed unlikely that he knew he had even fathered a child with Leah before returning to America.

'We never knew him,' said her grandfather, 'but we do know he was the man who led to your mother taking her life.' A comment which effectively precluded any further discussion.

By the time Esther was fifteen, her grandparents had lost control of their granddaughter, and she had become involved with a troublesome crowd. She stayed out late and was smoking and drinking. The balance had tipped, and her ageing grandparents were no longer able to discipline her.

At sixteen, and by now regularly truanting from school, where her work had all but been abandoned, it came as no surprise – and in truth was something of a relief to the couple – when she announced that she was leaving home to move in with a friend. It transpired that the friend was a man of twenty-three who had convictions for burglary, drug offences and car theft, and their flat was a squat in Cardiff's Canton.

And yet she still came home to them every two or three weeks, had a bath and took a few more of her possessions with her. Her grandmother, Bethan, knew very well that half of these things were probably sold before they even reached the squat on the other side of the city. But what could she do? What *should* she do? They were, after all, the young woman's own belongings. If she chose to squander them for another wrap of drugs, Bethan was helpless to prevent it.

One day, Esther said, perhaps in the next month or two, when she could borrow a friend's van, she would come over and take a couple more of the boxes of books that were still stacked in her room upstairs; more clothes than she could carry on the bus, and possibly even her mother's old computer.

If Esther was her mother's daughter, in nature, at least, the evidence for it was heavily disguised: whereas her mother had been conscientious, obliging and thoughtful, Esther was capricious, self-serving and impetuous. The women shared essential features, but on account of rangy, lithe, American Ethan's genes, Esther was taller at sixteen than her mother had been when she died in her twenties.

She didn't eat either regularly or well, and the drugs she took had ravaged her skin; but in spite of her dark brown eyes being set deep in her pale face, it *was* her mother's face, and one in which could still be glimpsed intelligence and sensitivity – despite all its privations.

And there was one other constant that had been passed between mother and daughter: a love of books. Had it passed in the family gene from Bethan and Elwyn to Leah, and now, in spite of everything, found its way through to their wayward grandchild? Nurture or nature? Whatever the reason, the young woman – just as her mother had done – still devoured books.

'Have you read this?' she asked her grand-mother now as she fished a crumpled paperback from her shoulder bag.

They sat together in the back sitting room, tea on the table, and kept an eye on Elwyn as he stood vacantly in the garden outside. 'It's really good,' she added.

'Well, well,' said her grandmother, looking at the cover of *The House of Loss*. 'Sarah was at college with your mother. They were on the writing course together.'

'Really?' said Esther. 'That's cool.'

'Yes,' repeated her grandmother, examining the book. 'We met her once.'

'And did you never read it, Gran?' asked the girl.

'No. It was too difficult. It was some years after your mother died, but it was too painful. I didn't want to stir up all those memories of her.'

'Shall I leave it for you now?' she said. 'It's really good; it's the best thing I've read for ages, and it was only a pound in the Oxfam shop.'

'Yes, OK,' she said. 'But doesn't ... Gareth

185

want to read it?'

'Gareth reads Japanese comics, Gran,' she said.

'I don't understand, Esther,' said her grand-mother. 'Look at you. You have so much to offer any boy...'

'Let's not go there again, Gran. Gareth's alright. He doesn't read books, but not every-body does. And anyway,' she said, 'I get that talk with you. If he read, we'd never have these chats, would we?'

'I suppose not,' she conceded.

'And my mum really knew Sarah Clement?'

'They shared a house in Stoke, before your Mum ... you know, before she became ill.'

'I'm going to contact her,' said Esther. 'I'll get her details from the publisher.'

Twenty-Seven

October 2006

'Guess what?' said Presley down the line. The amiable Brummie was Kavanagh's oldest col-league, a veteran of a dozen enquiries together. 'We've got your man.'

'Who would that be, El?' asked Kavanagh. With a peeping tom being sought, a couple of flaky suspects in the frame, to say nothing of one of Sarah Clement's former lovers, it could have been any one of a number of people.

'Your cyclist, of course. Who do you think?' boomed Presley, as if he didn't quite trust the BT connection to carry his words all the way down the line from Birmingham to Hertfordshire.

Kavanagh held the phone away from his ear and found himself shouting back. 'Excellent, mate. Who is he?'

'He's only a fucking TV reporter,' replied Presley, as if it could be safely assumed that the profession invited obloquy.

'A TV reporter,' echoed Kavanagh. 'How come? And where did you find him?'

'Didn't. He walked into the station, here in Brum, says he's only just sussed out that we're looking for him. He's spoken to his brief and she's on her way down. Told him to say nothing 'til she got here, apparently.'

'And you've got him there now?' asked Kavanagh.

'Downstairs, having a cuppa and looking suitably unhappy.'

Kavanagh lowered his voice, turned away from the room. 'What's your gut feeling, El, just between me and thee? Strictly off the record.'

'I tell you, Frank, if this guy's not in the frame, I'm not playing prop forward for Moseley Old Boys on Saturday.'

There was a pause. 'And?' said Kavanagh.

'It's the grudge match of the season, and I'll be there. This tosser's got something to hide. I'll bet you any money you like.'

'Well played, El. You're still an ugly bastard, but you're a fuckin' star, too.'

'Thanks a lot,' said Presley.

'We'll be up to question him just as soon as. Cheers,' said the inspector and replaced the phone.

As consumer affairs reporter for a regional television programme, it would have been very surprising if Marcus Breese had *not* known his rights. By the time Kavanagh arrived to interview him at Birmingham's central police station on Colmore Circus, his solicitor was with him. Breese and Ms Patel sat together on one side of the table, with Kavanagh and DS Joe Lavendar on the other.

The custody officer confirmed to Breese and Ms Patel that the man was present voluntarily, had come to the police station of his own volition, and was there merely to assist the police with their enquiries. He was not under arrest, nor had he been charged with any offence. The tape wound round in the machine as the red recording light glowed.

Although he'd done this a hundred times before, there was something so innately theatrical about the situation that Kavanagh was always a little self-conscious, like an actor at his first read-through of a new part.

He intoned, too deeply, 'Interview with Marcus Breese,' cleared his throat, and continued, more reasonably, 'in the presence of his solicitor, Ms Anan Patel,' and gave the date and time. 'Also present, Detective Sergeant Joe Lavendar. Mr Breese, you presented yourself at Colmore Circus police station in Birmingham this morning at approximately nine forty-five. Would you tell me, please, the circumstances that led to your doing that?'

Breese glanced at his solicitor, who nodded, and he began, 'Last week I was doing a long-distance cycle ride. For charity. By the time I got to London, the police were reporting a murder. Then, a day or two later, there was an appeal for a cyclist, and I became aware that you might want to speak to me.'

'Yes?' encouraged Kavanagh.

'About whether I might have any information...'

Ms Patel leaned towards her client and whispered, 'Just answer the question. There's no need to elaborate.'

'OK,' he said.

'How did you find out we were looking for you?'

'It was on the news, in the papers, that you were trying to trace a cyclist. I realized it might be me, and so I came forward, even though you never think that you could be the person involved...'

'Really?' said the policeman.

'Really. And then a couple of friends phoned. Work colleagues.'

'I see. And what did they have to say?'

'They were larking about. Joking. Said did I

know you were looking for a cyclist. Had I done it, that kind of thing.'

'Do you have many friends who joke about a woman having been murdered?' asked the inspector soberly.

'No, of course not,' said Breese.

'My client can hardly speak for what his colleagues do, or do not do, Inspector,' added Ms Patel.

Kavanagh nodded an acknowledgement and then went on, 'So, what did you do then, Mr Breese?'

'I called my solicitor.'

'Why did you do that?' he asked.

'I'm a reporter. I know about these things. I'm aware that the police can make mistakes.'

Kavanagh smiled at the implication. 'Can you tell me a bit about your cycle ride?'

'Of course. What would you like to know?' asked Breese.

'Where did you begin?'

'From near my home in Shropshire.'

'And you cycled all the way down to London?'

'Yes.'

'Did you enjoy it?'

'Enjoy?' he repeated. 'It was alright, I suppose.'

'Any problems?' pursued the inspector.

'Nothing unusual,' replied Breese.

'Could you elaborate?' said Kavanagh. 'I do a bit of cycling myself, you know, only to the shops, but I'm wondering, what kind of things go on when you cycle, oh, what is it ... it must be close to two hundred miles?'

'A hundred and ninety-three,' Breese confirmed.

'You have the exact figure?' said Kavanagh. 'That is impressive.'

'Not really,' replied Breese. 'It's on the 'net.'

'What about on your bike? Don't you have one of those little computer things? They calculate everything, don't they?'

'I did.'

'Did?' he enquired.

'It got damaged.'

'Really?' said Kavanagh. 'How?'

'I had some punctures. Turning the bike over to mend them, taking off the wheel a few times, it must have got broken.'

'And?'

'So, I got rid of it.'

'You took the trouble to take it off?' said Kavanagh.

'Yes.'

'Extra weight, I suppose?' said the policeman.

'Hardly. I just took it off. It was broken. I was pissed off with it,' said Breese.

'And?'

'And what?'

'And what did you do with your tiny computer, which records the miles, the distance travelled, but which got damaged?'

'I chucked it.'

'Really?' said the inspector.

'Really,' replied Breese, with reciprocal sarcasm.

'And where exactly did you chuck it?' asked the inspector.

'In the cut.'

'Not very environmentally friendly,' said the policeman.

'I suppose not,' said Breese wearily.

'And do you often lose your temper, Mr Breese?'

'I don't think my client said anything about losing his temper,' interrupted Ms Patel. 'Anyway, is this relevant, Inspector?'

'It might be,' said Kavanagh, refusing to be deflected.

'I hope so,' responded the woman.

'Where did you arrive? In London?'

'Regent's Park. On the Grand Union Canal,' said Breese.

'And where did you go from there?' asked the policeman.

'To my girlfriend's.'

'Your girlfriend? What is her full name, please, and where does she live?'

'Bernie. Bernadette Ford, and she lives in Primrose Hill.'

Lavendar jotted down the address that Breese volunteered.

'And what did you do when you got to Ms Ford's flat?' asked Kavanagh.

'Do?' asked Breese.

'Yes. What did you do?'

He glanced from the policeman to his solicitor and back again. 'We hadn't seen one another for over a week,' he said.

'I see. You ... spent some ... time together?'

Breese glanced again at Ms Patel. 'We went to bed. Why?'

'And your girlfriend will be able to confirm that?'

'I would have thought so,' he smirked.

'Presumably, you had your phone with you on the trip?' said Kavanagh.

'Of course,' said Breese.

'Would you be so kind as to let the sergeant here have it? We'll let you have it back, of course.'

'Why?' he asked.

'A woman's been murdered, sir. You are one of the few people whom we know was in the area. It's invaluable that we build up as full a picture of events as possible. Your phone records might help us. I'm sure, with your experience, you will understand that?'

'Yes, I know how these things work,' acknowledged Breese.

'What I don't quite understand, Mr Breese, is that we have spoken to several people who saw you for the first couple of days of your journey, but closer to the time that we are particularly interested in, no one's come forward yet to say they saw you at all...'

Breese looked to Ms Patel. 'Inspector, as I've just suggested, my client can hardly speak on behalf of people whom he doesn't know. If you need witnesses, I'd suggest, with respect, that it's your job to track them down. You can hardly expect him to speculate on why he was not seen by people who may, or may not, have been on his route at any one time.'

'Quite,' said Kavanagh.

The tape revolved and the index counter clicked as it monitored the silence.

'Tell me, Mr Breese, after you and your girl-friend had spent some time together, what did you do then?'

'We watched a DVD and went to bed. The next day, I came home. By train.'

'Did you know Sarah Clement?'

'Of course not.'

'Did you know *of* her? She was quite well-known, even famous, once.'

'I knew her name.'

'Have you read any of her books?' asked the inspector.

'No. I don't get a lot of time for reading. I haven't read anything longer than a magazine article for years.'

'But you did know of her?'

'I knew her name. I've just said so.'

'And did you know that she lived on the canal, at a place that you cycled past?'

'How would I?'

'How, indeed?' said the cop. He straightened his back in the upright chair. 'So, just to sum-marize, Mr Breese. Your cycle ride was largely uneventful, but you no longer have the computer that records the mileage covered, and so on. You didn't know Sarah Clement; you have never met her, nor did you know that she lived on the canal adjacent to where you passed, at about the time that we believe that she was killed...'

'Yes, that's right,' Breese said.

'I think that will be all for now,' said the inspector. 'Thank you very much.' And with that he recorded the time the interview ended and switched the recorder off.

Breese and Ms Patel got to their feet.

'Do you anticipate wanting to speak to my client again?' asked the solicitor as Lavendar opened the door for them.

'I think it very likely, Ms Patel,' said the inspector. 'One of my officers will be speaking to Mr Breese's girlfriend, and then I'm sure we'll need to speak to him again. But for now, of course, he's free to go. Good day to you both.'

Twenty-Eight

October 2006

'Why don't you quit? You only smoke three a day,' said Salt, getting into the car outside the Travelodge on the outskirts of Watford.

'We only have sex once a week, but I don't want to give that up either,' said the inspector. He leaned across and gave her a kiss. 'Friends?'

'Of course,' she said, after only a moment's delay.

'This one goes then,' he said, and crushed the butt of his roll-up in the ashtray as the BMW pulled away.

Kavanagh and Salt argued about all sorts of things – political correctness, psychotherapy, films, books, theatre and politics – but Kavanagh's smoking a few cigarettes a day wasn't usually one of them.

'Really, do you mind?' he asked as they joined the queue of traffic heading towards the town centre.

'I don't mind you smoking, Frank, but, strangely, I don't want you to die.'

'Me neither,' he added.

'You're an opinionated, red-neck pain in the butt,' she said, 'but for some odd reason, I quite like you.'

'Jane, can I just say, contrary to *Guardian* readers' folk lore, buying the *Telegraph* on a Saturday for the crossword isn't quite the same as being signed up to the BNP. I'm just an old, new man...'

'Yes,' she acquiesced without conviction. 'Actually, I shouldn't tell you this, Frank, but I quite like the smell of your tobacco. It takes me back to being sixteen, the last time *I* smoked.'

'Glad to oblige, Constable,' he said.

'*Do* we only have sex once a week?' she asked as they waited at traffic lights.

'I wish,' he said mournfully. 'Right now, that much would be nice...'

For the last week or so, conjugal relations between the couple were certainly some way down the agenda. Not only was Kavanagh staying in a decent hotel in the centre of town, whilst Salt was slumming it with a dozen other officers in the Travelodge, but the case was full on, with translators working out at Ellis's farm, interviews with witnesses and residents being conducted, and the results of forensic analysis of miscellaneous recovered items pending.

There was also the question of just who was playing peeping tom out at the farm, and whether he – or an improbable she – was involved in anything even more sinister.

And there was a thus far wholly failed attempt to try and discern even the possibility of a motive behind the gruesome murder of local bed and breakfast proprietor Terence May.

This man's macabre killing, only days into their investigation into the death of Sarah Clement, and just as the area was crawling with dozens of officers from every branch of the force, was in danger of making Kavanagh and his enquiry team a laughing stock.

The media loved a good murder, of course. Even in today's high-tech, high-speed, disposable society, a traditional murder still sold newsprint. And if it was true of one killing, two was even better.

But when, and if, the known facts of the matter started to pall, the tabloids, certainly, wouldn't be slow to play another of their favourite refrains: 'what a bumbling force/bunch of detectives/debacle this is'.

Everyone on the enquiry knew, therefore, and

none more keenly than Kavanagh, that they needed results – or at least tangible progress – sooner rather than later. Hence this morning's second full-scale update and briefing.

'Anyway, look,' she said, 'no matter how often we get to do it – or not – I'd just better be the only woman you're doing it with.'

'Jane,' he said seriously, 'if we're not straight with one another, what's the point? We're not kids.'

'The best part of me believes you, Frank, but when you speak like you did the other day about the voyeur thing out at the farm, I'm not so sure.'

'Let's not go there, eh?' he said. 'We've agreed to differ. It's not a deal-breaker for us, just a difference of opinion. And anyway, just because I have a view about certain blokes' behaviour, it doesn't mean I *endorse* that behaviour.' He slowed to let a car join the traffic from the left. 'And believe me, where you are concerned, let's just say ... you know I'm not good at the old three-word mantra ... but let's just say I'm really very fond of you.'

'Me too, you,' she said and reached across and put her hand on his leg.

'Oi, watch yourself,' he said, and accelerated away.

Kavanagh sat in the car and watched as Salt tapped in the security code and went in through the heavy door at the back of the police station. It was still a few minutes before nine and he rolled another Golden Virginia. He could chart his life, more or less, through the cigarettes and tobacco that he, and those closest to him, had used.

When he was a child, everyone smoked. Politicians and film stars in every film and newsreel in the cinema puffed away, and almost every member of the audience sitting there in the dark blew smoke back at them.

Aged thirteen, he'd buy five Park Drive, have one on his way to school, and another at his open bedroom window before his mother got in from work.

By seventeen, at his first job, before he'd signed up to train as a copper, he bought his first made-to-measure suit from Burton, his first car – a fawn Ford Consul – and smoked Rothmans from their sturdy blue and white flip-top pack.

When he'd first met his ex-wife, Rachael, she was smoking Players No. 6, but it wasn't long before she, too, started rolling her own, something which, to this very day, he still found incredibly sexy in just about any woman.

He stubbed his cigarette out, followed Salt into the building and took the stairs up to the briefing room on the third floor. The place was packed and noisy, but this was 2006, and there was not a skein of smoke amongst the many cops gathered there.

'Morning all,' said Kavanagh, and took his place in front of the computer-linked screen at the front. 'Right, ladies and gentlemen,' he called, raising his voice, and the room bubbled down.

ACC Hyland sat stony-faced in his pristine uniform at the end of the row, his grey hair curiously long, but immaculately cut. Kavanagh could feel the chill at ten paces.

'As you know, unfortunately, things have taken a turn,' the inspector began, glancing at Hyland. 'What was looking like a straight-forward homicide has now become, with the discovery of Terence May's body, very much more complicated. Just quickly, by way of summary, in case anyone's not been concentrating, first, Sarah Clement –' the PowerPoint guru flashed up a big photo of the slim, spiky-haired redhead with her forthright expression – 'disappears from her boat at the end of September.

'Her body is found in a nearby canal pound with an iron bar attached to it several days later by Jan McAvoy, a schoolteacher who spends her weekends working on canal restoration projects.

'It seems most likely that Clement was killed elsewhere then brought to the pound, where the weight was attached. There's very little sign of a struggle,' he continued, and pointed to a huge close-up of the slight bruising around her neck and scalp. 'There's no DNA available from her corpse to link her to an assailant – either there wasn't any, or the water's done its work – but the lack of restraint injuries or significant violence suggests that she might, possibly, have known her killer; as far as we can tell, there was no sexual assault.

'We've naturally done everything by the book: search area; reconstruction; house to house; looking for anyone in the area with a bit of previous; recently released offenders; strangers in that neck of the woods; family conflicts with the deceased, unresolved grief and business dealings – all the usual. Everything's been fed into HOLMES for cross-referencing and checking but, thus far, we haven't come up with anything particularly useful.

'Unfortunately, given that it doesn't appear that there was a sexual motive, and theft and burglary are definitely not contenders – unless robbers have suddenly given up half-inching laptops and iPods – we're still short of a motive. On the family front, Sarah Clement has a sister who lives in Hebden Bridge with her partner. They're gay.' Photos of Charlotte, the sister, and River, her girlfriend, flashed up on the screen.

'Sarah and Charlotte weren't particularly close, but there's no problem between them as far as we know. It's also unlikely that Charlotte's going to call the local police down here in Rickmansworth and ask them to check out her sister if she's the one who's involved with her murder. Possible, but unlikely, I'd have thought. Also, she and her girlfriend up in Yorkshire are living the life of Riley. River works in a whole-food shop, Charlotte's a van driver, and they're also in the middle of an adoption programme. Now, anything's possible, as everyone in this room knows, but I'd contend that this is hardly a picture of your usual murder suspects.

'So, basically, we're looking for a stranger in town and we're short of a decent suspect until this guy comes out of the woods.' A big publicity shot of Marcus Breese appeared on the screen, all sharp suit, TV smile and white gnashers. 'TV reporter Marcus Breese just happens to be cycling to London from his home up in Market Drayton in Shropshire. Between ourselves, this geezer's a bit of a pain in the arse, one of those self-righteous tossers who present all that consumers-being-ripped-off stuff – you know, *Watchdog*, *House of Horrors* and all that bollocks. Now, a blind man and his dog can see the whole cycling stunt's just a bit of PR for Breese himself, dressed up as charity do-gooding. His jaunt gets hardly any publicity, apart from up in Shropshire and on his own TV programme, but he does raise a bag of cash.'

'How much?' enquired one of the officers.

'Joe?' asked Kavanagh.

'About fifteen grand,' Lavendar confirmed.

'Anyway, Breese does the trip,' resumed Kavanagh, 'and we've got witnesses who spot him here and there en route. Except for a day or so round about the time when he'd have been near to Sarah Clement's boat. At just about the same time *she* goes AWOL, he slips off the radar, too. He says he was there, but if he was, how come no one sees him? Next, DC Salt speaks to his missus. What's the girl's name, Jane?'

'Bernadette. Bernadette Ford,' Salt called out.

'She backs up Breese's account of events but, guess what, she tells us the first thing young

Marcus does when he gets to her flat in north London is he dumps his trousers in the bin, and puts the rest of his stuff in the machine on a hot wash. Well, yes, OK, he's gonna be grubby after the best part of a week on a bike, but is this not a little odd for a young bloke who hasn't seen his girlfriend for a week?

'Finally, in the course of their searching for evidence at the crime scenes, forensics find an old orchard ladder in the undergrowth at Philip Ellis's farm. Now, it's only a few hundred yards from Clement's boat, admittedly, but I think it's unlikely that it's related to her murder, at least not directly, but that's only a hunch.' He glanced across at Salt. She responded with a raised eyebrow. 'It turns out there's been a bit of strategic pruning on a nearby beech tree, and that the ladder's been used by someone who's a bit nifty. This fella's been climbing up there and presumably having a dekko as the women who work on the farm take a shower in their accommodation block. The ladder's covered with prints, most of them belonging to the owner of the farm, Philip Ellis.

'Well, so what? It's his ladder. He doesn't deny it, just says he's no idea what it was doing out there in the undergrowth. And maybe he's telling the truth. Forensics are still trying to get prints from the tree, even checking it for DNA, but it's not easy and we'll have to wait and see.

'The farmer's recently taken up with one of his workers, a Polish woman called Katrina, and it seems that she's come in for a bit of resentment from some of the other workers on account of her newly elevated position, and there's a bit of a spite and envy thing going on there. Anyway, it's a line of enquiry we're following and when the interviews are completed with the migrant labour, we'll see if any of it adds up. That was about all we'd got – end of part one, if you like,' said Kavanagh, about to wrap up this part of proceedings.

'Nothing on the canal volunteers, then?' asked Scrivener.

'Gordon? Tony? Over to you.'

Tony Mullin got to his feet and opened his folder. 'We've had a bit of a look at them. All above board, just the usual kind of folk, you know, getting out of town for a bit of fresh air at weekends. They're all nuts about canals, and they seem regular, up-front folk. Somebody gave us a tip-off about this one bloke, a bit of a loner called Steve Pendle, so we had a closer look at him—'

'And?' said Scrivener.

'And nothing much. He's an IT programmer, chess player, never had a girlfriend, apparently, but isn't totally uninterested, not judging by the bits and pieces under his bed. Usual lads' magazines and stuff, nothing illegal, just the usual rumpy-pumpy. Speaking to him, I'd say he's just a bit ill at ease in company, but he's not a loony, not in my view, anyway, just a bit of a...'

'Loner?' suggested Kavanagh.

'Exactly,' agreed Mullin. 'Anyway, he's got

cast-iron alibis for the couple of days surrounding Clement's likely death.'

His colleague Gordon Wray chipped in, 'The only other thing we got was that team leader Jeff's been playing away a bit. Some of his accounts of his comings and goings didn't quite add up. Eventually, under a bit of pressure, he confided that about one weekend in four, when his missus thinks he's with the others digging mud out of an old canal someplace, he's actually bedded down in a Nottingham hotel with a woman he's been having an affair with for the last ten years. To make it all look kosher, he stops by at a field on his way home and gives his work clothes a good roll around in the mud ... Oh yes, and one other thing: one of the blokes in the group, Michael Dorling, his Toyota's got no tax or MOT.'

'Well, thanks a lot,' said Kavanagh. 'DVLA will be excited!' Then he continued, 'So, that was where we were up to, and then, last Saturday night, things get very complicated. The owner of the local B and B down on the canal, a gay fella called Terence May, gets killed in his bed. Someone breaks in and pours a jug of the man's own piss all over him. Unfortunately, his old electric blanket's switched on at the same time and May is electrocuted. All we know about him for sure is that he and his sick boyfriend moved down here six years ago, but we're struggling to find out much about his background before that – either he had some reason to cover his tracks, or he was a very private kind of guy. I don't know. What I feel sure about is that these two will be entirely separate murders. Having said that, in both cases, we're struggling for motives.

'In the Sarah Clement killing, our main suspect is still Marcus Breese, given his disappearing act. But what's his motive? Yes, he's a pain in the arse, but he's a young, fit, decent-looking pain in the arse, with a nice-looking woman in tow. And he's not got any previous.

'The only other lead that we're following up is a bloke who went out with Sarah years ago. She's had a lot of lovers these last few years, but this man – a bloke called Adam Shaw – became obsessive about her when she dumped him. He even stalked her for a while, and she had to resort to a court injunction to warn him off. My instinct is that as a suspect, he's a non-starter, what with it all happening so long ago. But we have to check him out, something which we'd have done already if Breese hadn't waltzed in for a chat. No matter; I've spoken to Shaw on the phone and we'll be on his case this afternoon.

'As for Terence May's murder, well, to be honest, we haven't got a clue. But we'll get there. If we just keep at it, we'll turn something up. OK, folks, that's me done. Any details, see individual officers on their specific areas. Log everything on to HOLMES. And for God's sake, don't miss anything. You know the drill, the innocent person you're chatting to right now could hold the vital piece of information that'll get us up and running, so make sure we log everything. We miss something at our peril. Let's not look back on this in five weeks or five years and say, "If only..." OK? Over to you. Any constructive thoughts and suggestions, I'd be grateful. Revelations and breakthroughs, I'll be euphoric. Good luck, everyone, and Joe, keep me informed of anything at all while we're up in Manchester, OK?'

Kavanagh would have liked to escape Hyland, but the man waited for him at the doorway of the crowded room.

'Sir?' said the inspector.

'Kavanagh,' replied Hyland. 'Notwithstanding your notion of discrete killings, you also said that the woman's murder was a one-off when we last spoke.'

'Yes, I did, and I certainly thought so, sir.'

'And now?'

'I still think we're dealing with two extant killings,' said the inspector.

'Frank,' Hyland said, exasperated, 'you're a very experienced policeman. We don't, I think, endorse coincidences. If we are dealing with separate murders, why did they occur within yards of one another, and within a week or so of one another?'

'I don't know, sir. And there's obviously some sort of causal link, but I still believe they're discrete.'

'Well, to say that I'm disappointed that things are making such slow progress would be an understatement; that they've become very much more complicated seems to me to undermine the premise of what you're suggesting,' said Hyland.

'Naturally, in the light of these unforeseen developments, I'll need to keep the investigation – and its conduct by yourself – under review. You do understand me?'

'Of course,' said Kavanagh. 'As ever, it's a little breakthrough we need; a witness to come forward, a bit of forensics, something that will just get us moving.'

'Yes, I dare say,' said Hyland, without conviction. 'Anyway, keep me informed if you'd be so kind. That'll be all for now.'

Twenty-Nine

October 2006

'Nice area,' said Kavanagh as he and Salt drove down one of the tree-lined roads that were a feature of the prosperous Cheshire town. 'What division are they in?' he asked.

'Sorry?' said Salt, holding the Manchester A–Z upside down as she tried to find Beech Grove.

'Altrincham. Are they Nationwide or Conference?'

'No idea,' she said, pointing to a road on their left. 'Here it is.'

The town centre had looked like any other, with McDonald's, Blockbuster and Specsavers now housed in the Victorian pale-stone buildings that had once been home to outfitters, grocers, butchers and furniture retailers.

But the nearby suburbs, only a five-minute walk from the centre, were unusually quiet and spacious, the wide roads dotted with mature plane trees. The entire place harked back to an earlier age. Only the shards of shattered glass from the smashed street-corner telephone kiosk were a reminder that this was now, not then.

'Nice spot,' said the inspector again, and pulled the BMW alongside the kerb in front of Greystone Court, one of the many former merchant's houses which had been converted into spacious apartments.

Adam Shaw, in black Levi's and a blue V-necked sweater over a white tee-shirt, was in pretty good nick for fifty, Kavanagh reckoned. The inspector breathed in through his nose and pulled back his shoulders as the man led them through the terrazzo-tiled hall and on into his ground-floor sitting room.

The room, which doubled as a study, was filled with books and play scripts amongst the solid dark furniture and comfy sofa. A blinking computer monitor sat on top of the huge mahogany desk in the bay window where maroon velvet curtains were half-drawn against the afternoon sun.

The walls had numerous playbills pinned to them, testimony to the man's output but, curiously, the testaments looked like archives, museum pieces that appeared dated even when the show they advertised was only three months old: a production at Bolton's Octagon or Stoke's Victoria Playhouse the previous year might just as well have been a Terence Rattigan revival from a decade ago.

Near the desk was a kit bag with squash rackets and shoes, shorts and tee-shirts spilling out on to the floor.

'Can I get you something?' Shaw asked, offering them seats on the sofa and the adjoining well-worn reading chair.

'We're OK for now,' said Salt, speaking for them both.

'As I said to you on the phone, Mr Shaw, it's about Sarah,' Kavanagh began.

'Please, do call me Adam,' he interrupted.

'Adam, we need to find out as much as possible about Sarah's background. You knew her well, I believe?'

'Oh, yes, I knew Sarah well,' he said. 'And, of course I'll do anything I can. I was so sorry to hear about her death, and especially for her to have died in such a terrible way.'

'You and she were together for some time?' ventured Salt.

'Yes, we were,' he said. 'A long time ago. Anyway, it's all in there.' He gestured to the crowded bookshelves that lined the wall adjacent to his word processor.

Salt looked across the room and saw that what she had assumed to be twenty volumes of George Eliot or Charles Dickens were, in fact, identical red one-year diaries.

'You keep a journal?' she asked, intrigued.

'Well, they're my workbooks, really. But, you know, work, life, for a writer, it's pretty much inseparable. Saves on therapists, too,' he added. 'Why pay thirty pounds an hour to talk to someone on a Tuesday afternoon when I can put it in those, and I might even get a play out of it, too, if I'm lucky.'

Who kept a diary these days? Kavanagh wondered as the man spoke. He associated the practice almost entirely with schooldays. And that was *his* schooldays, when, like most kids, he guessed, he wrote up his adolescent fumblings and teenage angst in some sort of rudimentary code.

'And Sarah?' asked Salt.

'What about her?' said Shaw.

'Was she the same?'

'Journal-keeper? I'm not sure,' he said thoughtfully. 'I wouldn't be surprised, though. The thing about writers is that they're always afraid that they'll forget the best idea they've ever had. And also, you never know what's going to take root, sometimes from the most inauspicious little notion, so you've got to jot stuff down. "Get it written, don't get it right," I often say to budding playwrights ... You've seen an anemone corm?' he went on, warming to his theme. 'Shrivelled, woody, stunted little thing.

211

Put it in a pot with some earth, give it a drop of water and, a few months later, the most beautiful flower you can imagine comes up. I grow some every year, just to remind myself that that's how things can begin.'

'It's a nice idea,' said Salt. 'And Sarah, then?' she went on. 'You think she might have been a diarist?'

As well as her voluminous correspondence, some of it going back thirty years, Sarah Clement didn't appear to have deleted any of her personal emails since she'd first gone online. But whilst there were a dozen A4 workbooks charting everything from daily wordages to plot problems and character studies, scraps of prose, nifty observations and snippets of dialogue, they had not yet recovered anything that resembled a personal diary.

'I don't want to speak ill of the dead,' said Shaw, 'and especially not Sarah, but the thing about writers is that they'll comfort their dying mother with one hand, and make notes with the other. I know. It's awful, and we all hate ourselves for it, but I'm afraid it's true. "The sliver of ice at the writer's heart", I think someone said. Graham Greene, I think. Anyway, as a writer, Sarah certainly had that, but she was a bit of a glutton, too.'

'How do you mean?' said Salt.

'Well, for most people, it's one thing or another, but Sarah was the kind of woman who would probably keep a diary *and* have a therapist. Do the yoga *and* the drugs. A bit of

everything, was Sarah. Well, not so much a bit –
quite a lot, really.'

'Go on,' said Kavanagh.

'You know – dope, drink, lots of lovers, and
still always working. Sarah hoovered up stuff.
She couldn't get enough, really. I guess it's why
she had so many partners; one man was never
going to be enough for her for long. Anyway, as
I say, more or less anything you want to know
about her, at least from our time together, I'm
afraid it'll be in there.'

'Afraid?' said Kavanagh.

'They weren't written for publication,' he said.
'They're private, or were supposed to be ... the
things we do, we say, we write, in private, you
know?'

'Of course,' said the inspector.

'I'm not keen on some stranger reading
through them. They're frank and so sometimes
they won't be very nice. But bear in mind, they
were never meant to be seen.'

'It's good of you,' said Salt. 'And it's not
something that everyone would do.'

'Yes,' he agreed, 'but when I knew you were
coming, what was I supposed to do? Hide them?
Pretend they don't exist?'

'A lot of people might have done exactly that,'
she said. 'But I give you an undertaking that
whoever gets to look at them will treat everything there with appropriate sensitivity.'

'Thanks, Ms ... sorry, what was your name
again?'

'Salt,' she said. 'Jane Salt.'

'Just don't let any writers see 'em,' Shaw said. 'I don't want any ideas nicked!'

'Not many Oscar Wildes in CID, I don't think – do you, Inspector?' she said.

Kavanagh was flattered that his policewoman lover was being flirted with by a decent-looking playwright, but he was not a little irritated that she seemed to be responding to his attentions with just a bit too much brazen enthusiasm. 'I doubt it,' he said. 'Not many.'

'What about a coffee?' said Shaw brightly, also clearly enjoying the exchange, and went through to the adjoining kitchen.

Kavanagh gave Salt a raised eyebrow, to which she responded with wholly affected ignorance.

'My memory's shot,' called Shaw from the other side of the open kitchen door. 'I can tell you Shakespeare's birthday, when Ibsen died, and when the first performance of *Waiting For Godot* was. But my brother's birthday? Not a chance.'

'May I look at one of these, please?' asked Kavanagh, gesturing to the journals.

'Sure, go ahead,' Shaw responded.

The inspector took down a volume at random and flipped it open. In a tiny, immaculate hand, there was the startlingly frank, raw material for a dozen exchanges in a novel or play: spats with friends and couplings with lovers; opening nights and rehearsed readings; rage as actors bumped into props and forgot their lines.

Getting drunk and being ill; who phoned and

wrote; royalties owed and cheques in the post, and even the results of his twice-weekly squash games were recorded with an almost forensic approach to detail.

Whilst the policeman absorbed this minutiae of another man's life, Salt read the bits and pieces that were stuck on the pin board above the word-processor. Amongst the postcards and telephone numbers, receipts, quips and quotes, was a picture of Sarah Clement. She was looking tanned and happy, her look towards the camera direct, challenging.

Shaw carried the tray of coffee into the room and set it down on the floor between them.

'Your new play is in rehearsal at the moment?' asked Salt.

'Yes,' he said, 'down in Chester. I'll let you have a couple of tickets for the preview if you like. It's taken ages to get it on, but it's finally going ahead.'

'Do you write for TV as well?' asked Kavanagh.

'No, I don't,' said the man.

'How come?' asked the inspector.

'I prefer working in the theatre,' he said. 'I don't really want to end up on a production line writing for some TV cop show year after year ... Do you like football?' he continued rhetorically. 'You go to all those matches just to see one good game on a rainy Wednesday evening. Theatre's like that. You just never know when it's going to be a great night.'

He poured them coffee and Salt pointed to the

pin board. 'You still have a photograph of Sarah, Adam?'

'Yes. I should take it down, really. But it's been there so long, and it seemed a callous thing to do right now.' He paused. 'And before this happened, I'd always left it up there ... sort of ... to remind me.'

'To remind you?' encouraged Salt.

'To remind myself...' He paused. 'That she was ... that she was kind of nuts. I don't mean to be cruel. She's only just died – in a terrible way – but she was crazy, even then.'

'Would you like to elaborate?' said Kavanagh.

'Sarah was two people. I know, I guess we all are, but what I mean is, she's this nice-looking, intelligent, passionate woman, but like a radio that's just slightly out of tune, there was always a little buzz there, too.'

'Go on,' said Salt.

'She was obsessive. OK, you've probably got to be a little bit that way if you're a writer. But it's a thin line between being driven and, well, being driven crazy. You know what I mean?'

'And you're talking about your time together, before her success with *The House of Loss*?' Salt asked.

'Yes, that came later, well after we'd split up. When she and I were together, it was the barren period, before the milk and honey.'

'She was struggling?'

'We all were. All young. All trying to get published, or get our work put on. There were a few of us up here in Manchester then, a sort of

216

writing mafia, supportive, yes, but, deep down, competitive too. I hadn't had anything much on. Just a couple of local productions. Sarah was hawking her stuff everywhere. She never stopped working, every day, every weekend, she never stopped. Writing for her really *was* an illness – or the opposite perhaps, like breathing or eating.

'And so every time she got knocked back, it was a killing blow, a real dagger through her heart. Everybody wants to be successful – your first book, your first play, we all want it – but, my God, Sarah wanted it badly. Maybe too much. She knocked on doors, she carried her stuff, literally, to a couple of publishers, ambushed the editors on the steps of their offices. They must have thought she was mad. The same with agents: she hand-delivered her manuscripts on several occasions. She must have written to every publisher in the book.'

'And those earlier books didn't get taken?'

He nodded his head from side to side. 'It was pitiful to see. She was like a broken thing. When a manuscript came back, rejected, she'd disappear into her room, smoke all day, drink a good bit, and then, maybe a few weeks later, she'd start again, a new book, and she'd be back to working all and every day, convinced that this was the one, the one that would see her into print...'

'What did you think of her work?' asked Salt and, recalling tutor Tom Hopwood's words, added, 'Or was she just unlucky?'

'Well, I liked Sarah's stuff. It was ... OK. Really OK,' he said. 'Trouble is, lots of people can write OK. Her books were *alright*. But alright's not good enough. No, what you've got to be today is pretty good, and lucky, too.'

'But she got there in the end?' said Kavanagh. 'The big book was better than OK?'

'Yes,' he said, 'it certainly was.'

'And yourself, too,' added Salt supportively.

'Well, I never had success on Sarah's scale, but people produce my stuff. My plays are on, not exactly the West End maybe, but it's OK.'

'Can you tell us a bit more about your relationship with Sarah? Outside of the work, the emotional side of things?' asked Salt gently. 'And how you two broke up?' She'd read the bitter exchanges that marked the end of their relationship, and her question was largely rhetorical, but she knew that there was nothing like hearing it from the person himself.

'Like I said, I don't write cop dramas, but I know that if you've been doing your job – and I'm sure you have – you'll know most of it already. But yes, I'll talk you through it.' He put his coffee cup down. 'It was a very difficult time, and I'm not proud of what I did. In fact, I'm ashamed.'

'Go on,' said Salt.

'But I'd never known anything like it. We were doomed, the relationship had been a roller-coaster of passion driven by our work and terrible fights and falling outs. We both knew we couldn't go on. But when we did finally agree to call it a day and part, she crucified me by saying I couldn't be in touch with her – not at all – for six months.'

'Why?' said Salt, intrigued.

'You tell me. *Six* months. Not five or seven, but six months. After you've been that close to someone for years, they're suddenly telling you that you can't phone, you can't speak or write, even. Nothing. I found it impossible. I couldn't cope with being cut off in that way.'

'And?' said Salt.

'I tried to deal with it, and I swear to you, I didn't want to be in the relationship as it had been, but equally I couldn't cope with this rejection, either.'

'So you did try to be in touch?' said Salt.

'Yes,' he agreed. 'I called and I wrote. Many times. She'd often said I was crazy. But was I? Or was she *making* me crazy by her behaviour?'

'You followed her, too?' said Salt tentatively.

'I shouldn't have done it,' he conceded, 'but I did, just to be near her.'

'You stalked her?' said Kavanagh bluntly.

'Yes,' he said, 'I'm afraid I did.'

'And?' said Salt, even though she knew very well the outcome of his obsessive behaviour.

'She took out an injunction, and I was threatened with prison if I breached it in any way. I went away. Went and stayed with a friend in Italy for a couple of months, tried to work over there. It was difficult, but yes, I stopped of course, and that was that, but it was a very hard time, and I still don't really understand why she needed to act in that way. I wasn't going to hurt her; I didn't want the relationship back where it had been. I just didn't want to be rejected. No one does, I suppose.

'When I got back to England, I saw a therapist for a few months, and do you know what he said? The thing that finally helped me through? He said, "Adam, everything you've told me about your relationship with this woman tells me it was an erratic, unpredictable love affair. But when it ends, you seem surprised that it follows the same irrational pattern." Somehow, these were the breakthrough words, the little bit of light that helped me through the darkness. It made sense, and I started to cope better. Eventually, I got back to work properly, and it was the beginning of my recovering from the whole thing.' He sipped his coffee.

'And more recently, you hadn't been in touch with Ms Clement?' Kavanagh asked.

'I haven't seen her for years,' he said. 'People I know, other writers, they tell me she'd become almost a recluse, more or less withdrawn from life.'

'You are sure about that?' said Salt directly. 'There's been no contact at all?'

'Sure,' he said. 'None.'

Kavanagh got to his feet and said, 'If you don't mind, Mr Shaw, we'll have to take your diaries with us. They'll be invaluable in helping us piece together this part of Sarah's past.'

'No,' he said, 'go ahead. But do look after

them, please.'

'Just one other thing I wanted to ask you, Adam,' said Salt as they started to pile the volumes on the sofa.

'Yes?' he said.

'I believe Sarah had a friend at Keele, a woman called Leah?'

'Yes,' he said. 'I never knew her. But Sarah talked about her sometimes. I think they were friends at about the same time Sarah was going out with a local guy, a roofing bloke called Nick Cherry.'

'Nick Cherry?' repeated Salt, and jotted down the name.

'Yes. Great name, isn't it? I've always remembered it 'cause I thought it was so good I'd use it in a play one day.

'And did you?' asked Salt.

'Not yet,' he said. 'But who knows?'

'And what about Leah?' said Salt. 'What can you tell us about her? Her name's cropped up a couple of times.'

'Well, I think her death affected Sarah very badly. She took her life, you know?'

'Yes, I believe so,' said Salt.

'When Sarah got low, and things were bad on the writing front for her, she'd say what a waste this woman's death was. What she could have done if she hadn't died. But I never met her, it was before Sarah and I were together.'

'You've been very helpful, Adam. Thank you,' said Salt, and extended her hand to the man.

Shaw fetched them some carrier bags from the

221

kitchen and Salt and Kavanagh carried his journals to the car parked outside.

'What do you reckon?' Kavanagh asked as they pulled away.

'I liked him,' she said.

'Yes, I could see that,' he said. 'But did he get back into stalker mode and pop down south to kill his ex-woman?'

'Of course not,' said Salt.

'*Of course*? Why so sure?'

'He's just told us more than most people would tell their best friend. Is he going to reveal all that pain if he's still doing it? I don't think so.'

'You know, Jane, people don't always fit boxes quite so neatly. Sometimes bits stick out, where the lid doesn't quite close, you know?'

'I'd put my life on his not being involved,' she said. 'And you can't lock him up just because he was hitting on me a bit,' she smiled.

'Why are you suddenly speaking American?' he said. 'You've been watching too many DVDs.'

'Anyway, look, I know how these things work—'

'What things? Murder?'

'Blokes. I'm no Renee Zellweger, but this much I do know: if another man fancies your woman, don't get tetchy; get chuffed.'

'I guess it depends on your experience,' he said seriously. 'When someone fancied my ex,

222

Rachael ... well, you know ... it always ended in tears. Usually mine.'

'Yes,' she said. 'But look, Frank, I'm not your ex.'

'Sure,' he said, and they drove in silence for a while, letting the exchange percolate and settle. Eventually, Kavanagh said, 'Is it just me, Jane, or are there too many writers in the world? I mean, who actually gets around to reading all this stuff? It takes me a month to read one week's Sunday papers.'

'I guess it's a small world,' she said. 'Cops and docs, you know: they all know one another.'

'And who was the other woman you mentioned, Leah something?' he asked.

'Yes, Leah Porter. Tom Hopwood, the lecturer I spoke to up at Keele, he talked about her, too. He's an alcoholic now, but he remembered her, reckoned she was the best writer he'd ever supervised. Not long afterwards, she had a breakdown and killed herself.'

'Right,' he said.

'I think we should go and speak to her family.'

'Why?' said Kavanagh.

'Friend of Sarah's; Hopwood mentions her, now Adam Shaw does too, *and* she took her life. It's a bit of a catalogue. She could be a bit of the jigsaw.'

'Maybe,' he agreed, 'but there's plenty to do back at base.' He indicated the carrier bags on the back seat. 'And someone's got to plough through that lot.'

'I'll make time,' she said. 'I'll track down her

223

family and have a chat with them.'

'Up to you,' he said as he accelerated up the slip road and on to the M56 for the journey back down south.

Thirty

October 2006

'Inspector?' called DC Scrivener from across the humming incident room. 'Call for you.'

'Can you take it?' said Kavanagh. 'I'm up to here. Put someone else on it...'

Scrivener put her hand over the mouthpiece, gestured an apology and said, 'Says he'll only speak to you.'

'Fuck,' muttered Kavanagh, nodded to the woman and picked up his receiver. 'Yes? DI Kavanagh speaking,' he said irascibly.

'Frank Kavanagh?' said the voice.

'Yes, this is Frank. Who's this?'

'You don't know me. I'm Chris Fenton, retired from the Met last year. I used to work out of Paddington.'

'What can I do for you, Chris? Things are pretty busy here.'

'I think it's what I might be able to do for you,' said Fenton.

'Oh, yes?' said Kavanagh, appropriately

sceptical.

'How's the enquiry on the bloke who was murdered down at the canal?' asked the man, without ceremony.

'May? Why?' said the inspector.

'Yes, Terence May, that's his name,' replied the man.

'Well, for a start, the enquiry's confidential, of course, and secondly, I wouldn't discuss it on the phone even if it weren't.'

'Yes, sure,' said Fenton. 'But you'll want to hear what I've got, I assure you.'

'I hope you're right,' said Kavanagh wearily. 'Give me your number and I'll call you back. No offence, but you know...'

Fenton gave him his landline number. Kavanagh dialled it immediately and the former cop picked up.

'OK, so what were you saying?' said Kavanagh. 'You've information about the man who was killed down at Rickmansworth?'

'What do you know about his background?' said Fenton.

'Not much,' said Kavanagh. 'He used to be in the art business and retired down here with his boyfriend about six or seven years ago. We're looking into him. You know the ropes. You know how these things work.'

'Sure,' said Fenton.

'Though we are running into a few dead ends, so whatever you've got could be useful. Go ahead.'

'On this one, Frank, you'll struggle to find the

real story. His tracks were pretty well covered, otherwise I wouldn't have been doing my job. You getting any warmer yet?'

'No, not really,' said Kavanagh, intrigued. 'Go on.'

'Terence May was on the WPP, and it was me who put him there. I was his liaison.'

'The Witness Protection Programme?' said Kavanagh. 'Are you serious?'

'Absolutely. It was me who cut the deal with him. Have you ever had any dealings with the programme?'

'No,' said the inspector. 'But I've got a good idea of what's involved.'

'It's dealt with by the least number of operatives who can arrange it,' said Fenton. 'It's strictly need-to-know stuff. If no one's been in touch with you about May, that's the reason why. No one knows who the fuck he is. The more people there are in the know, the greater is the risk of things leaking. You know how it is: if the pay day's big enough, someone, somewhere, is always going to talk. And we only need to get a bit porous and the whole thing would lose credibility, and then the programme would be history.'

'I see,' said Kavanagh. 'And what was May involved with that necessitated his having a new identity?'

'Art fraud. And his name was Neil. Neil Grainer. He was quite a player in a fine-art auction house scam operating out of London and Edinburgh. They were selling the supposed

226

work of some recently deceased artist or another at artificially inflated prices and then taking huge commissions as well. It was all very low-key and plausible. A formerly unknown piece by this or that sculptor or painter coming discreetly to market. Maybe it was an early piece that had disappeared, or something that had never been seen or had been in a private collector's hands for decades.

'They never brought so much out as to raise suspicions, but just enough to feed the greed factor amongst buyers and collectors. We're talking very big bucks,' said Fenton.

'Right,' said Kavanagh. 'And you cut a deal with him?'

'Yes, eventually. Their whole operation was watertight. Unless we could lean on someone to speak, we'd no case, just bits and pieces and a lot of circumstantial. The DPP wouldn't have taken it on. The best we could have hoped for would be picking off a few of the foot-soldiers, squaddies going away for eighteen months while the main players didn't even get their fingers burnt.

'But we got lucky when we had something on Neil's boyfriend, a bloke called Robbie. He'd been dealing in biggish quantities of amyl nitrate and so we were able to pressure him; we let him know he was definitely going away for a decent stretch. Robbie wasn't happy, and Neil definitely didn't want his boy being fucked by half of Wandsworth nick. After he'd had a bit of thinking time, he came to us with a deal.

Basically, he sold us the main man, a bloke called David; David O'Connor...'

'And Neil Grainer needed to disappear?' said Kavanagh.

'He most certainly did. There was always going to be a stiff sentence, 'cause there was a feeling that this kind of white-collar crime was getting out of hand and pretty well going un-punished, as if it was just a bit of a game between the cops and the bad guys in Armani. Drug importers and armed robbers were getting put away for years, but what about the VAT fraudsters and the high-end antiques and art house scams? So, the special art treasures unit was set up and we went after these guys with a big budget and a more or less tacit under-standing that if we got them to court, the beak would let 'em know what was what.'

'It must've been very big bucks?' said Kav-anagh. 'I don't know the figures, but change of identity isn't gonna come cheap...'

'Somebody in the Home Office will have done the sums, but it probably comes out at about five hundred grand to set the thing up, and then at least forty or fifty grand a year for life.'

'I knew there was something wrong with that queen when I saw his shorts,' said Kavanagh. There was silence on the other end of the phone. Fuck, thought Kavanagh. 'You were saying, Chris?' he said, wincing at his own ineptitude.

'You know, it's 2006, Frank,' said Fenton, with a hint of admonition. 'I thought we'd left all that kind of thing behind. People have got a right to live their lives—'

'Yes, of course they have, and I'm sorry. It was a stupid thing to say, and it doesn't reflect my feelings at all. Really, I've no problem with gay people—'

'Don't tell me,' said Fenton, 'half your friends are queers, and those that aren't are black!'

'Well, not quite, but I do apologize.'

'Accepted,' said Fenton.

'But you gotta agree,' added Kavanagh, 'it was a dodgy haircut. I hope that wasn't your doing?'

'I warned him against it. Get it cut short – a number one, a little stubble cut, and face to match – but he would have it long *and* dyed. He looked terrible, but it was what he wanted.'

'What else?' asked Kavanagh.

'We took him to Hungary for a couple of days for a bit of a nose and neck job. Coloured contact lenses are standard, of course, and then we got him out of Hoxton and up to Rickmansworth. He'd been on holiday there when he was a kid. He could have gone abroad – Spain and Portugal are popular, for the climate, but we do the States too; we've got a reciprocal arrangement with the FBI. But Neil had got it into his head that he wanted to run a B & B out in the sticks. Robbie was already HIV positive, and he reckoned that if and when the worst happened, the guests would be some sort of company for him.'

'How do you reckon O'Connor fingered him?' asked the inspector.

'I'm only guessing, but I reckon when your writer was murdered, someone with connections to David O'Connor must've got a quick look at him on the telly. People get casual and relax after a bit because they think they look completely different as soon as they get a haircut and a decent set of choppers. But they've still got the same build, the same gait, they're recognizable to people who've known them well, and always will be. The last thing I ever said to him was to keep his head down, but there you go – not careful enough, and it cost him big time.'

'And not a nice way to go, either,' said Kavanagh.

'Yes,' said Fenton. 'Pissed over by the very geezer he'd shat on.'

'Right,' said the inspector, 'thanks a lot, Chris. I'll get some of our people on to it straight away.'

'You're welcome,' said Fenton. 'You've got my number if you need it.'

Thirty-One

October 2006

The silver birch sapling that had been planted to commemorate Elwyn Porter's retirement from St John's School in Cardiff was now a sturdy tree, with a girth of nearly two feet. The little brass plaque at its foot had tarnished to dull indecipherability, the metal surrounding the engraved letters eroded by the sun and wind and rain in the years since his departure.

Many of the newer members of staff had no idea that this tree was any different from any of the others in the school grounds, and it was almost certain that no one who had arrived since the turn of the century was even aware that there was a brass plaque screwed to the little timber plinth down amongst the mulch and wood chippings.

A very few of the more senior members of staff, however, did remember with affection their long-serving Head and his dedicated work during some thirty years at the school.

But nowadays, alas, Elwyn had very little idea that he had once administered a school at all, let alone a well-regarded place of education for

231

eight hundred pupils, and a teaching staff of seventy. Erstwhile governors' meetings, appointments committees, school inspections and imperative business about bullying, lunchtime supervisions and playground litter duties, were all as nothing now. For shambling Elwyn, they might as well have never happened at all. Even the foggy amble around his suburban garden of a few months ago was now a thing of the past.

Some five or six years after his retirement, he began, just occasionally, to forget the word for the most familiar of objects. One evening, he found he couldn't ask Bethan to pass him the salt, but just pointed to it, and could not muster the word.

A month later he found himself in the supermarket trying patiently, doggedly, but wholly without success, to recall what it was that Bethan had sent him down the aisle to find. He stood there, looking at the bottles of Worcester and soy sauce, but just could not remember what it was that she had sent him to find. Later the same year, one autumn morning, he sat down for breakfast at the kitchen table fully dressed, but had buttoned up his cardigan whilst still wearing his pyjama top. Neither of them laughed any more.

Bethan made an appointment with their GP of thirty years who arranged for them to see a consultant at Cardiff's University hospital. And a few weeks after that, they sat with Mr Brewer who talked them through the brain scans, X-rays and myriad test results that lay spread on the desk before him.

The diagnosis was exactly as they had expected; they were not foolish people. The cure was non-existent; the prognosis, bleak. Like thousands of other people every year, seventy-one-year-old Elwyn was suffering from Alzheimer's disease.

He deteriorated at an alarming rate. This or that course of drugs possibly arrested the progress of the illness by an infinitesimal degree, but the malaise was inexorable. At first there were visits from friends and neighbours and former colleagues. But the deterioration in the man was so marked that very soon there was little comfort to be derived from even these gestures. The visits ceased completely until Bethan alone, with daily visits from a health worker, shouldered the burden of her ailing husband's care.

And now, the man's long days were a muddled round of being dressed and fed, helped to use the lavatory and then, propped up in his high-backed chair, sitting in front of seamless television. Grave news from Iraq. A bomb in London. A World Cup win or an Olympics bid. Stabbings on the streets of Manchester or Hackney. They were all as one for Elwyn these days as he slumped in front of the TV.

The family, whose future had once been so robust and propitious in every way, had somehow segued into a domestic catastrophe. Their only daughter had had a disastrous love affair, fallen into depression and eventually taken her own life, leaving the late-middle-aged couple to raise her infant child.

Esther had struggled throughout her childhood and adolescence with the legacy of her mother's untimely death. And now the cruel illness that had afflicted Bethan's kindly husband was destined to be a bleak final act in their tragedy.

It had not been difficult for Jane Salt to track down the Porters, for even now, in some quarters of the city, they were recalled fondly by parents who now had children of their own at the school where Elwyn and Bethan had ruled with a sort of benign authority for what seemed like time immemorial.

They sat together in the front room of the big Edwardian house opposite Roath Park. The woman was frail in body but still bright in mind. Her husband might no longer have any idea which country he was living in, but Bethan could have told you who was holding the Presidency of the European Union, as well as the shadow chancellor's name, and probably, given a few moments' thought, who had won the Six Nations Rugby the previous year.

Her mental acuity wasn't the result of following the advice of TV's pop psychologists, or government surveys that advised eating this much fish, that much fruit and those four daily vitamins. No, Bethan Porter had simply maintained the way of life that she had followed, more or less, for all of her seven decades. She'd always eaten some fruit (her mother had told her to), drunk a glass of water at morning and evening and a small glass of wine with supper. She fell asleep after she had read a few pages of the novel that she picked up after she had prayed each night beside her bed. The fact that her husband had followed a more or less similar regime (bar the bedside praying, perhaps) and yet was now unable to use the lavatory unaided, and took his strained food from a plastic spoon held by another, had not escaped her notice, however.

'It's about Sarah Clement, Mrs Porter,' Salt said now. 'As I told you on the phone, we're trying to find out about her background...'

The woman seemed pleased to have company, someone to chat with. 'Sarah,' she repeated. 'Yes, of course. Poor thing. I remember her, she and Leah were friends.'

'I'm so sorry to have to ask you these things, Mrs Porter; it must be painful for you, on account of...'

'Yes,' said the woman. 'The death of a child before its parents is against nature, and we have never got over it. But, bless him,' she went on, 'I'm sure Elwyn isn't even aware of it any more. Every cloud...'

'Of course,' said Salt. 'Leah and Sarah, they were close at university?'

'Yes, they were,' said the woman. 'They lived together in Stoke.'

'We're looking at every aspect of Sarah's life to see whether there is anything there that might provide a clue to her death.'

'I see.'

'And did you ever meet her?' asked Salt.

'Yes, when we went to collect our daughter from the house they shared. Leah had become ill and we had to bring her home. She was a husk. Our lovely girl had completely disappeared inside herself. Sarah carried a few things out to the car for us. Leah was helpless, she couldn't do anything.'

'And you had no further contact with her?'

'No, none at all. She wrote, but I know the letters went unanswered.'

'Your daughter's funeral? I'm so sorry to ask you these things, but she didn't come?'

'It was only immediate family. Leah wasn't in touch with any of her former friends. It was a complete nervous breakdown. She hadn't been out of the house for a year. She hoarded her pills and had tried to take her life twice before, but we managed to get to her in time. One day, though, we were out for just an hour, and she got into the garage, somehow found the spare set of car keys and sat there with the engine running. She was dead when we returned from the shops with Esther.'

'I see,' said Salt. 'I'm so sorry. And then it fell to you and your husband to bring up your granddaughter?'

'Yes,' said Bethan. 'Social services were involved, of course, to see that we were fit and able, but Esther had had such a terrible start, the stability that we could give, even if our age was not ideal ... I don't think there was ever any doubt that we would do it.'

'It must have been a challenge,' said the policewoman. 'How did you cope?'

'Esther was only two when Leah took her life. But because of her illness, we'd already played a big part in the child's life and so the change wasn't as great as it might have been. We did our best, but it wasn't easy. The irony is we'd both spent most of our lives with children. Between us, we'd probably dealt with every type of child you could imagine, but when it came to our own granddaughter, it was a very different thing. She was a troubled child; you could see it in her little face, even at that age. She didn't sleep well at night, never seemed really happy, and after her mother's death, things got worse.

'Even at nursery school, she was behaving badly. And later, at primary school, we had to go and collect her many times. She was wilful, but what was worse – and it so grieves me to say these things about my own flesh and blood – she wasn't just a naughty child, she was devious, too. And, of course, none of it was her fault, not really. Every child needs her mother, and her mother's love. Esther had never properly known that.

'She saw a child psychologist. And at home, here, we tried everything: encouragement, bribery even, cajoling, threats, carrot and stick, everything. We talked to her for hours, but all to no avail. She wasn't really there. She'd agree, she wouldn't argue, but then she would truant, steal when there was no need, smoke cigarettes. At fourteen, she was getting drunk and, of course, we were constantly worried that she, too, just as her mother had, would repeat history and get pregnant herself...'

'But she didn't?' said Salt, glad to find something to applaud.

'No, she didn't. I've no idea why. She had started taking drugs, and possibly it was those that made her less fertile than she might have been? In any event, thank God for small mercies, she didn't become pregnant, or if she ever did, she must have had a termination.'

'Where is she now?' asked Salt.

'She comes to visit occasionally. It might be just a few weeks, but I haven't seen her for months. The last time, I'd asked her to come round because I'd told her I was going to have to leave this house. I don't want to, but I can barely get Elwyn up the stairs now. I just can't manage him any more and he's going to have to go into care. I've found a retirement flat for myself. It's all a sad ending. But at least we have had some life. And anyway,' she said, focussing on the manageable practical issues, rather than the too-painful emotional ones, 'there are far too many rooms. They get dusty even if I don't use them, and the heating bills are huge.'

'I understand,' said Salt.

'The last time she was here, just after Easter – I'd still got her egg for her, I always get one – she lent me a book by Sarah Clement. I'd never read it. I suppose the connection with Leah was too painful, but I've read it now. I thought it was very good.'

'Did you tell Esther that Leah and Sarah had known one another?' she asked.

'Of course. She said she was going to contact Sarah's publisher and get in touch to tell her who she was ... I'd asked her to come and see if there was anything she wanted before I got a dealer in to take the furniture that's too big for the little flat; the rest I'm going to give to the church.

'She borrowed a van and came round. She was in the top room for ages, just going through things. In the end, she took a couple of her mother's dresses, some books and shoes, and Leah's old computer.'

'And do you know whether she did get in touch with Sarah?' asked Salt.

'No, I've no idea,' said Mrs Porter.

'Where does Esther live now?' asked Salt, her notepad open.

The woman smiled. 'You wouldn't be welcome, dear. It's what they call a squat. In Canton, on the other side of the city. Do you know Cardiff? It's one of the districts that's due to be developed shortly. The docks are now a marina with new apartments, the Welsh Assembly building, all that kind of thing. Tiger Bay's been gone for years, of course, and Canton's next, apparently. There are lots of old houses that have been compulsorily purchased by the council, but they're still awaiting demolition. Esther says they are good homes, and why shouldn't people live there. She has a point, I suppose, but we both know that she's living there because of the way that she and her boyfriend live; they would never get a landlord to give them a proper home. She wouldn't be able to get a mortgage or keep up the rent on a flat. It's true she had a terrible start in life, but now drugs have destroyed all her opportunities.'

'Can I take the address?' asked Salt. 'I'll be discreet, I assure you.'

The older woman wrote down the address and escorted Salt down the wide, sunny hall. Standing at the front door, she said with feeling, 'When I think of the happy times that we had here when Leah was a child, it breaks my heart.'

'I'm sure,' said Salt, and took the woman in her arms.

'Just before I go,' she said, 'do you mind if I ask what happened to Esther's father?'

'No, I don't mind you asking,' she said. 'He was a postgraduate student at Bangor in North Wales. Over from America for the second year of his doctorate. They'd first met there, in New England, when Leah was at Smith College for a year. But when he was over here, they broke up, and he went back home.'

'And that was it?' said Salt.

'He wrote to Leah for months. Letters would arrive here direct, or be forwarded from her university. But she never replied. She didn't want anything to do with him.'

'Why not?' asked the policewoman.

'Have you ever known anyone with depression, Miss Salt? Leah had lost all will to live; she had disappeared into a dark, unreachable world. It was a terrible thing to see. And yet, you know, before all this happened, she'd been so happy. I really think they had been in love.'

'So, what had happened between them?' Salt gently probed.

'I don't know exactly. But we think he had an affair, and that's what brought her illness on. It was a trigger, if you like. If you have a predisposition to that kind of illness, it can be anything. A lot of people, apparently, become ill after their defences are lowered. After a bout of flu, for example. Leah was such a trusting person, and with such an imagination, she would have been devastated.'

'And she never responded to his letters?'

'No, I don't think so.' Then she added, pensively, 'Did you know that she was a talented writer?'

'Yes, I did,' said Salt. 'When I spoke to one of Sarah's supervisors, he spoke very highly of your daughter's work.'

'Such a waste,' said the woman. 'Such a terrible waste.'

'I'm so sorry,' said Salt. 'Thank you so much for your help. I really am grateful.' She took the woman's hand. 'I hope things work out for you in your new home, and for your husband. Goodbye.'

Thirty-Two

October 2006

'Joe, can you get this out to the troops? I've just had a call from Anan Patel—'

'Who?' said Lavendar.

'Patel. Marcus Breese's solicitor. Apparently, he wants to come in for a chat.'

'Right,' said Lavendar, unimpressed.

'Cheer up, Joe. This is breakthrough time. He's a had a bit of time to think things over and you'll see, his brief's made it clear, he'd do better to come clean now...'

'You reckon?' said Lavendar.

'A small wager?' suggested Kavanagh. 'She's told him a bit of coming across now and he'll be looking at a reduced sentence for a guilty plea. We may not be home yet, mate, but we're heading there.'

'And what about down at the farm? The spying set-up?' said Lavendar.

'You know I never bought that stuff,' said Kavanagh. 'Just cheap thrills for some loner. The guy who's up that tree's a peeping tom, that's all. If he's a murderer, I'm Simon and Garfunkel,' and he began to sing a fairly difficult and completely tuneless couple of lines from 'Homeward Bound'.

'And the Leah Porter–Sarah Clement connection that Salt's hot for?' said Lavendar.

'Well, she's out there checking the angles,' replied the inspector. 'All we know for sure is that Leah had a breakdown on account of her no-good American boyfriend cheating on her. It's not the first time that a vulnerable person hasn't got over being cheated and lied to. She's talented and highly strung. She cracks up and eventually takes her life.'

'And Sarah? Where does she fit in?'

'She's a writer, and everyone agrees most of them are barking. Adam Shaw says she struggled for years, then she has a hit, and then it's back to the doldrums. I guess she, too, falls into a kind of wasteland, only hers is booze and dope and blokes.'

'Alright, so if Breese is the bad guy, why do you reckon he's killed Clement? What's his motive?' asked Lavendar.

'I've no idea, Joe. But one thing's certain: Sarah Clement died and yet offered little resistance. And Breese is about to tell us why.'

'No sexual? No previous? No theft? I don't see it, Frank,' challenged Lavendar.

'You watch the news, Joe? Last week, a woman was killed over a parking dispute with her next-door neighbour. A couple of years ago, a guy killed his wife because she turned the radio off when he was listening to the cricket. People, you know, half of them are nuts, and the

243

other half are crazy ... What do the advertising whiz kids say? "Think outside the box." Let's think outside the box; let's push the envelope and break through that glass ceiling! There'll be something that explains it all, it's just that we don't know what it is yet,' he said, and began singing again, this time 'Bridge Over Troubled Water', but still hopelessly flat.

Breese had lost a little of the confidence and swagger that he had displayed in his previous interview, and there was no trace at all of the sanctimonious man known to half a million viewers in the Midlands TV region from his appearances on *Monday through Friday*. Now, sat hunched in the chair beside his solicitor, he was looking wan and not a little afraid.

Salt and a couple of other officers observed him through the one-way glass of the room as Kavanagh began the interview, Joe Lavendar at his side.

'Ms Patel, Mr Breese. Thank you for coming in,' said the inspector. 'You know the procedure, of course, ma'am,' he said, and went through the mandatory recording formalities. 'You have something you wish to add to your previous statement, I believe?' he began.

'Yes, my client wishes to elaborate on a detail or two,' said Patel on Breese's behalf.

I bet he does, thought Kavanagh. 'Please, in your own time,' he said politely, 'perhaps you would just like to tell us what happened?'

'The thing is,' began Breese, 'I didn't really

tell you the whole truth when we last spoke...'

There's a surprise, thought Kavanagh, and nodded acknowledgement. 'Please, go on.'

'My journey to London, the cycle ride, it wasn't exactly as I had planned; it wasn't as easy as I had imagined it would be.'

'No?' said Kavanagh.

'As I said to you last time we spoke, there were problems with the bike – punctures and so on – and the camping was pretty unpleasant, what with a thunderstorm and all, and people weren't as friendly as they might have been. Kids, you know, throwing things, bits of abuse. It sounds nothing now, but at the time it was all a bit difficult.'

'I see,' said the inspector. *For heaven's sake, man, get on with it, cut to the chase*, he thought inwardly. 'And how does this relate to Sarah Clement?' he asked.

Breese took a deep breath. Kavanagh had conducted a lot of interviews in his time and he knew the form. Guilty parties invariably needed to approach their actual confession with a measure of circumlocution.

'Please, continue, Mr Breese,' urged the inspector.

'I couldn't sleep...'

Tick the box: sleep deprivation, not fully in control. Here we go with the extenuating circumstances that he and his brief have cooked up together.

'Yes,' he said, 'go on.'

'Punctures every day, horrible food; I got

soaked a couple of times and I was always tired...'

Come on, man, thought Kavanagh, *get it out*.

'I did a dishonourable thing,' continued Breese.

Dishonourable? Kavanagh repeated to himself. *Call yourself a reporter? You need a thesaurus. 'Dishonourable' is not the first word that comes to mind to describe a murder.*

'The fact is, at the time that I would have been near the murdered woman's boat, I wasn't on the canal.'

'Really?' said Kavanagh. 'So, where were you?'

'I was on a train.'

'Yes?' said the inspector, intrigued. 'How do you mean?'

'I was due back at the office by Monday lunchtime. Things hadn't gone well. I needed a good night's sleep and a decent meal but I still had a fair distance to go. So, on the Sunday morning, I decided to skip the last bit and get on a train.'

'You got on a train?' repeated Kavanagh, not even trying to disguise his complete scepticism.

'Yes. I'm ashamed to say it, but I did.'

'Why didn't you tell us this before?' asked the inspector.

'I was trying to protect my pride, my reputation,' he said.

'And now?'

'Now, unless I'm mistaken, you seem to think I was involved with the woman's murder. Of course I wasn't, but the only way I can convince you is to tell you what I was really doing.'

Kavanagh thought for a second, looked across at Lavendar who was keeping a straight face, but was almost certainly regretting that he'd not risked a tenner against the inspector's claims of an hour ago that they were, without doubt, about to hear a murder confession.

'Well, Mr Breese, your claim that, rather than being close to – or even at – the murder scene, you were on a train, won't make a great deal of difference unless you can substantiate your story. Did anyone see you on this train? There must have been witnesses. We've put out plenty of appeals. How come no one's come forward?'

'I don't know. There was a bloke at the station,' he said.

'Oh, yes? And where was this?' Kavanagh asked.

'Cheddington.'

'Right,' said the inspector. 'There was a bloke at Cheddington station who can verify your being there?'

'I guess so.'

'Would you like to describe him?'

'He was a traveller. You know, like an old hippy. He had a dog with him and a bag, a sort of old rucksack.'

'Right,' said Kavanagh. 'And this is the man who is going to back up your story?'

'Yes,' said Breese. 'I hope so.'

'Anything else, besides his dog and a rucksack, that might help us to trace him?'

'He had dreadlocks.'

'Oh, right?' said Kavanagh. 'He was a black guy?'

'No, he was white,' rejoined Breese.

Kavanagh looked at the man with contempt for his audacity and said, 'A white bloke with dreadlocks? Anything else?'

'He was about forty, tall and pretty thin, and he asked me if I could spare him a quid.'

'Did you give it him?' asked Kavanagh.

'Yes, I gave him a two-pound coin.'

'And I suppose there was no one else at the station? Except yourself and a forty-year-old hippy with dreadlocks...'

'And his dog,' added Breese.

Kavanagh smiled, in spite of himself.

'It was a Sunday morning, early, there was no one else there,' Breese added.

'And where do you think we're going to find this bloke?' asked Kavanagh innocently.

'I've no idea,' said Breese. 'Perhaps he uses that train regularly.'

'You reckon?' said Kavanagh as he leaned back in his chair and looked at the man. Years ago, that round-the-world sailor who'd moored somewhere and pretended to be winning the race had done something like this. Bigger scale, but similar deception, shabby and cheap.

Kavanagh knew for certain that he was dealing with a deceitful, ego-driven man, and in recent days, he'd grown inclined to believe that he might, possibly – even probably – be dealing with a killer. He had all but convinced himself

248

that this was some sort of latter-day Flashman. And now, the man opposite him was telling him he was nothing of the sort, but was, in fact, no more than a bungling Bertie Wooster.

'So you got on the train at Cheddington. Then what?' asked the inspector.

'I came into London, got off the Metropolitan line at Baker Street, and cycled up to Regent's Park. I phoned Bernadette and she came along to meet me.'

'And does she know about what you're telling us you did?'

'No, I never told her.'

'Like I say, Mr Breese, without independent verification, without a witness, what you're telling us holds no more water than your previous account of events.'

'Yes, I realize that,' he conceded.

'And tell me again, if you don't mind, why exactly didn't you own up to this previously? Can you imagine the time and resources that have been expended searching for witnesses as we looked into your earlier account?'

'I was cycling. The whole point was that I was supposed to be roughing it for charity. My friends and colleagues had sponsored me for a lot of money. How could I then tell people I didn't do it? They'd feel cheated. Especially with my ... you know ... my profile and my job. I felt crap about the whole thing. I still do.'

Kavanagh preferred the man when he had been arrogant and bullish; he'd been much easier to dislike then. This poor sap was almost sympathetic and, unfortunately, there was the possibility that he was telling the truth. Unlikely, but possible.

'Right,' said Kavanagh. 'We'd better get down to Cheddington and have a look. There's bound to be CCTV there. Meanwhile, if you would give Sergeant Lavendar here a full description of your traveller friend – what he was wearing, what he looked like, that kind of thing.'

'Will that be all?' asked Ms Patel.

'We'll have to look into your client's story, ma'am, and then we'll be in touch again, no doubt. But when Mr Breese is done with the sergeant here, yes, he's free to go. For now.'

Thirty-Three

October 2006

The squat on the busy road in Canton, down in Cardiff's ripe-for-development district, was even less propitious than Esther's grandmother had described it. The once-substantial houses were now boarded up and forlorn. The heavy-gauge metal sheets, all secured with big, con-cealed-head fixings, and screwed to every window and door frame, were formidable obstacles to any would-be intruder.

And if these things were not sufficient

deterrent, there was a tatty board warning off thieves and trespassers that claimed threats of video surveillance and regular dog patrols. *Yes, sure*, thought Salt as she stepped through the front garden's chip papers and pizza boxes, buddleia and scrubby elder, that was also home to mattresses, broken electric cookers, a refrigerator without a door, a smashed and heavily stained toilet bowl and several carpet pieces.

She picked up a gas-ring burner from among the clumps of long grass and rapped it several times against the metal frame that concealed the former front door. Nothing. She clambered over the junk at the side of the building and followed a trodden route to the back of the house.

Here, where once there had been a small garden, there was now a three-foot-high canopy of fearsome-looking brambles and a decent crop of dusty blackberries. Across the back door, the sheet of metal had been peeled back a couple of feet, providing entry for anyone prepared to crawl through the gap.

She stood in the sunny quiet of the back garden. She shouldn't be here. It was a Clarice Starling into-the-pitch-black-warehouse-alone type of stupid move.

In the movie, the audience tut-tuts its collective head and vetoes her folly. Don't do it, Clarice; don't go in there alone! Then they settle back into their seats for the vicarious thrill of her inevitable comeuppance.

I know better than this, thought Salt. Dodgy premises, iffy, dope-dependent folk – this is definitely not text-book. There should be half a dozen officers, armed with a warrant and Kevlar anti-stab vests, possibly following a couple of days' patient surveillance.

But that would take forever, and she was on a roll after her exchange with Bethan Porter and, more importantly, she was here right now. She took a deep breath, kneeled down, and squeezed her way in.

It wasn't exactly something from *Grand Designs*, but, compared with the desolate scene outside, it was some improvement.

The trouble with junkies – one of the many troubles with junkies – was that they were un-predictable. Often – usually, in fact, experience had taught her – they weren't violent. But some-times, just occasionally, they were. It depended entirely upon where they were in their medica-tion cycle: the need, the fix, the blissful answer of that massive need met, the gradual coming-to, followed by the beginning of the nag for the next fix. And on it went, the never-ending cycle. Feed the beast, and all was well. But, unable to fulfil that disabling craving, addicts could certainly turn nasty.

'Hello?' she called, her voice more timorous than she would have wished. 'It's the police. Is anyone there?'

The house felt empty. Sort of. But she'd been wrong before.

'Esther? Is there anyone in the house? It's DC Salt. I have to speak to you. Hello?'

Nothing. Silence. A board creaking, maybe?

The noise of the traffic outside, a little muted now, but still audible.

'We're coming up. Everything's OK. There are officers outside. We just want to have a word with you.'

She put a foot on the wide staircase. The banister, the newel posts and spindles were completely missing, looked as if they'd been broken off, leaving splintered, jagged uprights. Maybe they'd been used for firewood.

'I'm coming up now,' she said, with as much bass in her voice as she could muster.

She started to climb the bare treads, making as much noise as a pair of size four and a halfs could.

At the top of the landing, she stood silently, breathing heavily. The bedroom doors were missing. Maybe they'd been looted? The mid-Victorian house would have had substantial panelled doors, worth quite a bit in an architectural salvage yard.

She took a couple of steps towards the door opening and read the scene there: cold ash and sticks, the remnants of a fire in the little hearth, a couple of sleeping bags and a grubby duvet close to it. A few bits of improvised furniture: upturned cardboard boxes, some cups and bottles; the scorched silver paper and spent matches, teaspoons and syringes of the drug-user's life. Books, some on the mantelpiece above the fireplace, a few piled in the corner, along with an ancient computer and some disks in a clear, plastic box, and more paperbacks beside one of the sleeping bags on the floor.

The afternoon sun poured into the room through the grimy sash windows. She took another step through the gaping doorway into the room and stood there in the silence.

She felt even more uneasy, standing amongst these few things belonging to other people. As any number of householders had found, it was one thing to be burgled, it was quite another to come face to face with a stranger in your house. In spite of oneself, the resident's instinct was invariably to confront the intruder.

She backed out of the room. There were two other open doorways on the landing. She felt a growing sense of unease but took a few steps and approached the doorway adjacent to her. She put her head round the corner and recoiled.

The inert figure huddled there had his eyes almost closed, his head collapsed on his chest, the paraphernalia of his recent deed lying beside him on the bare floorboards.

'It's OK,' said Salt, her voice trembling. 'It's OK.'

The man raised his head a few inches and looked at the policewoman uncomprehendingly.

'DC Salt,' she said. 'I just need to ask you a couple of things,' she added, by way of an explanation.

The man ignored her and reached out towards his tobacco tin. With his eyes barely open, he rolled a cigarette as she watched.

'What the fuck do you want?' he slurred finally.

Salt knew this man. Well, not *this* man, perhaps, but his tribe. Every young copper had seen his type strut into the local magistrates' court – for dangerous driving, drug use, burglary or whatever – and then, half an hour later, he would swagger away from the place, cigarette in his mouth, community-service order or an ASBO tag against his name and a smirking two-fingered salute to the bereaved family or aggrieved householder.

'I'm Detective Constable Salt,' she said and, rather redundantly, took out her warrant card to show him.

He sneered. 'Right,' he said. 'Right,' and dragged on his cigarette.

'And you?' she asked. 'Who are you? What's your name?'

'Gareth,' he said.

'Is Esther here?' she asked.

'No,' he said without elaboration.

'Where is she?' asked the woman.

'Court,' he said derisively.

'Court?' repeated Salt. 'Why?'

'What do you think?' he asked.

'I've no idea. Why is she in court?' she asked again.

'Shoplifting. Magistrates' court. Two o'clock. Today.'

'I see,' said Salt. 'Did you not go with her?' she enquired, stating the obvious.

'She's better alone,' he said, 'without me. They'll only give her a bit of community, if she signs up to rehab. She'll be alright. Got a good

255

probation officer. She'll be alright.'

The man got to his feet unsteadily. 'Gotta have a drink,' he murmured and nodded to the room next door. He swayed past the woman and she followed.

Next door, he lowered himself down on to one of the sleeping bags, leaned against the wall and sipped from a cola bottle. Salt stood against the door jamb.

'What do you want?' he said.

'Esther went to her grandmother's recently,' she said.

'So?' he said.

'And took some things away.'

'So what?'

'What did she take?'

'Why? The old bird gave the things to her. Said she could take what she liked. She didn't nick anything.'

'I know that,' said Salt.

'Just books, some clothes, bits and pieces...'

'That?' said Salt, pointing to the computer.

'Yes,' said Gareth.

'What did she want it for?'

'Fuck knows. Why not? It's a fucking antique. It was her mother's.'

'What's on the disks?' asked Salt, pointing to the box.

'How the fuck should I know?' he rejoined.

'You haven't looked at them?'

'No.'

'Do you know if Esther has?'

'Yes, she took it all round to a mate's. We

haven't got all the services connected here,' he said sarcastically. 'Hey, look, I'm done with all this. Have you got a warrant to be here?' he said, getting to his feet.

'Sit down,' she said firmly. 'This is off the record. Just a chat. And anyway, who's given you permission to be here? We're investigating the murder of a friend of Esther's mother's, Sarah Clement. Do you know of her?'

'No,' he said.

'You haven't heard it on the news?' she continued.

'The news?' said the man. 'This is the news.' He gestured to the room.

'She was killed recently. She and Esther's mother were once close. We think there might be a connection.'

'Yes?' he said.

'Sarah Clement was a writer. Do you know her book?'

'I don't read books. Esther reads, not me.'

'Her mother was a writer. Well, she wanted to be. Did you know that?'

'Yes, Esther's told me.'

'People say she was a very good writer. But she never got published. She took her life before it could happen.'

'Too bad,' he said.

'Yes, it was,' said Salt. 'Esther was only a little child.'

'You think she hasn't told me?' he said. 'You know what they say: shit happens.'

'It certainly does,' she said, and pointed to the

257

disks in their plastic box. 'I'd like to take those with me.'

'I don't think Esther would want you to do that,' he said. 'They're hers. They were her mother's. What if I say no?'

'If you say no –' she took out her phone – 'I'll call the station and they'll send over half a dozen of my colleagues with a warrant. They'll take everything away from here and secure the place. You'll have nothing, and you'll have no-where to stay.'

Gareth nodded towards the box. 'Take 'em,' he said.

Salt picked up the box of disks and said, 'Don't worry, I'll look after them.'

'Worry,' he said. 'Oh, yes, I'm worried.'

She backed away through the doorway, down the open stairs and out of the house.

Thirty-Four

October 2006

It wasn't going to be easy to find an Amstrad computer; the last one had rolled off the production line some twenty years previously.

The once-innovative machine had originally been advertised by high-profile, personable writers. The campaign implied that not only could any idiot type a few pages on the green screen but with one of these on your desk, you too might knock off a best-seller between breakfast and supper.

It had been a veritable success and former East-End barrow boy, Alan Sugar, had sold hundreds of thousands of the things and made a decent fortune. Sugar might not have been much of a reader himself, but his PCW 8512s had, indeed, facilitated the writing of ten thousand mostly unpublishable novels.

Back at the incident room, Salt briefed Kavanagh and her other colleagues on her meeting with Bethan and her subsequent visit to Esther and Gareth's squat.

'And those?' he asked.

'These are the disks,' she said.

'And you're going to have to plough through all those?' he asked despairingly.

'Needs must,' she said. 'There's some sort of connection, Frank. There's something between Clement and Porter, something beyond being postgraduate chums. Look,' she went on, 'two young women, two deaths – one violent, one by her own hand – both writers, one of them very talented, apparently, the other very successful – for a while, at least. There's something there, I know there is, and there might be a clue to what it was in here.' She patted the box under her arm.

'Good luck,' he said.

'Thanks,' she replied. 'And what's happening

this end?'

'We've put out a fresh appeal for the missing hippy at Cheddington, and they're including it in an updated *Crimewatch*.'

'What about the CCTV?' she asked. 'No good?'

'No good at all,' he said. 'It's one of the only stations on the line that's got no cameras. Quiet as a grave. Not many commuters, and neither the hippy nor Breese bought a ticket, of course, so there's no computer record of either of them having been there that morning. If there was a guard on the train, he was reading the *News of the World* rather than doing his job punching tickets. So, Breese might have been there, he might not. But I still think his story's iffy.'

'What about Terence May, aka Neil Grainer?'

'Hyland's handed his murder over to Ray Durham. With Fenton getting in touch from the WPP, he finally bought the idea that the two murders aren't related, so it's a separate enquiry now, and there's no point tying up our people on it.'

'And the farm?' she asked.

'Yes, good news. At least we've got some movement there. We'd got Ellis's prints all over the ladder, just as he'd said they would be, but that meant nothing until forensics got something from the tree.'

'DNA?' said Salt.

'Exactly,' he said.

'What?' she asked, although she suspected she knew the answer.

'You want to guess?' he asked.

'I see,' she said.

'We confronted him with the evidence of his own ejaculations, gave him the odds against it not being his – up there in the high millions – and he owned up. He's been at it for years, apparently. Even did a bit of spying on Sarah Clement, but he swears that's all. When he started to employ migrant labour who needed accommodation, it was just too good an opportunity for him to resist. He even wired up some little cameras in the bathroom, but they kept steaming up...'

'Shame,' said Salt facetiously.

'Lighten up, Jane. I know it's serious, but it does have a funny side.'

'I think we agreed to differ, Frank.'

'Anyway, he's involved with the Polish woman now. She knows what he's been up to, and she's standing by him, apparently. She's also his alibi for the time around Clement's murder.'

'I just hope she proves me wrong,' said Salt. 'You know the figures on sexual deviants? They're the most recidivist criminals, the least likely to change their ways.'

'Well, Katrina says she's going to stand up for him in court. She reckons his extracurricular activities are history now that they're fettled as a couple ... I quite like the bloke to be honest,' said Kavanagh apologetically, fearing Salt's wrath. 'He's a nice guy who's just got this one hang-up. After all, it could be anything, and for him, it's looking at women. "There but for the grace of God..." '

'We'll see,' said the DC, unmoved by his forgiving stance and token appeal.

'Anyway, the DPP are preparing the case,' he concluded.

'What's the charge?' asked Salt.

'Sexual Offenders' Act, 2003,' he said.

'Right,' she said. 'I'd better get on with this lot.'

Salt wasn't looking forward to having to spend a day on eBay getting hold of an old Amstrad but thankfully Joe Lavendar saved her the ordeal. His brother, Sweet, a collector of junk, had made a good living for the last few years hoarding what people were short-sightedly throwing away today before it became collectible tomorrow.

He had missed the piano-smashing sixties, when you couldn't get your iron-frame Joanna taken away for love nor money, but which now sold for a minimum of two hundred quid. But he had no intention of making the same mistake with antique word-processors: he was certain that Amstrads and Sinclairs and Viglens – junk that had been tipped into landfill sites throughout the country since their demise – were, one day soon, going to rise again.

'Sweet' Lavendar might be right – although his brother, Joe, was extremely sceptical – and he had, in pursuit of his belief, acquired every machine he could lay his hands on for the last twenty years. He now had a south London lock-up stacked floor to ceiling with the things.

The man was convinced that sooner rather than later, a terrorist plot would disable all electronically linked business and commerce in the West and the entire communication network would collapse with catastrophic and immediate effect. OK, his humble antique machines would never be able to send an email or receive a scrap of internet information, but they could, and would, he was convinced, remain sacrosanct and viable word-processors, unsullied by the all-pervasive internet.

A hundred times less powerful than a Mac or PC, but a dozen times better than the snail pace of a typewriter and carbons, the Amstrad would have its day once more.

Lavendar popped round to see his brother in Stockwell, gave him twenty quid, and returned with a grubby grey machine a couple of hours later.

Salt sat in front of the thing on her desk and switched the monitor on. The screen came up green. And she waited. And waited. There was no sign of anything happening but for the very green screen glowing there.

She flipped open the plastic box and leafed through the disks. At the back was something called Locoscript Start-Up. She pushed it into the slot and the machine fired up, the screen filling with myriad word-processing options. The rest of the disks – a couple of dozen in total – were numbered, and some were dated, but there was no list of contents on their labels.

She plucked one at random and inserted it. The documents on the disk came up on the screen – undergraduate essays, notes on poems and literary texts, and miscellaneous letters.

She pushed the little button that ejected the disk and inserted another, this time from the following year. She scrolled the documents and opened a few at random. These were business letters – to Leah's bank and the local authority, grant applications for postgraduate study funding, travel scholarships for her sandwich year in the USA. And again there were detailed notes on plays, poems and novels, as well as essays in various states of incarnation. Typical undergraduate fare.

She pulled it out, inserted another. Much the same, including some letters home to her parents, copies of a few to ex-boyfriend Robert, and one to Smith College accepting their offer of a place for the following academic year.

The next disk, though, was quite different.

Shimmering there on the screen was a document that looked to Salt like something from a printer's catalogue. The font sizes were different from one another, and some of the text was in bold, some in italic, some in regular. The words shimmering on the screen had a familiar ring to them.

As she read several pages, it became clear that the paragraphs in different text styles were, in fact, re-workings of the same idea, often the very same words and phrases, but in either a different tense or using direct speech, rather than third-person narration.

Other chunks of the novel – for that's what it appeared to be – were alternative versions of similar events. So this is how a writer, or at least this writer, fashioned her work? Not satisfied or content with the initial depiction of this or that event, she was trying it in several different forms.

Salt scrolled through a few pages until she arrived at a more or less extant chunk of the book, a place where there were very few alternative versions of the text, and the extract could be read coherently.

As she leaned back in her chair, the monitor turned towards her, tea cup suspended in her hand, she realized exactly what it was that she was reading there. She knew this book. The words on the screen were from *The House of Loss*, a book which Salt had read when it came out ten or twelve years previously.

So how come they were on Leah Porter's old Amstrad? Had she and Clement shared the machine when they were living together way back when, in Stoke? Had they shared disks? Had Clement written the book, for some reason, on Leah's machine? Or maybe they kept copies of one another's work, a sort of early incarnation of backing up your stuff for safe-keeping? Maybe the disks had simply got mixed up?

And then another thought occurred to Salt, and this was not so much intriguing as alarming. She removed the disk from its slot, turned off the machine, and put the remaining disks back in their box.

Thirty-Five

October 2006

'Hi, Nick. Is that Nick? Nick Cherry?'

'Yes, this is Nick. Who's this?'

'It's Ethan, man. Ethan. How you doing, Nick?'

Nick had quite a few friends, but not one of them spoke with an American accent. And no one had called him 'man' for decades.

'Ethan? Ethan who?' he said.

'How many guys you know called Ethan, Nick? It's Ethan Colley. It's been ... what ... twenty years? You remember the union bar? The pub, what was it called, the one at the end of William Street? Me, you, Sarah and Leah—'

'Fuck me gently, is that you, Ethan?' said Cherry. 'Leah's bloke? Well, fuck me!'

There had been a lot of changes in the last twenty years, and in roofer Nick Cherry's view, almost all of them were bad. Immigration, crime, a wimpy Labour government that spent most of its time working out how to give big chunks of dosh to people who didn't deserve it.

Streets full of yobs and tossers who wanted to scratch his £75,000 4x4 Porsche Cayenne with its tinted windows and private number plate wherever he parked it.

And it was getting worse. Now people had started to actually give him the finger as he drove past them or stopped to buy petrol just because of this climate-change bollocks. And it *was* bollocks. The fuckers on the pavement giving him grief with their pushchairs and hordes of kids, or the tossers in their fuel-efficient Ford Fiestas, they were all just jealous, he reckoned. If they'd tried driving one of these bad boys, they'd want one too, and not a poxy Ford.

There were only two things he could think of that were better now than they had been way back when: the mobile phone in his hand, which sounded as if Ethan Colley was in the very next street, and the fact that, in spite of all his whining about tax and VAT and health and safety regulations bollocks and the myriad things that were difficult about running a very big and successful business, Nick Cherry Roofing was exactly that. In the north-west Midlands there was no bigger roofing contractor than NCR.

Cherry had a web site, a full-time accountant to ensure that he paid as little tax as possible, a workforce of forty full-time blokes – decent lads, *Sun* readers who knew what was what and had plenty of tattoos and mostly shaven heads, blokes who could wield scaffolding poles as if they were toothpicks – and as many casual labourers as he needed when the job was even bigger than the run-of-the-mill jobs that he always had on the go.

Hayley, his tanned, paper-thin wife, was on the board and kept an eye on the office and did the wages. They had a villa tucked away next to the El Paraiso golf course in the hills behind Estepona on the Costa del Sol which they visited several times a year, even though he really much preferred being on a bustling site and keeping an eye on the job.

Cherry didn't manoeuvre poles and sling chunky brackets or shoulder Welsh slate himself any more. But he could have done. He'd started that way twenty-odd years ago, and he reckoned he was still the equal of any of the blokes working for him.

So, the phones worked well – much better than in the old days, in fact – but just what the fuck was the American Ethan Colley phoning him for after all this time?

So what is it, Ethan? You got a roof job for me?'

'Sorry?' said the man from Boston.

Twenty years and still no sense of humour, thought Cherry. 'Joking, mate. How you doing?'

'Oh, right, yes. The roof's fine,' said Colley, catching on and laughing self-consciously. 'Nick, I'm calling you 'cause I wanted to say how sorry I am about Sarah.'

'Sarah?' said Cherry.

'Yes, Sarah. Sarah Clement. I read about her over here in the *New York Times*.'

'Blimey,' said Cherry. 'It was in the American

268

papers?'

'Sure. Not much. Little paragraph on page eight or something, but you know, she was ... well, she had been – a famous writer.'

'Right,' said Nick.

'So you two ... you weren't ... you know, any more?'

'You're jokin'? I hadn't seen her for twenty years,' said Cherry.

'I see. Anyway, I'm sorry, mate,' said Colley in a woeful attempt to employ the vernacular.

'No worry,' said Nick. 'So, how you doing?'

'I'm OK, man. How about you? A successful way of business, I guess, judging from that web site of yours.'

'Yes, we make a crust, you know.'

There was a silence on the line as the forced jollity of their exchange slipped into the chasm of the intervening years.

'There was something I wanted to ask you, Nick,' began Colley.

'Yes?' said Cherry.

'You know Leah? You remember her? I've always wondered what happened to her. We lost touch, you know, after we had that ... well, I don't know what it was, but some kind of falling out. She didn't want me to be in touch. I tried, again and again. But, at the end of the semester, I had to come back to the States. I wrote, of course, but I never got a single reply.'

Cherry paced the scaffolding planks that had already been fixed halfway up the massive four-storey factory outside Leek, some seventy feet in the air. The wind gusted around him and he walked with one hand on the safety bars, the other with the phone clamped to his ear as the wind blew.

'I don't know what happened to her,' said Cherry. 'She got ill, didn't she? Sarah and me was still going out, but when you and Leah broke up, and she got sick, it was never really the same for us after that. We sort of faded out, really. I think she finished that writing thing she was doing and went back to Manchester. That was it for me. With her at least. I got the business going and she went off to be a writer. It's what she'd always wanted to do.'

'Well, she sure did it,' said Colley. 'She wrote a best-seller. She was famous.'

'Not in West Bromwich,' said Cherry, deadpan.

'Right,' said Ethan. 'And Leah? What happened to Leah?' he asked.

'No idea, mate. I never heard of her again. Sarah and me lost touch. You know me, I'm not one for writing, and she'd left Stoke. We never spoke or anything. I saw her on the telly once, flicking between channels I was. She was talking about books with some brainy fuckers. I couldn't understand a word of it. She looked alright though. All I thought was, *yes, you bet, mate: I've been there*. Didn't say a word to the missus, I can tell you. I don't read books. What's the point? I'd rather live life, not fuckin' read about it. Tell a lie: I read one last summer at the villa. Bloke in the place next to ours gave it to me. About the SAS it was. Took me a week to read it.'

'And so you know a bit about Sarah being killed?' asked Colley.

'Well, I know the cops reckon it was murder,' said Cherry. He knew that this was a moment for a second's appropriate pause, and he held the phone a little way from him. 'They reckon she was killed on the boat where she was living, or just near there. The police are all over it.'

'Why would someone want to kill her, Nick?' Colley asked, almost as if the roofer might have an entirely reasonable answer for him.

'Dunno, mate. Like I say, I hadn't seen her for years. I just hope they get the fucker what did it.'

There was another silence across the ocean. Eventually Colley began again, 'Anyway, I'm so sorry to hear about it. I really am. Are you married yourself, Nick?' he asked brightly.

'Fuck me, you're not proposing, are you?' said Cherry.

'Not exactly,' said Colley, 'but I am free as it happens. My divorce came through about two months ago.'

'Right,' said Cherry.

'Second marriage. First lasted about seven years, this one nearly ten. Twenty years, two marriages, three kids. And all the time there was that nag at the back of my mind about what happened to Leah.'

'Sure,' said Nick, stopping at the end of the old industrial building that was soon be sixty luxury apartments, and looking across to the Derbyshire Peaks in the distance.

'The thing is, Nick, Leah and I, you know, it wasn't just some college affair. I really loved her, and I think she loved me. I *know* she did. It's not everyone that I'd say this to,' he continued.

Cherry took the phone away from his ear and scowled. He didn't talk about his feelings, and he wasn't at all comfortable with a bloke he'd known over twenty years ago talking to him about his.

But Colley continued. 'But I think even through those two marriages, there was a part of me that was still with Leah. I never really let her go, you know.'

'Right,' said Cherry, wincing. 'I don't know what to say, mate. I believe you, but I don't know what to say.'

'I'm trying to find her,' said Colley. 'I already called the university, but they wouldn't tell me a thing. Something about the Data Protection Act. "What about freedom of information?" I said. "Have you heard of that?" I told them it was really important I get in touch with her. Do you know what the woman said? She said to me, "Have you tried Friends Reunited?" For fuck's sake, Nick, I'm not looking for an affair on a fucking web site. I just want to know what happened. In a way, it's about wanting to put the whole thing to bed. Do you know what I mean?'

'Sure,' said Cherry, and kicked a lead roofing strip off the scaffolding plank and watched it

272

plummet to the ground below. He felt that he had to try and say something, anything. He had a very awkward sense that the bloke on the other end of the line might even be going to cry. 'All I know is ... sorry to say this, mate, but all I remember is, you'd been ... you know, you'd had it off with some bird over at Bangor. That's what Sarah told me anyway. There was a lot of crying in the house they shared, and then Leah comes over to see you late that night.'

'Yes, that's right,' said Ethan. 'But we made it up. Really. We had a great night. I'd done ... I'd done wrong, but we made it up, big style. It was just about the best night we'd ever had together. I can still remember it.'

'Anyway, she comes back the next morning,' Cherry went on, 'and she's had that accident—'

'Accident? What accident?' said Colley.

'You know, she ran Sarah's old car into the back of a truck. On the A5 somewhere. She'd stopped at road works and hit the back of this lorry. Driver didn't even feel it, and anyway, she's a nice-looking bird, and he just says, "It's alright, forget it."'

'I didn't know this,' said Colley.

'Anyway, the driver's not bothered; no damage to him or anything. When Leah gets back, though, she's right upset. The car's had a bit of a bump at the front, and it's not even insured for Leah to have been driving...' He paused.

'Yes?' said Colley.

'And that was it,' he said inconclusively.

273

'Why didn't she ever tell me?' asked Colley, bemused.

'No idea, mate.'

One of Cherry's workmen down on the ground gestured a mug of tea to his boss seventy feet above him. Cherry gave him a thumbs-up acknowledgement.

'Ethan, mate, look, it's great to talk to you, but I've gotta go. I've gotta meeting, you know?'

'Sure,' said Colley. 'It's good to speak with you after all this time, Nick. Let's keep in touch.'

'Sure,' said Cherry and, without ceremony, folded his phone into his pocket.

Thirty-Six

October 2006

Josh Frampton had always been a loner, and for the last four years, after years of solo travel in Europe and the Far East, he'd found a place where he could pursue his solitary life almost undisturbed.

On the very edge of the Chiltern Hills he'd found an area where, a century ago, charcoal burners had made their homes and eked out a paltry living. In a sheltered pocket of woodland on Berkhamsted Common, tucked away from

274

public paths and hearty ramblers, he'd built his yurt and made a home.

Wood was plentiful; he drew water from the nearby spring and cycled twice a week to the village a couple of miles away where he bought food. Every few weeks, with his Border Collie on a rope lead, he took the train up to London, had lunch with his mother in Richmond, and returned the following day. These occasional trips were more than enough to reassure him that his Thoreau-like life was the one that suited him.

He practised simple woodcraft, fashioned a wattle fence to surround his few pots and pans and provide shelter for his fire. He had made a pole lathe and could now turn spindles and stakes, should he need them. He collected dead wood for his fire, pollarded the odd willow and copsed the woodland saplings. And that was how he spent his days.

In the evening, until the natural light made the task impossible, he read eastern philosophy, works that tended to espouse the very life that he was living. In keeping with the earth's diurnal rhythms, he bedded down at dark, and woke with dew and birdsong shortly after dawn.

He rarely begged, but would occasionally approach a stranger and ask for a little change to support his unobtrusive lifestyle. He was living the life of the sannyasin.

Ironically, given that he certainly wasn't leaving one, he had never even heard the words 'carbon footprint', had no idea just how close many of us had come to perishing, unprotected, in an outbreak of so-called 'bird flu', and he certainly had no idea at all that, with a Russian billionaire's rubles and a Portuguese maverick's idiosyncratic charm, Chelsea had won the Premier League title in the previous two years.

These things were wholly unimportant to him. He was living in harmony with nature and hoped to die that way. The football league, pandemics, even global warming were things of an ephemeral nature, and concerned him not one jot.

There were many things that Josh didn't do: he didn't go to work, and he didn't claim benefits (his mother gave him fifty pounds whenever he visited, which lasted him until his next visit). He didn't have a girlfriend, and he didn't wash or cut his hair. And, these days, he never heard or saw the news.

Buying birthday presents for people is always a nightmare. Who knows what someone really, really wants? And what do you give to a man who already has nothing, and has made it clear that he wants nothing more?

The only way that Josh's mother had tried to get round the dilemma was to give her son something on his birthday that she, herself, would have liked to receive. Admittedly, she had never given him a cosy nightdress or a boxed set of Frank Sinatra CDs, but Josh had taken home to the woods with him, over the last few years, tins of extra-virgin olive oil, boxes of

Terry's All Gold chocolates, a Harrods selection of very nice soaps, and two white Christy bath towels.

These things sometimes looked a little odd amongst the more serviceable, practical items around his Mongolian tent – the battered and blackened saucepans and kettle, the chipped and stained mug and cereal bowl – but eventually the chocolates got eaten, the olive oil was consumed, and the towels became an integral and grubby part of their surroundings.

But this year, his mother had been inspired. She'd seen a TV programme about Trevor Baylis, the man who had invented the wind-up radio, and she immediately ordered one for her son. Next time Josh came home, she showed him this piece of low-tech technology and he was, to her slight surprise and not a little delight, entirely taken with it. Josh could just as easily have taken against it, complained philosophically about the earth's diminishing resources that had been used in making another piece of frippery. But no, he wound it up immediately, and listened with a kind of wonder to the words issuing forth, as if by magic.

The idea of, very occasionally, having just a little music in the evening back at his camp was appealing. 'Thank you, Mother,' he said, gave her a kiss, and wrapped the machine carefully in his rucksack.

Admittedly, just a little troubled on the way home on the train the following morning, using a formula of his own devising, he tried to do a rough estimate of just how much oil had been used in the machine's manufacture, but he found it nigh on impossible, and eventually gave up.

And so, since that July day, a wind-up radio could now, occasionally and very quietly, be heard issuing from this particular bit of Buckinghamshire woodland. Mostly, Josh listened to Radio Three. He invariably turned down the volume when the news headlines were broadcast every hour or so. But sometimes he listened to Radio Four and tut-tutted at man's follies. The more remote he had become from that world, the more insane it seemed to be. The news, and the news magazine programmes, had started to resemble an extended version of that completely insane early evening show that he had sometimes heard in his former life, *Just a Minute*, the sole premise of which was the requirement of one of the panel to say anything whatsoever, on a particular topic, for one minute. That was it. Seamless inanity rewarded. It was, indeed, just like the news, and he reckoned that he was very well away from it.

Iraq, North Korea, the Middle East, the dollar and interest rates, and then, barely audible, hardly listening at all, as a sort of footnote to this global snapshot of woe and avarice, Josh caught some words that made him listen: 'The BBC announced today that, pending the outcome of the current police investigation into the death of the novelist, Sarah Clement, and irregularities with regard to television consumer affairs reporter Marcus Breese's fund-raising cycle trip from his home in the Midlands to London, Mr Breese will no longer be contributing to the programme and has been suspended from his post until further notice. Police are still trying to trace a man whom, it is believed, might have been seen with Mr Breese at Cheddington railway station in Buckinghamshire early on Sunday morning, the first of October. The man they are looking for is described as a "traveller", aged about forty, and wearing his hair in what is described as "dreadlocks". BBC Radio Three news. And now, this evening's concert comes from the Birmingham Symphony Hall—'

A sense of schadenfreude could be felt throughout the region where Breese had, until recently, worked, not least from those viewers who were not even aware of the meaning of the word, and certainly couldn't have spelled it.

Josh turned the radio off and pushed his fingers into the long matted ropes of his hair. 'Good Lord, that must be me,' he said under his breath.

Thirty-Seven

October 2006

DC Scrivener called out to DI Kavanagh across the room. 'Hey, Frank, we've got a match.'

People immediately stopped what they were doing and descended on the screen that was flashing up a DNA match. The name Esther Porter was highlighted and blinking on the HOLMES 2 database.

'Esther Porter?' said Kavanagh, reading from the information on the screen, and speaking for the half dozen cops who stood gathered around the monitor. 'Matching DNA sample pertaining to items recovered from the scene of newspaper boy Jack Gillespie's disappearance on November 3rd 1986.'

'Fucking technology,' said Kavanagh. 'It does not know when to stop being smart. In 1986, that girl wasn't even born.'

'Hang on,' said Salt. 'She's just gone on the database, right? Convicted of shoplifting offences.'

'So?' said Kavanagh, and began to turn away. 'She still wasn't born at the time of the Gillespie boy's abduction.'

'No,' said the DC. 'But her mother was.'

The factory conversion site on the outskirts of Leek was a hive of activity. Scaffolding poles on ropes pirouetted up the side of the building with as much finesse as the acrobats unfurled from the roof of the Dome on Millennium New Year.

Radio One blared out from battered radio/tape players as the entire building was gradually cloaked in a fretwork of poles and boards, an elaborate undergarment prior to its disappearance behind a cloak of thick blue plastic tarpaulin.

A year or so later, an entirely different beast would emerge. Once a brewery, now dozens of apartments at £150,000 a throw. Magic.

'Health and safety,' said Nick Cherry, pointing to his yellow hard hat and leading Kavanagh and Salt away from the noisy activity towards his Porsche. 'You two should have 'em on, really. I could get a fine.'

He opened the doors to the Cayenne and invited the cops to step in to its luxury leather interior. Kavanagh sat in the back seat, Salt up front with Cherry.

'You know what this is about,' said Kavanagh and, barely waiting for an acknowledgement from the roofing magnate, continued, 'Sarah Clement, the murdered woman, you went out with her I believe, some years ago?'

'Blimey,' said Cherry. 'Word's out then...'

'How do you mean?' said Kavanagh.

'Well, I had a call yesterday from a bloke I haven't seen for twenty years, and now you two

281

are here.'

'Who was that?' asked Salt.

'A Yank. He used to go out with Sarah's mate, a woman called Leah.'

'Really?' said Salt, glancing back at Kavanagh.

'He was trying to get in touch with her. He'd read about Sarah being killed, and so he phoned me.'

'And?' the constable prompted.

'And what?' he said. 'I've no idea where she is. Haven't seen her since ... God knows when.'

'Right,' said Kavanagh. 'We'll talk about Leah later, but for now, would you fill us in on your time with Sarah?'

'Bleedin' hell, how easy's that?' he said.

'Meaning?' said the inspector.

'Meaning it was a long time ago, you know.'

'Yes, I'm sure,' said Salt helpfully, 'but do your best; there may be things you can help us with.'

'Right, I'll try,' he agreed. 'What is it you want to know?'

'How did you find her? Sarah?'

'Down the union bar—'

'No, I didn't actually mean that,' interrupted Salt. 'I meant, how did you *find* her. What kind of person was she?'

'She was good-looking,' he said. 'Slim. I wasn't bad myself, either, then,' and he patted his paunch to acknowledge the change the years had wrought.

'And you met her in the union bar, you say?'

'No, that's not right, it wasn't the union,' he said, as he conjured the scene. 'It was a student pub. I was there for the cheap beer on a forged student union card. Ready to take the piss out of these kids coming away from home. Me and a couple of mates, working guys, ready to have a pop at these poofters with their long hair if they gave us a chance. But it didn't happen that way. I was up at the bar getting the beers in, and when I turned round, this woman with short hair and a tee shirt and jeans was right behind me. I spilled some beer on her. At first, I thought it was a bloke and I was gonna make trouble, even though it was my fault, and then she smiled, and I saw that it was a girl, but a girl with a small, you know ... chest.

'She says it's alright – about the beer – and we get talking and I buy her a drink and then she goes back to her friends and I stay with mine. I look up a couple of times, and she's looking at me and trying not to make it obvious, but she smiles a bit, and this mate of mine, Decker – he's in a wheelchair now, fell off a roof in town – Decker says to me, "You've pulled there," and I says, "Fuck off,", but when we leave, I go over and give her one of my business cards with my number on it.

'I was just starting out on my own then – I must've been twenty-two or -three, but I was gonna do it right and I was proud to have a card with *Nick Cherry Roofing* printed on it. Cost me twenty quid for five hundred, I remember. She must have thought "what the fuck's this?" But I gave it her anyway. Two days later, I'm amazed: she phones. And that was it, really. We start going out together. Must have been the best part of a year. I don't know why. I had a bit of money and I suppose I could be a bit of a laugh, but I always expected her at some point to tell me to get lost, 'cause she was at university and all that, and I was just a local bloke who didn't even read what she called a proper paper.'

'And the woman she lived with, the one you mentioned a moment ago, Leah, you knew her too?' asked Salt.

'Yes, I knew Leah a bit. And the other girl that lived with them, Cath.'

'And did they all get along?'

'Yes, mostly – you know what women are like.'

'No problems that you were aware of between Leah and Sarah?'

'They did have a bit of a fall out once.'

'Go on,' urged Salt.

'The thing about Sarah was, although they were friends – she and Leah – I always thought Sarah sort of resented her. It wasn't that she was better looking, 'cause she wasn't. Like I say, Sarah wasn't every man's cup of tea. She was...' He hesitated, glanced at Salt, as if to seek her permission. 'She was a bit ... you know what I mean? She didn't have much up there...'

Salt nodded, a sign that she was keen that the man continue his account, even if it did include personal details of his former girlfriend's bosom. 'Please, go on,' she said.

'Leah was a nice-looking girl, but she always had that – what's the word – privileged feeling about her, you know? And she was a tasty-looking woman. Small, with a nice figure. Sarah was more boyish really, but there was something about her that I found ... well ... she did it for me, that's all I can say.'

'So, what happened?' Kavanagh pressed. 'What was their row about?'

'I remember like it was last week,' said the roofer. 'They got on OK, but, like I say, I think there was something about Leah that bugged Sarah a bit. I suppose it was a class thing, really. I know all about that. I'm not an oik or anything, but I never went to college. In a way, I shouldn't have been going out with her. She should have been with some smart tosser doing his degree, and I wouldn't have got a look in.

'But Sarah was different from most women. She did her own thing. It didn't bother her that I didn't use big words all the time. I was her bit of rough, she said, and she was my posh totty. Yes, they were good times,' he said thoughtfully. '*Really* good. Maybe 'cause we both knew it wouldn't last.

'Well, what I was saying is, in the same way that Sarah was above me, if you like, I think Sarah thought that Leah was a bit above her. And she was, really. You could tell by the way she spoke. She'd been to a good school and her folks were teachers. Her dad was a headmaster, I think, and they had plenty of cash. And on that writing course they were doing, whatever it was,

Sarah said Leah was the star. There was nobody even near her. So, you know, there was a bit of jealousy, I think.'

'What was the row about?' asked Kavanagh again.

'Blokes, of course. Leah was going out with this Yank, a fella called Ethan – the guy who phoned me yesterday – a right good-looking twat he was, too. He was alright, typical Yank, I suppose. He thought we all had terrible teeth and that we was dirty 'cause we only had a bath – not many people had a shower in them days. He was OK, but me and him, we had nothing in common. He was fuckin' hopeless at footie. I took him out for a kick around with the lads once and he was diabolical, but we had a laugh.

'We all went swimming once, the girls and us two, down the local baths, and he couldn't believe that people swam in that, you know, that chlorinated water. Sarah told him, it's 'cause everyone here takes a piss in the water, and he was like, "I'm not fuckin' going in there." He rented a car once to have a bit of a nosey round, up in Wales, and he drove it around in first gear all day, just waiting for it to shift up. He'd never come across a motor that wasn't an automatic. For a bright bloke, I tell you, he was barking.

'But really, we were only together because the two women were mates. We'd make up a four-some, go for a drink or a Chinese or whatever. Like I say, there was nothing much for him and me. He didn't know about pointing chimneys and I didn't know fuck all about what he was studying – what's he called – Freud?'

'And the two girls? You were saying?' said Kavanagh.

'Yes, there was something about another woman up in Bangor. I think Ethan had got off with this other bird. He must have told Leah – or she got wind of it, I dunno – and anyway, one weekend, he doesn't show up here to see her and there's nothing but phone calls and tears, and Leah and Sarah talking for ages and me being told to get lost 'cause they'd got women's stuff to talk about. Eventually, Leah decides she's gotta go over and see him. Trouble is, it's about one in the morning and she hasn't got a car herself, and there's no way I'm driving her in the van – apart from anything else I've been drinking since seven and I'm well over the limit. So, she asks Sarah if she can borrow hers. Leah's the person who's got, like, everything and she's asking Sarah if she can borrow *her* car.'

'And?' prompted Salt.

'Leah, 'cause she's got rich parents and all, she doesn't understand that Sarah's had to work nights at some chippy back home in Manchester just to earn the money for that old car. It was a wreck, really, a tatty old Fiat, but she's proud of it. It's like, it's her car. Anyway, Sarah levels with her, tells her, not nasty or anything, "I don't want you to take it. I need it to go home at the weekend, and what if you wreck it? And anyway, it's not insured for you." So she feels crap, and Leah's well upset, 'cause she knows – well, they both do really – that if it was the other way round, Leah would just say, "Sure, take it." In the end, Sarah feels so bad she agrees and she says, "Oh, take the bloody car, but for God's sake, be careful."'

'And that's what happened?' said Kavanagh.

'Yes. She goes off and sees Ethan and spends the night and all, and then, coming home early the next morning, she runs into the back of a truck at some lights on the A5.'

'Really?' said Salt.

'Yes. But when she gets back here, between them, Sarah and Leah, they sort out a little scam. I was quite impressed to be honest, being women and all – they decide to wreck the car a bit more so they can get it written off, get the insurance and get Sarah a new motor.'

'And it had only been a minor crash, you say?' asked Kavanagh.

'Nothing. Bit of the wing and the bonnet and a crack on the windscreen. Didn't even mark the truck, Leah said. All repairable for fifty quid.'

'So what happened then?' asked Salt.

'That's why they need me. When I get back from playing football that morning, they ask me to take 'em out and trash the car some more, so it's a write-off.'

'And you did?'

'Why not? Look,' he said seriously, 'this is now, and that was then; it's a long time ago. I'm helping you, but I don't want to get in trouble for something like this all that time ago, you know? Things were different then.'

'Don't worry,' said Kavanagh, 'no one's going to be after you for anything you tell us that'll help with this enquiry. Please, go on.'

'What exactly did you do?' asked Salt.

'We took it down to a bit of woodland and I rammed it a couple of times to smash it good. It was a bit of a wreck anyway, only worth a couple of hundred quid, tops, so it didn't need much to make sure it wasn't worth repairing. By the time I'd shunted it into a tree, it certainly wasn't.'

'Just the front?' asked Kavanagh.

'Yes, Sarah said it was best if we just did the front, make it look like she'd skidded and hit a tree on some quiet road somewhere.'

'What about the back? Did you open the boot?' asked Salt.

'The back was locked. I remember, 'cause I was gonna get a tyre lever or something to smash a headlight with, and Sarah said it was wedged shut or something, and she told me to forget it and leave it alone.'

Kavanagh and Salt exchanged looks. 'And after you'd damaged it, what then?' asked Salt.

'I drove it back to the house. Couple of days later, the insurance assessor takes one look at it and he writes it off.'

'And what happened to the car?' asked Salt tentatively.

'The insurance company's not interested as long as it doesn't come back on the road. I think they took a few quid off the settlement figure and let her keep it for spares. Next day, I drive it down to the local scrappy. He whips the wheels and battery off, and then we all stand there as he takes it up in the grab and drops it in the crusher. A couple of squeezes in those hydraulic arms, and five minutes later, all that's left is a block of metal with bits of wire from the electrics and fluid coming out here and there. It was alright, I tell you. I like watching them do that. I still do, to be honest.'

Kavanagh and Salt looked at one another again.

'What's all this about?' asked Cherry. 'Why do you want to know all this now?'

'It's just that it might tie in with Sarah's death in some way,' said Kavanagh.

'What? After twenty years?' said Cherry, sceptical.

'You say Ethan called you yesterday?' Salt said non-committally.

'Yes. Said he'd been trying to get in touch with Leah. He's divorced and I think he was looking for a bit of old-flame stuff, you know. He asks me if I know what happened to her and if I know how he can get in touch. I told him, "I've no idea, mate, all I know is she got ill before me and Sarah broke up." That's the last I ever knew of her.'

'And he knew about Sarah?' asked Salt.

'A bit. He'd read it in the paper over there, what with her being a writer and all. I told him what I know, from the papers here, and then he asks me about Leah. I said something about the accident, when she was coming back from seeing him that day, and he says he never knew about that, and he can't understand why she didn't tell him. He says he wrote and called her loads of times, but she never replied, and then, after a while, he had to go back to America...'

'The thing is, Nick,' Salt interrupted, 'we don't think Leah ran into the back of a truck.'

'How do you mean?' said the roofer. 'I saw the motor.'

'Yes, it was damaged, I'm sure,' said Kavanagh. 'But we've recently acquired a DNA profile which tells us categorically that Leah couldn't have been on the A5 that day, she was on another road in Shropshire, further north.'

'Why?' he asked.

'We're not sure. Maybe she fancied a change of scene? If she went cross-country from Bangor to Keele, she could have taken a short cut on a quiet stretch outside a village called Overton.'

'So?' said Cherry.

'On that road, on that day, a child went missing, and was never seen again.'

'You what?' he said. 'What you on about?'

'You might remember the case. He was a lad called Jack. Jack Gillespie. A newspaper boy.'

'Yes, I remember that,' said Cherry. 'It was in all the papers.'

'They thought he'd been abducted,' continued Salt. 'They found his bike, but nothing else.

'We think Leah might have hit him. Presumably killed him. Because the car wasn't insured for her, maybe she panicked and put the boy's body in the boot.'

'Jesus,' said the man, 'I can't believe I'm hearing this.'

'You never looked in the boot of the car?' asked Salt.

'I've told you,' he said. 'It was locked. Or it was wedged. That's what Sarah said.'

'So anything could have been in there when it was crushed?' said Kavanagh.

There was a silence as Cherry saw in his mind's eye the magnetic grab collect the old Fiat and drop it into the hydraulic arms of the crusher. In only a few minutes, the steel jaws had boxed it up into a cube of metal just a few feet square. He'd watched, fascinated, as it was slung on to the pile of similar former cars as they awaited collection on a low-loader before being shipped to China. A year or so later, they'd return to the west as children's toys, pots and pans, bicycles and cheap tin trays.

'Jesus Christ,' he whispered, the enormity of his actions brought home to him. 'How could I have known?'

'Leah took her own life three years later,' said Salt.

'You what?' said Cherry.

'After that boy went missing, she went into depression. Our guess is that she killed the boy, and never got over it. She tried to take her life several times, and she finally did it when her own child was only two years old.'

'She'd had a baby, then?' he said, surprised.

'She must have been pregnant the day all this

happened. Ethan Colley's almost certainly the father,' said Salt.

'Bloody hell,' said Cherry.

'We don't think her suicide had anything to do with his having an affair. It was all to do with what must have been her accidental killing of that little boy,' added Salt. 'Once she was in depression, perhaps having a baby of her own was the final straw, a terrible reminder of what she had done.'

'How come Ethan didn't connect the disappearance of that kid with Leah?' asked Cherry.

'Even if he knew the geography,' said Kavanagh, 'which sounds doubtful, he thought she was on an entirely different road – the A5, the main road back to Stoke. And anyway, he doesn't even know about her supposed accident. She doesn't tell him. So why's he going to make any connection between his girlfriend and a child's disappearance miles away?'

'Jesus,' said Cherry. 'I don't know what to say.'

The cops got out of the roofer's car. 'You've been very helpful, Nick,' said Kavanagh. 'We'll need to speak to you again, but for the time being, thanks.'

'I'm shattered,' said the man. 'I'm really fucked by this.'

'I'm sure,' said Salt. 'But if you've told us the truth, I doubt that anyone's going to suggest you knew any more than you've told us. Jack Gillespie's parents have been desperate to know what happened to their child for twenty years, and

your version of events might at least help them
come to terms with their loss.'

He walked with them over to their car. 'Before
you go,' he said, 'where does all this tie in with
Sarah's murder?'

'That's a whole different story,' said Salt, 'and
we can't go into it right now. But we believe
there might be a connection. Goodbye for now.
We'll be in touch.'

'Yes. Sure. See you,' Nick said, and stood
there bewildered as they drove away.

Thirty-Eight

October 2006

Sarah Clement's novel was every bit as good as
Salt remembered it, possibly even a little better.

'So, who wrote it then?' asked Kavanagh.

'Who, indeed?' she echoed. 'It's on Leah's
machine, or at least on her disks, but Clement
published it. Leah was battling full-scale depression, and her mother describes her as being
completely helpless. The last thing she's going
to be able to do is get a book published, no
matter how good it is. But all the time she was
doing the writing course, and even when she
was in America, according to her mother, she
was always working on something, something

she was reluctant ever to talk about. A couple of years later, she kills herself.'

'And then?' said Kavanagh.

'Well, four, five years later, this comes out. I don't know, Frank. It's speculation, but maybe Sarah knows about this book, knows just how good it is, and after all her own rejections, she puts it out as her own?'

'Go on,' he said. 'I'm impressed.'

'It's not cast-iron, all I'm saying is it's a *possibility*,' said Salt. 'The only two people who've said anything about Leah's writing – Tom Hopwood, her tutor on the MA, and playwright, Adam Shaw – said she was the one with the talent. Hopwood suggested she was Mozart to Clement's Salieri.'

'Yes, but you also said that the man was a drunk,' said the inspector.

'He is,' said Salt, conciliatory. 'But he's not a falling-over drunk, and he does know about these things.'

Kavanagh breathed the heavy, thoughtful sigh of acknowledgement. 'And then Leah gets sick...'

'Depression, followed by a complete breakdown. It's more common than cancer. What are the figures? Something like one person in four will, at sometime during their life, suffer some sort of mental illness.'

'It's such a nice idea, Jane, it belongs in a book. But let's say you're right for a minute. Where does that leave us as far as Clement's murder is concerned?'

'A few months ago, Esther took her mother's computer away from her grandmother's house. There's no electricity at the squat, but she eventually got a look at the disks round at a friend's place. She's read *The House of Loss* already, we know that, and she'd lent it to her grandmother before she even knew that her mother and Clement had ever known one another. So, as soon as she reads the stuff on disk, she puts two and two together and surmises that her mother's had her work stolen by her best friend.

'Esther's lost her mother in circumstances that have never, adequately, been fully explained. She has no knowledge of the accident and the little boy, and so she quite reasonably assumes her suicide must have been something to do with the appropriation of this manuscript. She's also, incidentally, lost all the rights money that would have come to her if her mother *had* published the book. Esther's already struck up a bit of a friendship with Clement after her gran told her that her mum and Sarah had known one another at university. If she now suspects all this, maybe she goes over there and confronts Clement with it? She might not even be right, but if she believes she is, she's got a strong motive for wishing to harm her.'

'And if Sarah did help Leah get rid of the dead child,' added Kavanagh, 'maybe in some odd way, Sarah feels that she is owed something? We'd better get young Esther in for a chat. See where she was around the time that Sarah Clement died.'

Thirty-Nine

October 2006

'Esther, we think there are some things you'd probably like to tell us,' said DC Salt bluntly. 'Things about Sarah Clement, you know?'

The young woman sat there in something of a daze, the station's appointed duty solicitor at her side.

'Yes,' she said. It wasn't clear whether it was question or affirmation.

'On the night that she died,' continued Kavanagh, 'you went to Sarah Clement's boat?'

She didn't answer.

'We have a sighting of the vehicle you used, Esther. It's on a dozen CCTV cameras from Cardiff to the M25, all the way into Rickmansworth—'

'I haven't got a car,' she said, a half-hearted, token defence, a contradiction almost for the sake of it.

'No,' said Salt. 'The van is registered to your friend, Ryan Haines. We know that, but he's not driving it. We have video of you at a petrol station on the M4 buying fuel...'

'So what?' she said defiantly. 'I borrowed it.'

'Please,' said Salt again, 'why don't you tell us what happened, Esther? It's the easiest way.'

Her head was slumped down halfway to the table top. She lifted it and looked up at her solicitor. The woman in the dark suit looked back at the girl.

'Can I smoke in here?' Esther asked.

Kavanagh pointed to the sign. 'Health and safety,' he said. 'Sorry.'

She fingered her tobacco tin, tapped its lid with her broken nails, then began, 'We used it whenever we wanted it. Gareth, you know, he'd let him have a little bit of gear in return. The deal was we'd just take it if we needed it. He leaves the key under the passenger seat.'

'Was Gareth with you?' asked Kavanagh.

'No.'

'Are you sure?' said Salt. 'This is very important.'

'I went alone. It's nothing to do with him. It's all my stuff. I had to talk to her. I had to find out what happened.'

'Go on,' said Kavanagh. 'What did happen, Esther?'

She breathed deeply. There was a resignation about her that suggested that she just could not be bothered to lie, to try to defend herself with a cloak of fabrications. Perhaps she sought the relief of the confessional? And anyway, even in her state, she knew that CCTV wasn't going to lie. They hadn't made that up.

'I had to speak to her, find out what it was she'd done to my mother. And why. Once, she was just a kind of acquaintance, but for months now, she'd pretended to be my friend.' She revolved her tobacco tin on the table top. 'You know –' she choked on her husky words, trying to hold back the tears – 'except for my grandparents, everyone in my life has let me down. I've never even known my own father,' she sobbed. 'How can a man have a child and not want to know her? My mother killed herself when I was only two. And now this woman pretends that she's a friend, when really, all the time, she's cheated my mother, and now she's lying to me.'

She pulled a tight ball of tissue from her jeans pocket. Salt passed her a big box of the things from beside the recording equipment.

'I parked near the bridge,' she continued, the tissue held to her eyes. 'I'd parked there a couple of times before, when I'd first visited her.'

'What time was this?' asked Salt.

'Half-eleven? Twelve? I don't know. It was quiet.'

'And?' said Salt.

'I walked down the path. It's always quiet there, and I stood by her boat. I could see her inside, sitting there, smoking, a glass in her hand. No music, just sitting there, drinking and smoking. I watched for a long time, listened to the water, the little waves slapping against the side of the boat. I didn't even know what I was doing there. I didn't know what I was going to say. After a while, I stepped on board. She heard me and got up. "Hello," she said. "Who's there?" I opened the hatch doors. "God," she said, "Esther. What are you doing here?" I just looked at her. "What is it?" she said. And then she looked at me, and in that one look, I could tell, she knew. "Come in," she said, and offered me a drink. "I want to use the toilet," I said.' She glanced up at Salt. 'I needed a wee. I went to the toilet and she poured me some gin. She wanted me to sit near her, but I didn't want to. I took a kitchen stool instead. "I guess you want to talk?" she said. I asked her what had happened, how she could have done that, how she could have stolen my mother's book. "I could try and explain," she said. I told her she should. "What do you know?" she asked me.

'"What do you mean, what do I know? I know that *The House of Loss* was my mother's book, and you stole it. What I don't understand is why. Or how. And why you've lied to me and pretended to be my friend. How could you do that?" I said.

'"Could I do anything else?" she said. "Was I supposed to turn you away? Say that I didn't want to speak to you? Just imagine..."

'"Imagine? I can't imagine," I said. "You've got to tell me." She told me she thought I probably understood about being a writer. I'd shown her some of my poems after we first met. I said to her, "You going to nick those, too?"

'"No, I'm not going to steal your poems," she said. "But because you write, perhaps you can understand what it's like wanting to be published?"

300

'"Yes, I'd like to be published one day," I said, "but I wouldn't steal someone's work to do it."

'"It's a sickness," she said. "Your mother used to talk about having the creative virus when she was writing. And it was the same for me. It's nothing to do with how good the work is; it's the doing of it. You become driven. You become obsessive."

'I asked her: "So, what's this got to do with my mother's book?" She said that after she'd finished her MA, she completed her own book and sent it out. She'd written and rewritten it, again and again. Some drunk who'd taught them, I can't remember his name, had apparently always praised my mother's work, but had never been enthusiastic about hers, or anyone else's in the group. This man had always told them, no matter how good you were, you had to have some luck, too.

'Anyway, she got her degree and went to live in Manchester with another writer. She kept sending out her book, but it kept coming back. No one took it. No one said it was terrible, but no one took it, either. She got letters out, showed them to me, letters that said things like "we need to be one hundred per cent behind our clients, and in this case..." and "literary fiction is particularly difficult just now..." or "the market for adult women's fiction is very depressed at the moment..." In the end, she puts the book away and begins a new one, and this one, she's convinced, is good enough to make it. But the same thing happens: she sends it out, and back it comes.'

Esther paused, dried her eyes and blew her nose. 'Can I have a cup of tea?' she asked.

'Sure,' said Salt, 'I'll have someone bring us some. Do you want to carry on until it arrives?'

'Yes,' she said. 'Anyway – and this is years after my mother became sick – one day, she's checking stuff on the disks on her old computer, seeing if there's anything there she needs before she chucks it out, when she comes across some files of my mother's. Either their disks have got mixed up, or they were copies. She says she doesn't know, she'd thought my Gran and Granddad took the originals when they took all my mother's things away.

'She reads the book on the screen, and she knows it's good. But her own stuff's good, too, she believes. And she'd sent that out, and back it had come. So, just how good was it? She feels wronged; she's still had no success, even though she believes her work is good enough. My mother is dead, and no one knows about this book of hers. She decides she'll send it out. She reckoned that agents and publishers always miss lots of talented writers. She told me about people who never got published for years, and then went on to sell lots of books. Really, it's like an experiment for her. To justify her own rejections. So, she sends it off.

'But it doesn't come back. An offer to publish it does. She says to me: "What was I supposed to do then, Esther? Sell a story to The *Sunday Times*: frustrated author sells deceased friend's book to publisher? Or do I just go along with the fraud?"

'I told her, "It was never your book to sell. It was my mother's." But she did it anyway. And she said the reason why was so that once this was published, at least her own future work would be recognized for what it was.'

There was a knock on the door and a DC brought in a tray of tea.

'Go on, please, Esther,' said Kavanagh.

'On the strength of *The House of Loss*, they gave her a two-book deal. The second book was published a year and a half later. Apparently, it was slaughtered by the critics. I told her, I just said, "I'm so fucking glad."' She sipped her tea.

'The book was remaindered within a couple of months and, apart from a few bits for magazines, she's done nothing since. But my mother's book still sells,' she said, unable to conceal her pride.

'What about the royalties?' Salt asked.

'Oh, yes, the royalties,' said Esther bitterly. 'She gives most of the money away. *My* money. Just keeps enough for drink and bits and pieces. I said to her, "Am I supposed to feel good about that? My mother's book, and my money?"

'She said none of it had given her a shred of happiness. She broke up with the man she was with – she's had tons of blokes, but no happiness – and now she just pretends she's working on a new book. But she's not working on anything at all. She's just drinking and getting wasted. Same as me, I s'pose. She told me if she had the

303

courage, she'd have done what my mother did, and kill herself.'

'I see,' said Kavanagh. 'What happened then?' he asked, sensing the final act's approach.

Esther sighed, swirled the tea around the bottom of the mug and said, 'She was drunk. She said she needed to get some air. She pushed past me and out through the little doors. I stayed there and rolled a cigarette, got another drink. After a bit there was a noise outside. I came out – I was a bit drunk, too – and she was lying half on the lockers, half on the floor where she had fallen. She tried to get to her feet, but she fell back down...'

'You didn't try and help her?' said Salt.

'No. I did nothing. She struggled to get up, and when she was on her feet again, she stood there for a moment, and then she just fell backwards over the edge of the boat into the water, like a kid might, for a joke or something in the swimming pool. I watched her rolling there, with my knee resting on the lockers. She lifted a hand out of the water and reached up to me. The side of the boat was a long way above the water line. "Esther," she said, and lifted her arm up to me. I just looked down at her. I didn't help.'

There was a silence as the young woman ran the picture in her mind.

'Go on,' said Salt quietly.

'She was rolling about there, spluttering and gasping for breath. I leaned right over the side, reached down and grabbed her wrist.'

'Yes?' said Salt.

'With her wrist held in mine, I put my other hand on top of her head and held her there.'

'You held her under the water?' Kavanagh asked, trying to hide his incredulity.

'Yes.'

'She struggled?' Kavanagh asked.

'Not much,' she said. 'Hardly at all. She slipped free of my hand once, and her head popped up like a balloon, but I grabbed her hair and held her down again. And after a bit, this time, she didn't come up.'

There was silence in the room. Kavanagh took out his tobacco pouch, pushed it across to the young woman. 'Go ahead,' he said, and they both rolled cigarettes as the tape wound round.

'What happened next?' Salt asked.

'I went and got my drink. I sat there in the quiet with the water lapping, and her floating there. The water was still, but her body bumped against the side of the boat every few minutes. Eventually, I leaned over, reached down and tried to lift her. But it was impossible. The side of the boat was too high. I went into the cabin to look for a rope or something, but I couldn't find one. I looked through the drawers and found a long silk scarf. I leaned right over the side and grabbed her, pulled her arm up, tied the scarf around her wrist, and then tied it to one of those things where you ... you know, one of those things...'

'A cleat?' offered Kavanagh.

'Yes, a cleat,' she agreed. 'I looked inside the boat, checked there was nothing of mine there,

305

emptied my ashtray over the side, and then I picked up my glass and threw it into the water as far up the canal as I could. I locked the doors, untied the scarf and walked round the boat, pulling her behind me in the water. At the front of the boat, I stepped down and began to walk up the path, pulling her body behind me.' She took a long drag on her cigarette. 'A couple of hundred yards up the path, I drew her body into some sort of ... I don't know ... a little bit of water off the canal. There was a pile of girders and I lugged one to the edge of the water and knotted the scarf to the middle of it. I pushed the iron bar over the edge into the water, and it yanked her body down. It felt alright, like I'd done a good job.'

There was a long silence in the room. Eventually, the young woman looked up at Kavanagh. 'You asked me,' she said, 'and that's what happened. She deserved it. She'd pretended to be my mother's friend, but she wasn't. All she did was cheat her.'

Salt got up and opened the heavily reinforced window a few inches.

'She *did* steal your mother's work, Esther, of that there's almost no doubt, but we are certain that there is more to your mother's suicide than you know.'

'How do you mean?' said the girl.

'As far as we've been able to determine, your father, Ethan, did have an affair, a relationship with another woman. But he says that he and your mother sorted things out between themselves, and we think it might be true.'

'And?' said Esther.

'Well, we've always been given to understand that it was as a result of his affair, and their subsequent break-up, that your mother went into depression.'

'What do you mean, "given to understand"?'

'We know that Leah, your mother, drove to Bangor to see your father. He was a postgraduate student there. The following morning she was coming home from seeing him, back to her college in the Midlands. We believe she left the main road and took a diversion, went a cross-country route. What we'll probably never know is why. It's a quiet road today, and it was even quieter twenty years ago. Maybe she just wanted to be off the main road for a bit. Anyway, she drove near a village called Overton. It's in Shropshire. She was in Sarah's car.'

'So what?' Esther asked.

'The car wasn't insured for her. That much we do know.' Salt paused. 'Your mother hit a young boy from the village who was out delivering newspapers. She killed him.'

'My God,' she said. 'How do you know this?'

'We know it because of you, actually,' said Salt.

'What do you mean, because of me?' she said, shocked and totally confused.

'When you were recently prosecuted for shoplifting, your DNA was automatically entered on the national database.'

'So?' Esther said.

'One of the things that the system threw up was a familial match of your DNA with something recovered from the scene of a boy's death all those years ago,' Kavanagh explained.

'Mine?' she said.

'It couldn't have been yours; you weren't born,' said Salt. 'But your mother was. A DNA match between a mother and her children is not identical, but it's very, very close. The odds against it not being your mother's DNA at the scene of Jack Gillespie's disappearance are literally millions to one.'

'My God,' said Esther.

'For twenty years, it's been assumed that the boy was abducted, and probably murdered,' continued Salt. 'Now, it seems that his death was a tragic accident.'

'Oh, my God!' said the girl again. 'But what happened to him?' she asked, afraid of what the answer might be.

'We think that your mother panicked, drove home with his body in the car, and then Sarah and her boyfriend probably helped her to get rid of it,' said the inspector.

'And that's why my mother had a breakdown? Why she took her life? Nothing to do with my father?'

'Yes, we're almost certain of it,' said Salt. 'And he almost certainly never knew that your mother was pregnant with you when he went back to America. Giving birth to you, seeing you grow, perhaps these things didn't bring her the joy they might have done, but only sorrow for the tragic accident that she'd had.'

'And Sarah tried to help her?' mouthed Esther through the tears that rolled down her cheeks.

'We think that she helped your mother get rid of the boy's body, and the car, yes.'

'I've helped kill her, and she was trying to help my mother?' she said.

'The boy's parents have had the loss of their son to bear all these years,' said Kavanagh. 'In all that time, because of Sarah's silence, they've had no idea what happened to him. But yes, it is true, Sarah was trying to help her, and without gain. At least, not then.'

'Why didn't she tell me this?' said Esther. 'If not before, when I came to tell her that I knew about the book? If she had told me ... everything would have been different.'

'Maybe she didn't want to interfere with a course of events that she anticipated, possibly even wanted,' said Kavanagh.

'Oh, God,' Esther said again. 'I killed her, and she was only trying to protect me.'

Forty

November 2006

Of course, an unsolved murder case is never closed.

In 1987, after months and months and months of diligent work, with dozens of detectives investigating the disappearance of the newspaper boy Jack Gillespie the enquiry was quietly scaled down.

There was no announcement of such a thing, and the skeleton team which remained on the case for the best part of another two years revisited old avenues, explored new, ever more unlikely scenarios and attended people in prison and bail hostels, people who were only remotely known to them, but had not yet been interviewed.

Lines of enquiry that had once looked promising, but had turned out to be dead ends, cul-de-sacs that led nowhere, were trawled through again.

And even today, twenty years on, that information was still there, not on disk or floppy, but on the many thousands of sheets of paper filed in wallets and stored in stout boxes that languished in the basement of West Mercia

Police HQ in Shrewsbury. Not only did such cases remain officially open but, with new DNA and other scientific techniques, police officers revisiting dormant cases of murder, rape or child abuse were becoming increasingly common.

Men – for it was usually men – who might have spent the previous twenty years with their feet up on the sofa, the family cat nestled in their crotch, had begun to dread every knock on the door.

Some had ended marriages and discreetly relocated to distant spots in South America and Asia; others had changed their names, taken advantage of cosmetic surgery, acquired new National Insurance numbers, and moved to the south coast from Scotland, the bleak flatlands of East Anglia from the noisy West Midlands, in their attempts to stay out of the reach of the police.

For these were diligent people, people who liked nothing more than to knock on the door of a killer of yesteryear, now an ageing family man, perhaps, but with a secret so dark and so distant that it had all but disappeared into the backcloth of his life.

And there were circumstances, occasionally, when a case would suddenly be reopened. Perhaps a deathbed confession from some hapless soul; a prisoner revealing something to a cellmate, that cellmate then spilling the old beans to a tabloid newspaper on his release from custody.

Very rarely, incompetence or maladministration might be suspected, and then an entirely new team, with a new chief investigating officer, would be assigned to the case. Fresh eyes and a fresh approach would be brought to bear to re-examine all the evidence in the search for the detail that might have been overlooked in the original enquiry.

The Home Office Forensic Service itself, after all, had missed the spots of blood found on the trainers and tracksuit bottoms of the assailants in the Damilola Taylor murder case in Peckham, south London. Only when a newly appointed senior detective arranged for items of clothing to be sent to an independent testing laboratory was the incriminating evidence found and linked to the killers, whose convictions eventually followed.

Way back in the late eighties, the case of the early-morning disappearance of the newspaper boy on a quiet Shropshire road had, of course, been covered extensively, and made the news for many weeks as sightings were claimed and fruitless leads followed. Although there were repeated appeals to his assumed abductor for his safe release, experienced detectives knew that the likelihood of the boy still being alive – and released – having been held against his will and forced into God only knew what levels of depravity, were remote.

They appealed to anyone who might have noticed odd or suspicious behaviour in a partner, lover, husband, wife, friend or colleague. And, of course, as ever, they didn't reveal all they knew. The template was established, the familiar procedures followed. The deranged attention-seekers who wanted to have their fifteen minutes' of fame, and could barely wait to confess to anything at all, had to be weeded out in the usual way: they would lack the critical information that was known only to the police and the killer.

Whatever had happened to Jack Gillespie, it had been violent. His blood on the tarmac showed as much. Plaster-cast impressions from the tyre tread marks on the soft verge had soon facilitated identification of the make and size of the car's tyre. But the Dunlop brand was so common that it had advanced the investigation not one jot. Given a suspect, it might prove a useful piece of supporting evidence; but as far as *identifying* that suspect, it was useless.

And, yes, there were skid marks on the road that suggested violent braking, and of course the boy's cycle had suffered some sort of glancing impact. But how persuasive was this? A person with the abduction of a child in mind was unlikely to be deterred from his objective simply because it might require him to fell that child in some violent way.

But if it were an accident, a genuinely tragic mishap, had the car driver simply panicked and taken the boy away from the scene? The cops didn't believe this hypothesis for one moment, but they did publicly promulgate it as a way of trying to suggest to the abductor that, perhaps he or she might take advantage of the suggestion as a way of trying to cover his or her crime in this proffered cloak of threadbare justification.

The police also stressed repeatedly, on television and in the press, that anyone coming forward with information would be treated in the most sympathetic way, for it was the boy's parents' most solemn wish that, if their son was no longer alive, they learn what his fate had been and afford him a loving burial.

But all of their pleas, all of their appeals had failed.

Jack's parents were now divorced and living miles apart from one another.

Kavanagh sent a car for the boy's mother in Nottingham; his father drove across from Overton, the Shropshire village where he still lived.

For the first year or two that had followed their tragic ordeal, united in their grief, the couple were actually brought closer together than they had ever been prior to their son's disappearance. But as the years stretched on, and their other children left the village and began to make their own lives away from the family home, an atrophy developed between them that neither of the parents had the wherewithal to heal. Theirs was a creeping sickness of an estrangement: there was no third party, no thrill or excitement of clandestine meetings in pub or supermarket car park. Just a slow falling apart.

And, as the years passed, and the anniversaries of the day that their son had cycled away, never to return, came and went, they all but gave up hope of ever learning of his whereabouts.

Twenty years later, they had reconciled themselves to a life entirely without him – without even knowledge of his body's resting place.

His father, Tom, continued to drive for a local haulier, lugging massive tree trunks from the forests of mid-Wales up to Ellesmere Port. He had a game of darts, ate too much and not very well, and drank quite a bit most nights.

His ex-wife, Susan, had originally moved to Lancashire to be near her younger sister. She'd worked at a big conference hotel in Preston, and subsequently became involved with one of the chefs there, a Scotsman. The relationship had lasted several years but, like a lot of people in the hospitality trade, the man drank heavily and, when drunk, became violent and abusive. They'd eventually parted and Susan Gillespie was now alone again.

Twenty years down the line, and a Detective Inspector they'd never heard of was calling them for a meeting in Shrewsbury. And the detective who had led the original investigation, and since retired to Spain, was going to be present too. Was it a further ordeal, or some kind of revelation? Were they going to walk into the room and find their son there? A handsome lad of thirty-two, but with a boyish smile?

Of course not. It had been the first question that they had asked when Kavanagh had phoned. 'No, I'm sorry. The news is not good. It's not what you want to hear. We haven't found Jack. But we do have some information that might help to explain what happened to him.'

They sat in the family liaison room. Kavanagh introduced himself and Detective Sergeant Joe Lavendar. There were few civilities and no one talked about the weather. The divorced couple acknowledged one another like polite strangers, with neither rancour nor affection.

Before they had even taken their seats, Susan, unable to wait a moment longer said, 'Please, tell us what's happened.'

'Of course,' said Kavanagh. 'We believe we know what happened to your son. His death was an accident. He died when a car hit him. There was almost certainly no pain, and no prolonged suffering. The woman that we believe killed him panicked at what she had done, because she was driving a car that wasn't insured for her. We think she put him in the car, and took him away from the scene.'

'And ... and then what happened to him?' his mother asked tentatively.

'I'm afraid we believe the car was destroy-ed...'

'With ... Jack?' the boy's father asked.

'I'm afraid so,' said the inspector. 'I'm terribly sorry to have to tell you this. It must be awful...'

Susan Gillespie began to shake uncontrollably, and then she sobbed with a racked grief that came from deep within her. Her ex-husband stepped across the room, knelt before her and held her in his arms.

After a minute, Kavanagh said quietly, 'I know it's no consolation, but I think you should know that the woman who was responsible for the accident was very young. She took her own life shortly afterwards. We think it was because of her grief. Her remorse at what she had done.'

Half an hour later, the couple were on their way back to their respective homes. Joe Lavendar was downstairs in the canteen having a bacon sandwich and a cup of tea.

Kavanagh remained in the redolent empty room with its easy chairs, low table with an anaemic-looking spider plant and a box of man-size tissues on it. Standing at the window sill, he looked across to the Welsh hills and dialled Salt's number.

She picked up on only the second ring. 'How you doing?' he said.

'I'm OK,' she said. 'How did it go?'

'They were glad to know, I'm sure. But it was hard...'

'Are you OK, Frank?' she asked carefully.

'Yes, I'm alright,' he said. 'Thanks.' Then, after a pause he added, 'Jane, we should try to be good to one another, you know?'

'Sure,' she said. 'Let's do that.'

'Take care,' he said. 'I'll see you soon.'